CASS TELL

THE COFFEE LOVER

A Novel

Books by Cass Tell

Wings Series - Novelettes
The Brussels Atonement – Wings Series 4
The London Inferno – Wings Series 3
The Paris Crossing – Wings Series 2
The Prague Transit – Wings Series 1

Novels
The Coffee Lover
Dance With Poetic Sea
The Savant
The Cookbook
Pale Tides
A Smile Forever, A novella and short stories
Virtual Eyes
Social Code
Blue Fate 5: Pursuit
Blue Fate 4: Squeeze
Blue Fate 3: Dropout
Blue Fate 2: Buyout
Blue Fate 1: Startup

Children's Stories
The Wise Girl and Baby Yaga's Son

Children's Series - The Adventures of Amy and Jack:
The Insidious Hope
The Impossible Storm
The Amazing Rescuers
The Impossible Prize

COPYRIGHT PAGE

CONTENTS

DEDICATION

To all coffee lovers.

CHAPTER ONE

After stepping out of the shower, I caught the scent of freshly brewed coffee, like velvet maple drifting into my bathroom. So, with a need for caffeine, I quickly wrapped a blue towel around my wet hair, put on my cotton robe and headed for the kitchen.

There, I poured a fresh cup of coffee, raised it to my lips and took a sip. With that first taste, an unexplainable moment of pleasure filled my being, like someone saying, "Relax. It's all going to be okay."

The previous evening I had roasted green coffee beans using a high-end Ikawa digital roaster. It produced the most exquisite coffee possible. Then I poured the beans into my coffee maker and set the timer for eight o'clock in the morning.

The coffee beans originated from a remote area of the Ethiopian highlands. I had learned about this from a top chef in New York City and followed his example by investing in the coffee roaster. It was well worth it.

The chef taught me to program the roaster to bring out all the subtle flavors from the beans. Roasting at home was one of my few enjoyments, and while not an expert, I wanted to learn more.

I took a second sip, and my phone rang. After answering it, I heard the voice of Ernie Finkel, my boss.

"Zipper, where are you?" He never used Sarah, always defaulting to my family name.

"At home."

"You're late."

Ernie's statement was relative, as none of my colleagues kept a schedule. They were reporters, and there was no such thing as regular office hours. Even so, his reprimand rankled me. I had been up past midnight, working on a piece with a tight deadline.

"You should double my salary for all the time I put into this job," I countered.

"I need to see you in ten minutes," he said.

"It won't happen unless you get the subway people to speed up the trains." It was only a nine-minute ride from my 96th Street Subway Station to Grand Central Station, plus a combined ten minutes of walking on both ends. But today, no one would rush me.

I reached for the coffee cup, and in doing so, the phone slipped from my fingers, and I caught it before it crashed to the floor. When placing the phone back to my ear, I only heard the last part of a sentence. "And, we need to act fast on this."

"Sorry, I missed that. Can you repeat it?

"No. just get into the office and make it quick."

From experience, I knew that Ernie was impatient, and while challenging, I learned not to let it get to me. He ran a group of independent journalists, and it was not a simple task. More than once, I had heard Ernie say his job was like herding cats. That was an overused cliché, and he needed to find a better analogy.

"I'll get there when I get there," I snapped back, and then felt guilty. I owed the guy. Ernie had recently saved my neck from a stressful threat of a lawsuit resulting from an article I had written about a restaurant. I was forever grateful and at least had to humor the guy.

After Ernie hung up, I carried the cup to the living room of my small apartment, sat on the couch, and put my feet on a coffee table covered with food journals. To give my feet a comfortable place, I pushed some of them onto the floor. The coffee table only served as a storage place for magazines and newspapers, for recently, they held little interest.

Then, I took my time to enjoy this moment of relaxation. For the past weeks, I had worked sixteen-hour days and needed time to decompress.

My living room was tiny, and covering one wall was a set of bookshelves that took a day to set up. The assembly instructions were complicated and pieces missing, so it meant going back twice to the furniture shop. The second trip consisted of a lengthy argument with the store manager, and eventually, after much badgering, he sent someone who completed the task in about three minutes. It confirmed that I should never become a carpenter, mechanic, or engineer.

A small section of the shelves held my books from university, and the rest contained thick history books inherited from my father. He had been a professor of Jewish history.

My older sister, Naomi, received all his theology books, mainly long interpretations of laws in the Torah, written by famous past rabbis. Our mother had separated the books into two piles, the history books in one, and the religious books in the other. She knew the inclinations of each daughter and remarked that I was not the most observant, so the theology books shouldn't go to waste.

That comment about my observance to religious customs wasn't entirely accurate, for the family was not Orthodox, and we were not strictly Reform, with its progressive biases. The Jewish world was multifaceted, culturally and religiously, with all its fragmented groups and sub-groups.

My family tended to take a laissez-faire attitude to strict practices of rituals. My father had been philosophically oriented toward Zionism, that is, the right of a Jewish homeland. For my mom, the synagogue was primarily a place for social life. She sometimes laughingly claimed that our identity as Jews came from our collective membership in an *unorganized* religion. That was typically followed by, "whenever two rabbis meet, you get three points of view." My mother loved the rabbi jokes she learned from her brother living in Israel.

Naomi, my sister, married Daniel, a rabbi in training, and he made good use of our father's theology books. Daniel now had the aura of a learned academic with his impressive collection of authoritative tomes sitting on shelves behind his desk in his office.

When I finished drinking the coffee, I dressed in designer jeans that loosely fit my buns and legs. I went for comfort over the skin-tight look that squeezed every contour. I wore black sneakers, and a gray t-shirt trimmed with dark purple short sleeves. On the front of the shirt was written, 'Northwestern Wildcats Purple Pride.' I wasn't one to cling to the identity of my university, having graduated, and never returned to the place. Wearing the shirt was only a way of annoying Ernie when we debated the merits of our respective schools of journalism, Northwestern versus New York University.

I put on a light indigo cotton jacket that came from India. The label on the collar always brought a big smile for on it was written, *For Height 5' 8", Bust 34", Waist 24".* When I bought it, I laughed out loud, for I'd never seen such precision bestowed on any garment. Someone in India was setting a new standard, and maybe it was a new marketing trick. But indeed, the jacket did fit.

Today was a day to dress down, for I planned to spend it at the office and not out on the field.

When leaving my apartment, I questioned that strange demand from Ernie. What was so urgent?

* * *

Within the hour, I entered my office building, took the elevator up to the twenty-first floor, and walked down the hallway. At the end was a window with a view of the surrounding buildings. Whenever I came to the office, I paused there to look out at New York City. The varied architectural monuments stretched endlessly, and often I tried to think of a metaphor to describe them. It was a way to kickstart my writing juices.

The day before, I imagined those buildings as thick fingers pointing skyward. Today, they were church spires seeking the gods of materialism. The city was impressive, the center of mega-billion dollar companies operating in every form of finance and commerce.

The company I worked for was different. It wasn't mega-billion or even mega-million. I worked for Real Media, a struggling content provider that sold its services to a long list of magazines, newspapers, and desperate corporations. The journalists working for Real Media could write on any subject imaginable, each having a specialty. My forte was restaurants.

After graduating from university and joining Real Media, my first assignment was to generate articles for a large food company where I traveled the country writing about the production of cereal, canned vegetables, and frozen dinners. The topics were not exciting, the very opposite of what my university journalism classes had prepared me to cover, like serial killers and crooked politicians. Still, the food articles developed my writing abilities. I can describe a kernel of corn in a dozen different ways.

Then, Real Media switched me to restaurants. Over five years, I visited every dining place around, from gourmet eateries to food stalls. One discovery was that readers wanted more than the description of restaurant decorations, kitchen layouts, and the color mix in meals. They liked human interest stories about the chefs, the servers, the managers and owners, and anyone else working in a restaurant. That's where I once slipped up, resulting in the lawsuit.

A restaurant owner sued me because I called his place, "a terrifying encounter with slithering organisms emerging from mold-covered coleslaw. Someone should change the name of the restaurant from 'Le Palm d'Or' to 'Barf on the Table.'"

Okay, it was a bit over the top, written in a moment of exuberant literary creativity.

The owner turned out to be a wealthy, influential politician, and he reacted the only way he knew, in a court of law. He figured he controlled the judge. Ernie defended me and threatened to flood the media with insulting articles about the restaurant and the politician. Eventually, the whole thing faded away, as tomorrow's headlines quickly obliterate today's hot topics.

I learned a couple of things from this. First, be careful when dealing with influential people, and second, Ernie was a fighter. But, I still held to my original description of the restaurant.

After the first year of visiting restaurants and consuming endless calorie-rich meals, there was a scare when I looked in the mirror and realized my lanky, lean frame was going to pot. So, I joined a fitness club, and it worked, pretty much. Following countless hours of Zumba, exercise machines, and self-defense classes, at least I was now less clumsy, and could impressively thump a punching bag. Having learned

Krav Maga, an Israeli self-defense technique, in theory, I could break someone's nose. In reality, when it came to fight or flight, my preference was flight.

When considering my life, lately, I wondered where I was going. Writing about restaurants had become mundane, and my motivation was waning. While my articles ended up in newspapers, food periodicals, and inflight magazines, my existence had become excessively routine. The pile of food magazines on my coffee table was a depressing reminder of my insignificant contribution to the world. Did I want to cover restaurants until the end of my days? Definitely not, but opportunities for journalists were few and far between.

It wasn't that restaurants, chefs, and food were all that negative. Restaurant people worked their tails off for the benefit of others. Daily, I saw the joy many of them experienced from their work.

In my case, it was different. While my articles entertained readers, wasn't there something more meaningful to do with my skills? Journalism was supposed to be a way of accomplishing something significant, a means of fulfilling the traditional Jewish rubric *Tikkun Olam*, or "Repairing of the World." This wasn't happening. Should I change my profession altogether?

I was twenty-nine years old, and besides the unchallenging work, no romantic relationships were on the horizon, except for one possibility. Lately, there was a kindling flame with one of my colleagues, and I sought to pursue it. His name was Scott. In the office, I noticed the way his eyes lingered on me just a second too long, and several times we flirted with each other around the coffee machine. There was chemistry between us, and he was a nice guy, the kind you want to know better. We had agreed to go out to dinner when he returned from his latest assignment, and during the waiting period, I had a few bouts of fantasy, even imagining a life with him. I scolded myself when that happened, for I didn't want to be like a schoolgirl with a whimsical infatuation.

My mother had always insisted that I marry a doctor or lawyer from a good Jewish family, although lately, any doctor or lawyer would do. When I was twenty-three, my mother made a casual mention of a ticking biological clock. Now it was a broken record, for my mother wanted more grandkids. Was that a necessity? My sister, Naomi, had two kids with a third on the way.

For me, the right relationship never happened. Boyfriends along the way had turned out to be shallow and self-centered. Some lacked ambition, whereas others were obsessed with climbing up corporate ladders, wishing to define themselves through collections of material possessions. A couple of relationships had seemed to be going in the right direction, but they ended as disasters. Maybe the breakups were all my fault? Perhaps I wasn't that easy to get along with? Conceivably, a future with Scott could be different. Or, was I running ahead of myself?

I turned from the window and entered the Real Media office, an open plan space of irregularly sized cubicles. Sometimes I wondered if the interior designer was a fan of Pablo Picasso, with a concept that odd-shaped working areas stimulated minds. Instead, it had created a battleground between journalists who constantly clashed over ownership of the larger irregular shaped boxes. My space was against a window, and I fought with my life to hold that territory.

One of Ernie's jobs was to maintain peace among the occupants. Not all were full-timers with Real Media, as some top journalists used those spaces as a base when they came to New York. With mass media being an ego-driven world, many times, other reporters made me feel like I was a bottom-feeder in the journalism food chain.

While there was an inner-office clash over spaces, most of the time, the cubicles were empty because the journalists were out on assignments. Ernie's office was a cubicle off in one corner, about four times the size of all the others. He had a round desk covered with stacks of papers, and much of the time, he was on the telephone barking orders at journalists or engaged in verbal fights with publishers. There was also a couch where he slept when working late at night, which was often.

Ernie Finkle was small, nervous, and energetic, a super-charged New York Jew. Because of his Albert Einstein style of hair, I imagined he was born in the middle of a lightning storm.

As I walked toward my cubicle, Ernie's voice boomed across the room. "Zipper, get over here." No one would applaud him for his diplomacy.

I continued moving to my work area, put my computer-bag down on my desk, and then sat down.

"Zipper, I need to see you," he yelled.

I counted to twenty and then casually walked over to Ernie's corner. "What's up?" I asked.

He glanced at my t-shirt and commented, "That place produces fake journalists."

"If you remember the last data, Northwestern School of Journalism ranks higher than your New York whatchamacallit cartoon-writing school."

"Ranking is subjective," he countered.

"So, give me something objective."

"Are you going to waste the entire morning? We got an urgent one."

"What is it?" Urgent was Ernie's middle name, along with a lot of others.

"Scott Roberts was the lead on this one, but it seems he's tied up in California. You're the next logical choice because no one else is available. Is your passport up to date?"

"Yes, I think so." The mention of Scott caught my attention.

"Good. You're flying out today."

"What?"

"You're going to Tegucigalpa."

"Where's that?" I knew it was some city south of Mexico.

"Honduras." He answered.

Ernie was directive, rude, and annoying, but I had worked with him long enough to know I could turn him down. Ultimately, it was my decision on what assignments I took.

"Why, Honduras?"

"Coffee," he said.

CHAPTER TWO

An hour later, I was back at my apartment, packing a carry-on bag. Because of time pressure, Ernie wasn't specific about the assignment, saying he'd give more details *en-route*.

That was typical Ernie. He encouraged his journalists to discover the heart of a story creatively. What he meant was to write something no matter what. All I knew was that the International Coffee Organization and the Specialty Coffee Association had sponsored the project, whoever they were. As Real Media was always short of funds, this project highly motivated Ernie. It was an opportunity to make connections with "deep-pocket companies."

I suspected Ernie had little knowledge of the details of the project. He had too many irons in the fire to keep up with everyone, and it was Scott Roberts who landed this one.

Scott had a background in Economics, and possessing a curious mind, he often came up with the unexpected. His articles had a different focus than mine. I wrote about the colors and textures of food, the aromas of meals, and the décor of eateries, with a healthy mix of restaurant personalities thrown in. Therefore, I had some concerns about the purpose of this Honduras coffee article. If it were for a financial journal, then my piece would be a disaster.

Ernie tried his best to calm me, but our discussion resulted in a heated debate. The assignment, as Ernie struggled to explain it, was to spend a day or two maximum in the mountains of Honduras and then write an article about coffee farmers. It was straight forward, a simple no brainer for anyone with my extraordinary qualifications, so he said.

Initially, the thought of being stranded with no apparent objective in some unknown country didn't appeal to me, and I let Ernie know it.

Then I did a double-take. I needed a break from the city, and what could be better than a few days in a warm country? Although, whoever thought of coffee from Honduras? Most people would tell you that coffee came from Brazil or Colombia. My fundamental question to Ernie was, why would anyone throw money away on such an uninteresting subject?

Ernie wasn't able to answer. All he knew was that this assignment helped the Real Media bottom line.

After further thought, I saw a bright lining in the clouds. Sharing the project with Scott was a motivator. I wanted to get to know him better, and why not do it over a shared project? And, this was about coffee, and I was a coffee lover, so the idea of the trip intrigued me.

Planning for two days in Honduras, I packed a pair of shorts, a couple of tops, underpants, and a bikini in case there was a pool at the hotel, or even better a swim in the Caribbean Sea. Was Honduras even on the Caribbean Sea?

I changed my Northwestern t-shirt for a lime green one. The color of the shirt was similar to the color of my eyes. Everyone else in the family had blue or hazel eyes, and the theory of my mother was that the lime-green had slipped into the gene pool back in the middle ages when a traveling salesman had visited our ancestors' Slavic village. On the front of the shirt was the image of a colorful bouquet and small letters under the flowers saying, 'Home & Garden.' It came from a trade show on home appliances and garden tools, where I had written an article.

I went to the bathroom and quickly brushed my long, unruly brunette hair and applied a light cream nude lipstick to my lips and then wondered if it made me look like I just came back from the dead. Somehow the lipstick contrasted with my green t-shirt and the indigo jacket. One glance at my watch and color scheme didn't matter. A basic rule of travel is that flights don't wait. I was cutting it close.

As I quickly headed toward my front door, there was a knock. I opened the door, and it was Stanley Schultz, my neighbor, also known as Stan.

Uneasy to see him, I said, "Hey Stan, how's it going?" Discussions with Stan could last forever, and I needed to rush to the airport.

"Not good," he said, his fist trembling, tightened over something.

Stan was almost eighty years old, had penetrating gray eyes, and stood slightly hunched over. I figured he had spent too many years stooped over a typewriter and then a laptop. Stan had been a highly recognized journalist and had won the Pulitzer Prize for his reporting on corruption in the banking industry.

As a friend of the family, he helped in finding my apartment when I first moved to New York. It was in the same building as his, on the south end of East Harlem, just on the boundary with the Upper East End. It was a perfect location because of the quick subway ride to the Real Media office, and all the other media companies around Grand Central Station. Of most importance to Stan, the apartment was close to the nearby synagogue on Lexington Avenue, which also delighted my mother.

Stan was my mentor, and he relentlessly challenged me to do something more significant with my life, while reminding me that writing trivial stories about food-joints was beneath the dignity of a professional journalist.

Seeing Stan's trembling hand, I asked, "What's wrong?"

"Sarah, I need you to do something for me?"

I took a deep breath. There was a flight to catch. "Sorry, Stan, but I'm pressed for time."

"This won't take long." He reached toward me and opened his hand, and in it was a flash drive. He said, "Take this. It's imperative. I've been working on something that will save the world."

I smiled. Ever since first meeting him, he was working on something critical, and retirement hadn't stopped him from being an investigative reporter. I liked Stan and even adored him. He always had words of advice. We were both Jewish, and that gave us a unique bond. However, he was much more the practitioner than I. He went to the synagogue every Saturday and observed every religious holiday. I didn't have time for all that, but he brought me back to my roots, and that was appreciated. At the same time, I realized that most of his investigations were groundless conspiracy fabrications.

"What's going to save the world?" I asked, looking at the flash drive in his hand.

He grabbed my hand and placed the flash drive in it. "Take this and hide it in a secure place, but don't open it and read it. It will suck you into something terrible."

I reluctantly held it and asked, "What's so terrible?"

"I shouldn't tell you, but someone is trying to take over the world, to control everyone. I can't prove it yet, but I'm almost there. Well, not quite, but almost. I mean the entire world." His hands stretched out above his shoulders to emphasize the point.

I held back a laugh. How many times had I heard this from Stan? "Okay, I'll keep it, but what am I supposed to do with it?"

"Nothing for now. My life is in danger, and if they knew you had this information, they'd come after you. Just keep it safe."

"They who?"

"You don't need to know."

"Okay, but I've got to run." I bent down and kissed Stan on the cheek and said, "*Mazel tov.* I'll see you in a couple of days when I get back."

Stan blushed. "Do what I say about that flash drive. And, make sure you say your prayers. And, go to synagogue with me on Shabbat."

"Okay."

Stan turned, scurried down the hallway, and I put the flash drive into one of the pockets of my computer-bag. I shut the door to my apartment, pulled out the handle of my carry-on bag, and sprinted for the elevator.

Besides the anxiety of being late for my flight, uneasiness filled me when realizing I was on a trip to an unknown place, which was just a bit outside my comfort zone.

CHAPTER THREE

After eight hours of travel to Tegucigalpa, I left the airplane and walked down the stairway. The sun was low in the sky and reflected off the tarmac with engulfing heat. I followed the passengers to the airport terminal.

It was less hot inside the terminal building, where I followed signs that said, 'Salida,' which I remembered meant 'Exit' from my high school Spanish courses. It also helped to have 'Exit' written in smaller letters on the sign.

I passed through customs where they checked my passport, a simple affair. U.S. citizens didn't need a visa if staying for less than ninety days. I didn't have a checked bag, but stopped in the baggage claim area, took out my phone and dialed Ernie's number. I was relieved when it rang, not knowing if roaming on my U.S. phone would work in Honduras.

The phone rang five times, and he answered, "Ernie here."

"This is Sarah. I'm now in Honduras."

"Good," he replied.

"Now, what am I supposed to do?"

"Scott Roberts has all the information on the assignment."

"I already know that."

"I can't get a hold of him. He's gone off the map, and honestly, I'm not a hundred percent sure about logistics."

"You mean like who to meet with?"

"Don't worry. It will work out."

"That's helpful," I sneered. "Sounds like you're zero percent sure, which means you don't have a clue where I'm staying or what I'm supposed to be doing."

He fired back, "Not really, but we have the funding. So don't be difficult. Just wing it."

"What does that mean?"

"They may have sent a driver. Did you find him?"

"I'm not out in the general public area yet, and how was I supposed to know about a driver? I'm not clairvoyant."

"Relax, Zipper. Someone might be there."

"Might?"

"Well, maybe," he said. "If no one's there, just go find a hotel until we get this sorted out."

"Ernie, that's very comforting. You're a real jewel."

"Stay in touch," he said, and the line went dead.

I moved the phone away from my ear and stared at it. "You've got to be kidding," I exclaimed out loud. Two people passing by turned their heads and stared at me.

Ernie was known to have pulled off crazy stunts, but this one beat them all. This wasn't a picnic, like flying to Kansas. It was an entirely different country, hours away from the U.S., where I had a minimal understanding of the language. It was sending me off with the promise of, "I'll let you know when you get there." Well, he hadn't.

I decided the only course of action was to do what Ernie suggested, to find a hotel, and wait it out until I heard from him. And, for sure, it wouldn't be a flea-bag place. It would be the best hotel in town, one with a large swimming pool where I could lounge around in my bikini and drink one of those exotic tropical drinks.

Then, I smiled, realizing this could be a perfect holiday.

I lifted the computer bag onto my shoulder, towed the carry-on bag behind me, and headed out into the general public area where a crowd of people waited for passengers.

The first thing I noticed was that most people were shorter than me. Second, most had dark hair and Hispanic features. Well, what do you expect? You're in Honduras. You're on a fabulous, unexpected holiday. And most of all, Ernie is an imbecile.

There was a line of men in dark suits, white shirts, and dark ties holding small signs with neatly printed names, just like you find in airports all over the world. These were the pre-arranged chauffeurs who drove people to destinations. I certainly wished I had a destination, and the question of finding a hotel followed that thought.

I glanced at the names on the signs, Gomez, Thompson, Schmidt, a United Nations hodge-podge, and then I saw a sign held by a man that said, Scott Roberts. My heart jumped when I saw the name.

The name had been sloppily written by a worn-out permanent marker on a faded and stained piece of cardboard, as though someone ripped it from an old box in the backyard.

Scott Roberts. What was this? I hadn't seen him on the flight. All I knew was that Ernie didn't have a clue what was going on. In any case, someone was waiting for Scott.

I looked at the person holding the sign. He was much taller than the rest of the drivers, maybe six foot three or even six-four. With light brown hair and blue eyes, he stood out because of his worn khaki-colored Bermuda shorts, sandals, and a t-shirt. A quick age guess put him in his early to mid-thirties. On the t-shirt was written, *Café La Fuerza*. He certainly didn't look like a coffee farmer, but what were they supposed to look like?

The guy was gazing past me at other passengers, so I walked up to him and said, "I know I probably don't look like a Scott, but I might be the person you are seeking. I'm replacing him."

He froze for a moment with a worried look on his face, and then he relaxed, smiled, and in a perfect American accent, said, "That's a surprise, but if you're a writer, then follow me."

"I write," I said.

He nodded, reached down, and took the handle of my carry-on bag, slipped the computer bag from my shoulder, and transferred it to his, and then he led the way out of the airport terminal.

Just outside the front door of the terminal, he flicked the cardboard sign into a trash can. "Looks like Scott isn't a Scott," he said.

We walked along the airport sidewalk, and I tried to keep up with his long, athletic strides. He headed in the direction of a black limousine, stepped in front of it, and I had a quick hope of cruising the city as a dignitary.

Instead of stopping at the car, he moved into the street and proceeded toward the other side.

I waited to let a car pass while thinking there might be an assignment after all, whatever it was? At the same time, the idea of the swimming pool and the exotic drink regrettably slipped from my plans.

CHAPTER FOUR

The tall chauffeur was now in the middle of the busy road, dodging cars. I zigzagged while trying to stay up with him. All of a sudden, my timing was off when going around the back of a moving pickup truck. The driver of the next car had to slam his breaks as he honked his horn and yelled something unintelligible. Sometimes it was beneficial if you didn't understand a foreign language, although here, I was the foreigner.

The tall chauffeur seemed to have understood it and gave a hard stare at the driver of the car, who sunk below the steering wheel. I made it to the other side of the road as my chauffeur hurried on. I didn't feel like running after him like a dog following its master, so I deliberately slowed my pace. He'd just have to wait for me. What did he expect? I was a foreigner and hadn't learned the trickery of car dodging on a chaotic street. Most of all, he was just the driver.

That gave me a moment to think. It was evident my chauffeur was expecting Scott, and he was surprised to see me instead. Yet, the chauffeur didn't seem upset about that. His bosses might react differently, or whoever was behind this project?

Now, the pressing question was, what was the specific assignment? Mister *know-it-all* Ernie had blown it. If these worldwide coffee associations were behind this, then there must be documentation defining Scott's mandate. Those organizations wouldn't indiscriminately dish out money to send a New York journalist on a joy ride to a Central American country. Somehow I'd have to get my hands on the project documents to find out more.

I thought of Stan Schultz and how he might handle this. Stan said a reporter should always stay in charge. Sometimes you needed to act naïvely while asking carefully crafted questions. At other times, you took the offensive. He said, whatever you do, don't be like Barney Fife, the deputy sheriff from Mayberry on the Andy Griffith show. When Stan used that illustration, it showed the historical longevity of his experience. What he was saying was never to come across as half-witted.

But that was precisely the situation I was in, and it certainly felt uncomfortable. And where was Scott? One telephone conversation with him and I'd know what's going on.

Then I wondered if paranoia was filling my brain over something that wasn't that big a deal. Many times I had stepped into unknown situations and came away with terrific articles. I was a capable writer. Once you had a sense of what the client wanted, you could mold and bend the story from there. Ernie had said to relax, but that came from the most unrelaxed human being on the face of the planet.

The tall driver led me into a parking lot, and past a line of cars until we came to an open-topped Jeep looking like a relic from an ancient military campaign. He put my bags on the rear seat and pulled out a rope and a small tarp.

"What's that for," I asked.

"In this city, there are master thieves. They can snatch the watch right off your wrist. Occasionally they'll remove your hand to get the watch. Their knives can slice through any rope in a second, but with a bit of luck, we should make it."

"A bit of luck?" I exclaimed.

He had a slight grin. "There's something else to consider. This country gets torrential downpours, so I'll cover your bags." He placed the tarp over my bags and then securely tied everything down with the rope.

I looked at the open Jeep and asked, "And, what about us?"

"What do you mean?"

"The torrential rain."

"Did you bring a rain jacket?" He replied.

"Ah, well . . . no."

He smiled. "Then, what about a swimsuit?"

"Funny," I mocked. Was this guy dense? I hoped he wasn't a sexist moron.

"Get in," he directed.

I climbed into the rider's seat and looked for a seat belt, but couldn't find one. He sat in the driver's seat, reached under the dashboard, pulled out some wires, twisted two together, and touched the two with a third wire. A cracking spark shot out of the cables and the engine sputtered to life. The Jeep needed a muffler.

Over the extreme noise of the car's engine, I yelled, "What's your name?"

He looked over and loudly said, "Luke Cotton. What's yours?"

"Sarah Zipper."

Glancing toward me, with a raised tone, he asked, "Did you say Zipper?"

"Do you have a problem with that?"

"Not a bit. It's just ah, unusual."

"It's Jewish," I shouted. "And did you say Cotton? It's a bit, ah, different."

He grinned. "That's right. Goes back to 1185, where some guy known as 'the builder of churches' worked for an English king. He came from Cotham in Yorkshire, and his name got simplified to Cotton. And there you go."

Oh, this should be really good, I said to myself, a driver with a vague notion of history.

With a louder voice, he asked, "What happened to Scott?"

I yelled back. "He got delayed by another assignment."

"Do you work for him?"

"Same media group." How could I explain that in Ernie's organization, you hardly ever worked for or even with anyone? Each journalist was on their own unless you asked a colleague to check what you'd written.

"Are you up for this?" Luke asked.

"A piece of cake," I replied over the noise of the exhaust pipes, remembering Stan's advice to stay in charge, although the churning sensation in my stomach told me I didn't have a clue what I was doing.

The gears of the Jeep made a hostile grinding noise when Luke shifted into reverse. The Jeep backed up, and the gears crunched again when he shifted into first. The Jeep jumped forward, and we headed toward the parking lot exit.

"How far are we going?" I shouted.

"About two hours from here."

"Two hours in this thing?"

He yelled, "Pray, we make it."

CHAPTER FIVE

After leaving the city, the scenery quickly changed to rich green vegetation, villages, and small farms with vegetable gardens and banana plantations. Forests and jungles pushed in against the farms, as though in a land-rights battle.

Already, I was taking mental notes of the countryside to pad my article for the coffee organizations. My experience was that padding is an excellent skill to have when one is ignorant of a subject.

We traveled two hours on a reasonably good highway, and then Luke turned onto a bumpy dirt road. Luckily it didn't rain during the trip, although the wind devastated my long thick hair. It would take weeks to untangle.

I regretted not bringing earplugs, wondering if I would ever correctly hear again without a perpetual buzzing in my ears.

The dirt road was bumpy as it snaked into the jungle.

Because of the loud noise of cars and wind on the highway, it was impossible to converse. Now I was able to ask questions. With a loud voice, I asked, "Where are we going?"

Luke yelled back, "La Fuerza coffee farm."

"Where is it?"

"About five miles up this road. Hang on because this isn't exactly a super-highway."

The darkness of the evening descended, and Luke turned on the Jeep's headlights. During a few small stretches, he accelerated, but much of the way, it was slow rough going. I perpetually swung back and forth in my seat when the Jeep dipped through frequent pot-holes.

Eventually, we drove past a wooden sign with 'La Fuerza Coffee Farm' painted on it, and we went up a long driveway until Luke stopped the Jeep in front of a shack. One dim lightbulb hung above the porch. A teeming mass of insects circled it, like zillions of tiny dive-bombers seeking a landing site. In the darkness, I saw other shacks of various sizes, along with a big building that looked like a warehouse.

Luke stated, "Well, here we are, home at last."

I stared at the insects and then into the jungle darkness, wondering if it was possible to order a taxi in this area of the world. Wouldn't it be better to commute in the morning from a five-star hotel in Tegucigalpa?

Luke got out of the Jeep, untied the ropes from my bags and carried them toward the front door of the shack. I followed. He opened a squeaky screen door, and we went inside.

It was a simple room with wooden slat floors. A single bed with a yellow mosquito net was against one wall, and a worn-out couch sat against the opposite wall. A door led to a primitive-looking bathroom that contained a shower with a torn plastic curtain, a toilet, and a stained sink. A musty odor seeped out of the walls.

"What is this place?" I gasped while thinking it wasn't exactly my fantasized posh hotel with the pool and colorful tropical drinks.

"It's our guest quarters," Luke replied. "Sorry we can't do better."

He placed my bags on top of a table and said, "It's best to keep them up here and not on the floor."

"Why's that?" I asked.

"Cockroaches, especially at night, enough to carry your bed away. I'll get you some bug-spray that will help a bit, hopefully."

There was that *hopefully* word again. Instead of finding reassurance, a heavy uneasiness returned. Typically, I wasn't a fussy person, having seen rats in New York restaurant kitchens, but the idea of cockroaches transporting me into the jungle was beyond creepy.

Still wondering about my purpose in being here. I asked, "Is there someone who could help clarify my assignment? I have a few questions, and it would help make sure I'm on the right track."

Luke smiled. "It's outlined in the contract. Scott was already working on it."

I hoped Ernie had spoken with Scott. "Could you let me know if anything has changed, or if there's anything that's a top priority for my article?"

"Article?"

"About the coffee, ah . . . operations."

"The mandate is to write a series of articles."

"Oh?" In saying that, I was afraid I wasn't following Stan Shultz's advice about not coming across as a halfwit.

Luke frowned and looked at me with concern in his eyes. "Are you actually a writer?"

"Yes."

"It sounds like you aren't sure about the goal of this job."

"I work with Scott and am the most qualified person to replace him." It was a deflection to his statement. I added, "I'm just asking for some specifics to ensure we fulfill client requirements."

"Okay, we can go through all that at dinner. I have to check on a few things. Meet me in the dining area in fifteen minutes. It's two buildings over." He motioned with his hand toward the door and then to the left.

Luke left the room, and as soon as he shut the squeaky front door, I immediately took out my phone to call Ernie. There was no signal, which was inconceivable because my phone was my lifeline to the world.

I was not the type to have a panic attack, but my stomach felt hollow with the sudden reality of being cut off from humanity, combined with having little knowledge of my mission. This place was beyond my worst nightmare.

And, who was this Luke, and didn't bad things happen to visitors in this part of the world? What was that bone-head Ernie thinking by rushing me into this insane assignment? I imagined the torture I would put him through if I ever made it back to New York.

CHAPTER SIX

Fifteen minutes later, I stepped out of the moldy hut and ducked under the swarm of insects buzzing around the hanging light. As I turned left, darkness greeted me, and strange sounds arose from the jungle, a combination of birds and insects, and maybe something else? Perhaps out there was an army of cockroaches formulating plans to transport my bed into the jungle? I fantasized about what would happen when they carried me there. The whole situation gave me goosebumps.

Dim lights from two other shacks gave enough visibility to make it to the dining area. It was a rectangular wooden building with long rickety-looking picnic tables. At the end of the room was a kitchen area where a man washed dishes.

Luke sat at one of the tables, and he spoke with a man seated across from him. Luke raised his hand, motioning for me to join them.

I sat down next to Luke, who said, "Let me introduce you to Manuel Espinosa, who manages this cooperative. Manuel, this is Sarah Zipper, the journalist who is replacing Scott Roberts."

I guessed Manuel was in his late forties. He had dark, weather-beaten skin and lean muscular arms.

"How do you do," Manuel said, speaking with a Spanish accent.

"It's nice to meet you," I replied. Who in this modern era says, how do you do?

The man working in the kitchen area carried a tray to our table. He placed plates in front of us and then laid out another dish with a stack of flour tortillas and a pot full of beans. Then, he came with a cluster of yellow bananas still attached to the stalk, as though just cut from the tree.

"It's simple, but filling," Luke said, passing the tortilla plate to me.

The last food I had eaten was the meager meal served on my flight. I took a tortilla, positioned it on my plate, and then covered it with a helping of beans. Once Luke and Manuel served themselves, I took a bite, and it was tasty and filling. Being a restaurant writer, I conjured up descriptions of thin toasted flatbread, melting in your mouth, complemented by aromatic, spicy red beans providing a perfect balance to the tortilla, both visually and to the taste. It was wonderfully nourishing. Although, on the flip side, a steady diet of this would quickly become tedious.

As we ate, I said, "Scott Roberts got hung up in Los Angeles, so this morning I picked up the assignment. Can you provide details on the parameters?"

"What's your understanding?" Luke asked.

I hesitated, realizing that Luke was a man of few words by answering a question with a question, which was definitely a disadvantage to me. "Broadly, it's to write about coffee in Honduras." Broadly was the appropriate word, the best I could find, for there was nothing else to go on. I wondered if I would make a good politician, sounding like knowing everything when, in fact, you knew nothing.

Luke grinned. "I'm guessing someone quickly threw you into this."

"Yes, but that's okay."

"Okay? Are you a writer, like for newspapers and magazines and stuff like that?"

"For the past six years, my pieces have appeared in media all over the country, and *stuff* like that."

"Media? What does that mean?"

"I'm primarily a restaurant and culinary writer in addition to covering human interest stories that go along with food. Coffee is food." I found myself becoming aggressive, but why be so defensive to a guy who uses words like *stuff*?

He said, "This has been in the works for some time, and we recently got the funding. In the coffee trade, there are industry journals targeting coffee professionals. That's a specific group of people with advanced knowledge of the business, and some writers know how to speak to that audience. With them, it's primarily technical stuff. Your task is to write for a different audience, one that your company, Real Media, seems to know how to address."

"Which audience is that?" I asked.

"We need a series of articles that will be read by millions of coffee drinkers, people on the street. These articles will go into a nationally syndicated newsfeed."

The idea of the newsfeed caught my attention. Several times I had written pieces that went into newspapers across the country. "Which national newsfeeds?"

"In the human interest sections of Sunday newspapers, whatever they call it. It's those sections that talk about culture and food and travel, and things like that, and not the business section."

That gave relief, as writing business articles was not my talent. "So, what's the specific topic?" I wondered why Scott would be interested in a project like this.

Luke replied, "Coffee is a hugely consumed commodity, but most people never consider the origin. They don't understand that most of the coffee they drink comes from small farms around the world, whether in South America, Africa, Asia, or Central America. The people producing coffee tend to be extremely poor, whereas consumers in the developed world are willing to pay exorbitantly for a cup of coffee."

That was true. Often, I paid a bundle for lattes in New York coffee shops. "Exorbitantly is an appropriate word, but good coffee is worth the price."

Luke smiled. "I agree that it's worth it. , but there's an imbalance, which leads to the question of who benefits from the profit? We want you to write about the movement of coffee as it goes from producer to consumer. It's to give readers a better appreciation of a commodity they consume every day. In the end, we want more money to flow to the needy coffee farmers."

That was totally different from Ernie's explanation, but the new description of the assignment was interesting. For sure, Ernie had been in the dark on this one. I needed to speak with Scott to find out what groundwork he had done. Was he still working on this, and how could we collaborate? Scott was a good guy, but would he be upset knowing I was now in the mix? In any case, it would be reassuring to hear his voice. "I'll need more information on this," I said. "Is there anyone I can speak with?"

"You'll speak with many people," Luke replied.

I realized my question was odd. The long trip and change of environment had been tiring and was messing with my thinking. "What I meant is that I need a principal person."

"That's me," he said. "I'll be your counterpart through some of this project, maybe not all of it, because of my responsibilities, but you can run any major questions through me. If I don't have the answers, I can direct you to the people that do."

"Where do I start?" I asked.

"Tomorrow morning, Manuel will show you around the farm. During the coming days, we'll follow the trail of coffee from the farm to the consumer. Be ready to travel."

The idea of travel was a surprise, and I wondered what that meant, but rather than questioning Luke on everything he said, I replied, "Sounds good to me." At least I now had an outline for the assignment, and it was far more challenging than Ernie's "one or two days in Honduras." The possibility of drinking good coffee along the way was a bonus.

One problem might be the meager amount of clothing I had in my carryon bag. Instead of Ernie's quick visit to a picturesque coffee farm, this trip would go to more places, and it might take longer than a couple of days. Living in the same clothing over many days was not a cheery thought.

We finished the meal, and I asked, "I'm not picking up a phone signal. Is there a phone I could use, or any way to connect to the internet?"

"There's a fixed-line phone in our office and also an internet modem. You can pick up the WI-FI signal from your guest cottage. There isn't a password."

The sound of *guest-cottage* gave a lovely sensation, with the dreamy image of a quaint stone house in the English countryside surrounded by a white picket fence, and pink roses running up the side of the door. Instead, my shack was the front-line battleground of the cockroach world. Luke hadn't mentioned mosquitos, which were akin to the air force of the insect army.

After finishing the meal, Luke handed me a can of bug spray, and a small bottle of mosquito repellant. "These might help," he said.

The word '*might*' was not reassuring. His use of terms such as *might* and *hopefully* and *stuff* were anything but definitive.

I agreed to meet Manuel at six in the morning and then went back to my guest shack. I held the can of bug spray in my right hand and sprayed around the floor of the room. Then I looked at the label on the can and saw a skull and crossbones, and underneath in large letters was written, *Atención Peligrosa*, with a lot of small print under that. I surmised this substance was not meant to be inhaled.

I then covered myself with the mosquito repellent, which was sticky and oily, and smelled similar to turpentine

After removing my laptop from its bag, I turned it on, picked up a weak Wi-Fi signal, and then went to my email. There was a long list of messages, but one caught my eye. It was from Ernie, and the title was, 'URGENT!"

I opened it and read,

Sarah, I've got bad news to send. Scott Roberts is assumed dead in Long Beach, California. He was shot. I'm trying to acquire details. Get back to me as quickly as possible. Sorry to send you this news. Ernie

I read it a second time, and then again. After each reading, it was like being hit by a hammer in the chest. I took a breath and wondered if this was a joke. That would be perverse humor and not Ernie's style. It seemed unreal.

Feeling speechless, I sat down on the old couch. This was impossible to comprehend and a jumble of thoughts raced through my mind. It was as though a tornado suddenly swept up my expectations. For sure, this news couldn't be real.

I thought of Scott. He was so likable, and in some silly way, I had pinned my future on him. What happened? I knew that he was intelligent and good with numbers. Some areas of Los Angeles were dangerous, at least from my understanding. Was it also like that in Long Beach? What was he doing there? Was he merely in the wrong place at the wrong time? Or was it a deliberate act? I needed more information and especially more specifics on what he was investigating.

I tried to send an email to Ernie, but the connection was slow, and the message kept timing out. That left me frustrated, and the reality of this assignment made me angry.

This was too much. What was Ernie thinking, and who were the people that put me in this dump? Anger rose in me like hot waves.

I thought of going to the office, where there was a phone but didn't know my way around the farm's buildings. So, I left the shack and went back to the dining hall to see if Luke or Manuel were still there. The place was empty. I'd have to wait until the following morning to call Ernie.

Back in the guest-shack, I set the alarm on my phone for five-thirty in the morning, went to bed, my soul suffocating with grief. I endured a fitful night with little sleep while my mind scrolled through Jewish prayers looking for comfort.

CHAPTER SEVEN

My alarm sounded, and I looked at my phone. It was half-past five, and I had to meet Manuel Espinosa in thirty minutes. I turned on the light, and several cockroaches scampered for cracks in the floor, which gave me the creeps. At least the bed hadn't been moved.

That was immediately followed by the reality of Scott's death, which still was unbelievable. It gave a terrible feeling of hollowness, with the loss of a man I wanted to know better. We could have been friends and lovers and life partners and all the rest, but all hopes dissipated after reading a short email. I needed to contact Ernie. There was a two hour time difference between Honduras and New York, so it was seven-thirty in the morning in New York.

After a quick shower and then getting dressed in the same clothing I had traveled in, I skipped my routine of applying minimal makeup. My hair looked like rats had nested there for the night and I almost broke my hairbrush when attempting to undo the tangles. I gladly left my sleeping quarters and walked toward the dining area. The sun was still below the horizon. Upon entering the dining hall, I saw Manuel Espinosa and Luke Cotton. They were holding coffee mugs.

Luke smiled and said, "Good morning. It looks like you may have had a short night. How about some coffee?"

"Yes, please," I said, knowing my description of the night was horrendous and anything but *short.*

Luke went to the kitchen area and came back holding a coffee mug in one hand and a French press in the other. He pushed the filter down and then poured coffee into the cup and handed it to me. "Black, or with cream and sugar?" He asked.

"Just black." I took a sip and immediately tasted subtle flavors of tropical fruit and caramel. "That's amazing," I said. It gave a slight sense of comfort.

"The coffee from farms in this area is *excelente*," Manuel said, with a grin on his face.

"With coffee like that, I look forward to this assignment, but first, could I use your phone to call my boss in New York? I still don't have a phone signal, and the internet wasn't working very well. Something urgent has come up, and I need to speak with him."

Luke said, "For sure. Let's go to the office."

He led me out of the dining hall, and we went to the largest building on the compound. Inside, men loaded large brown burlap sacks into a truck. The pungent smell of green coffee beans filled the room. It was nothing like the scent of the final roasted product.

Luke pointed. "Those are bags of green coffee beans, each weighing sixty-nine kilos, or a hundred and fifty-two pounds. They are driven to the port, put in containers, and shipped. Most of it ends up in the U.S."

One man used a handheld trolly to move a bag, struggling to pull it up a ramp onto the truck. Two other men carried bags on their shoulders.

"That looks like hard work," I stated, with my mind somewhere else. I hoped my comment had come across as genuine.

"They work their butts off. On the front end of coffee production, it's nothing but toil with little reward. We'll have a chance to talk about that, but first, let me get you to the phone."

At the back of the warehouse was a small office, and inside a desk covered with a mass of papers.

Luke pointed to a black phone on the desk and then gave me the international dialing code for the U.S. He said, "I'll be out there if you need me." He walked out of the office.

I dialed Ernie's number, and he answered it on the fourth ring. "Ernie here," he said.

"It's Sarah. What happened to Scott?"

"The story is still developing," With Ernie, everything was a story. "I heard about it an hour after you arrived in Tegucigalpa and tried to call you but couldn't get through."

"There's no phone signal here," I said. "A driver was waiting when I arrived, and now I'm about two hours away from the airport, on a coffee plantation or farm, or whatever you call it. What do you know about

Scott?" Ernie wasn't aware that Scott and I had an attraction to each other.

"There's not much at this point. The FBI called me, Agent Cortez, who asked what Scott was doing in Long Beach. All I know is that he was working on this coffee assignment and not much more. As you've seen, I can't keep up with twenty or more unruly journalists. My inability to answer the FBI agent's questions made me look stupid."

"What do you think I've looked like down here? You gave me nothing to go on. And the living situation here is abominable. But that's beside the point. What about Scott?"

"It's an ongoing case, so the FBI Agent didn't reveal much. All I know is that it happened in the hotel parking lot where Scott was staying. Two shots into his body and one to the head. Then, he was thrown into a van and driven away. The hotel security camera caught it, and it seems there were a couple of witnesses. The FBI agent was not forthcoming. It's still nighttime in California, so I have to wait a few hours before calling Agent Cortez."

"Wait a second. You said the FBI. Why are they handling this and not the Long Beach police?"

"That's a strange one. Agent Cortez said they are working with the Long Beach Police Department, but the FBI is taking the lead. I couldn't get much out of him, but I'll keep trying."

I knew the FBI got involved in cases of terrorism, organized crime, and a bunch of other things. "Do you think this coffee assignment had anything to do with the shooting?"

"That's a long shot. Why shoot anyone over coffee?"

"Was Scott working on anything else?"

"Oh, probably. You journalists are always multitasking."

"Is it possible to get to his notes?"

"Who knows? Maybe there's something on his laptop. I'm sure the police or FBI now have it and are looking into it."

"What about the cloud?" I asked, thinking about the dedicated cloud site for Real Media journalists. That's where we were supposed to keep our drafts and final submissions. Lacking discipline, I rarely did that, instead, handwriting my notes on notepads, and then drafting the story on my laptop. Ernie wasn't strict about keeping to the rules, as long as submissions were on time.

He said, "I'll take a look at his cloud account. Scott was organized, so maybe we can find out what he was up to."

I was silent for a moment. "This is horrible, isn't it?"

"Unbelievable. It hasn't sunk in." He waited, as though searching for words. "Try and get through the day, or even take time off if you need it. It's tough to work with this hanging over our heads."

"Thanks, Ernie, but this assignment might be a good diversion to keep my mind on something else. By the way, it looks like they want a series of articles, which may take longer than we initially thought."

"Then go for it, but stay safe."

We hung up, and the oppressive reality of Ernie's description of Scott in Long Beach began to take effect, like a massive boulder sinking into a lake.

I somehow had to make it through the day. Even more significant, I needed more information on what happened to him, and why?

* * *

I left the office and walked back into the central part of the warehouse, where the men were loading the bags of green coffee beans into the truck. The acrid smell of green coffee still filled the room, but that now combined with the odor of working men.

Luke worked alongside the men, loading bags of coffee beans without the use of a trolley. With one swift motion, he lifted a bag to his shoulders and swiftly carried it up the ramp into the truck. The guy certainly had the strength to handle one hundred and fifty-two pounds like it was the weight of a tire.

When he walked out of the truck, he waved and came over to me. He wore a tank-top t-shirt that clung to his broad chest. The sinewy muscles on his arms were equal to any of the exercise fanatics hanging out in my gym back in New York, at least those going for strength and agility rather than massive bulk.

I noticed a round scar on his left shoulder, close to his clavicle.

He said, "It's tough work."

"That's some heavy lifting you're doing."

Luke laughed. "It's a way to get a workout, but these men are the ones to be admired. They keep it up all day."

"I'm impressed," I stated.

"For these workers, it feeds their families, and I wish we could pay them more. You'll find this same kind of work going on all over the world, people who live below the poverty line growing, preparing, and carrying coffee, all for the enjoyment of others."

The tone of his voice conveyed sincere compassion.

"Did you get through with the call?" He asked.

I hesitated for a moment, wondering if I should tell him about Scott, but decided otherwise. It was too painful to disclose. And, I didn't know Luke, so caution was best. "I spoke with my boss, to see if he was okay with the multiple articles, rather than writing the one story about coffee in Honduras. He said to go for it, so as of now, I'm all yours. Where do we start?"

With the back of his hand, Luke wiped sweat from his forehead. "I need to get a couple of trucks loaded, to drive to the port tomorrow. Manuel will show you around the farm. You'll find him in the building behind the warehouse. I suggest you take a look around to get first impressions and we can work out a strategy later on."

"Sounds good."

Luke went back to loading coffee bags into the truck. I exited the warehouse, walked along the side of it toward the back, and saw another building about the same size as the warehouse. After finding a door, I went inside and saw ten women standing by long tables. On the tables were mounds of green coffee beans.

Manuel stood next to one of the women while pointing to one of the mounds. I went to him, and he smiled. The women glanced at me, but then quickly went back to work.

He said, "I'll show you around the farm, but first you should observe what's going on here. These women are selecting coffee beans."

I watched the woman next to Manual, who had a flat layer of beans in front of her, and with quick hands, she picked out a few beans, placing them into different piles.

"You mean they pick the beans one by one?" I asked.

"That's correct. The beans have already been sorted by size, but this is a final quality control to separate out any bad beans."

"It looks tedious." I couldn't see myself doing this day after day.

"It can be monotonous. Coffee is a seasonal crop, so they do this for five or six months out of the year. Their pay is not much, but they appreciate having the work. Unemployment and poverty are realities."

I watched them while my thoughts drifted. It felt like sleepwalking in a daydream if such a thing were even possible. I tried to force myself to quit thinking about Scott, knowing I was on this coffee farm for a purpose. I needed background information for the articles.

Manuel continued, "Once the beans are separated, they go into the large burlap bags, which are loaded into trucks in the warehouse. Let me show you where coffee is grown."

He led me outside, and we walked on a path through a cluster of trees. The way opened to hills covered with rows of coffee bushes, each about eight to ten feet tall.

I found myself breathing heavily and asked, "What's the elevation here?"

He laughed. "Do you live at sea level?"

"New York City."

"You will feel the difference. In Honduras, coffee grows between nine hundred to sixteen hundred meters, about three thousand to over five thousand feet. We have a temperate climate, and Arabica coffee grows best in those conditions. We have several varieties of coffee. Location and soil conditions change the taste of coffee as you move around the country. Of course, the coffee from our farm and our neighbors is the best." He laughed with a broad smile. "Now, we must go a little higher."

I followed Manuel up a path, and my breathing became heavier. Finally, we came to rows of coffee bushes where men and women picked red beans from the plants. The reality of Scott's death flashed through my mind, as well as the words of Ernie when he questioned, "Who would shoot anyone over coffee?" It seemed such a farfetched scenario.

Manuel said, "We selectively pick from November to April, taking the larger red coffee cherries, while waiting for the green ones to mature."

"Cherries?"

"Not like from cherry trees, but it is what we call these."

"How do you get green coffee beans from that?"

"In the coffee business, it is called washing. The green beans are inside those cherries. I will show you later, but first, I must tell you that the best coffee is grown in the shade of trees." He pointed to the jungle and said, "The shade over there gives more time for the beans to mature, where they take in minerals and nutrients. The flavor is more full-bodied than the beans grown in the open rows. And, of course, over there, the jungle is preserved."

"So, each coffee has a different taste."

"Exactly. It is like wine. If you taste a Cabernet Sauvignon from France or Chile or California, they are different from each other. It is similar with coffee."

"Do you know African coffee, like from Ethiopia?" I thought of the coffee I roasted at home.

He smiled. "Ethiopian coffee is excellent, but so are others from African countries like Rwanda, Burundi, Tanzania, and Kenya. Each has a unique taste. In those countries, the coffee growers work just as hard as we do. They are poor, like our people. In Honduras, there are over one hundred thousand families growing coffee, and over ninety percent of them do this on tiny farms. It's like that throughout the world."

"Have you been to those countries?"

"Luke and I go there. Our association supports coffee farms and villages in some of those places, just like here in Honduras."

"Association?"

"We have a nonprofit organization backed by church groups."

"What do you mean by church groups backing coffee farms? How does that work?" I had never heard of such a strange thing. What would these religious people think of next?

Manuel laughed. "It doesn't always work, but we try our best. We are simply attempting to help improve the lives of the less fortunate. Now, let me take you to the washing station."

He added a new dimension to my article, a potential humanitarian component. That was my strength, portraying the human side of a story, entertaining readers, and even persuading them with trivial content, but was there something deeper here?

The mention of church groups brought images of religious cults from the United States ending up in South American jungles. Had Scott been working this angle and did that put him in danger?

It seemed farfetched, but I had to explore every possibility, because for now I had nothing to go on.

An uneasy feeling crept slowly through my body clouding the beauty of the colorful landscape.

CHAPTER EIGHT

Two thousand seven hundred miles away from Honduras, a woman with red hair and striking green eyes stared out of the massive window of her west-coast office. It had a panoramic view of the San Francisco Bay. Having been in the modern building for three years, her company had outgrown the place.

Her other office was in New York City, and each site had its advantages. On the west-coast, Silicon valley oozed with high tech companies and venture capitalists. New York City was entirely different, a concentration of wealth and power. She preferred New York, where she had a large house on the Upper West Side, not far from Central Park. It was ten minutes away from her office, and it employed several carefully chosen accountants.

Ten years previously, when she was twenty years old, Mira Brennen dropped out of university and moved to Silicon Valley to start a high-tech company, with a heartfelt desire to bring good to the world. With an exceptional ability to win the confidence of investors, she raised funding, too much funding.

Her high-tech startup underperformed, but creative accounting obscured reality, and more investors joined. With an excess of funds, she started a venture capital company. This transitioned into Lyra-Dominion, a holding company with investments all over the world.

Her underlying mantra was that *wellbeing* is a fundamental human right. It applied first to her investors and then to others. Unknown to investors, Lyra-Dominion paralleled her first high-tech startup. It underperformed.

Being creative, she and her closest staff found ways to meet the demands of investors. This involved off-the-book ventures where substantial profits flowed in through a complex web of accounts. That provided the cash for paying ample dividends to investors. The phony outstanding performance brought more financiers to the table, and Lyra-Dominion was now worth billions.

Because of her astonishing success, Mira Brennen became the role model for female entrepreneurship. Feminist groups loved her. Business magazines regularly featured her on their covers and television news programs frequently sought interviews with her. Politicians invited her to events where she received immense recognition. That gave her connections and power, and Mira craved for more. At thirty years old, she had skyrocketed to the heights of America's wealthy and influential.

As Mira stood by the window, her phone rang and she answered. It was Sai Bashir, her Chief Operations Officer.

Sai said, "It wasn't exactly as we planned, but the result is satisfactory."

Mira paused and breathed a sigh of relief. The plan had been to force the journalist into a car, and then make him disappear. Something different happened, but it didn't matter because Sai had safeguards in place. There was no way to track the event back to Lyra-Dominion.

"People who don't see the vision are obstructionists to the wellbeing of the future," she said, repeating a slogan she often used at employee events. It was a fundamental part of her belief system.

"We are still working on the other one," Sai said.

"Don't wait too long." They needed to be careful about what details were mentioned over the telephone.

Mira and Sai had a close working relationship and shared no secrets. She was the visionary Chief Executive Officer, and he was the Chief Operations Officer, the implementer.

"We are trying to complete the transaction today," he stated.

She knew what he meant. Another journalist was investigating the company, and the odd thing was that the two journalists had not known each other. It was surprising that their investigations came from two different directions.

Sai had removed one of the journalists. Now, they had to deal with the second one, who was an older man living in New York City. He had been a well-known reporter for major newspapers, and he had even won the Pulitzer Prize for one of his probes into the finance industry.

"This time, make sure it's a deletion, and take care of any offensive nuisance." That meant that the old journalist must quietly disappear, and to destroy any incriminating records.

"That's the goal," Sai confirmed.

"And, of course, remove any of his connections estimated to cause problems." It was unclear if the old reporter was working on his own.

"Someone is researching that," Sai said.

"That's good. Keep me up to date on how this develops."

"Will do," Sai confirmed.

Mira hung up the phone and turned to look out the window. With those problems eliminated, her power would stay intact and even increase over time. Her company could continue doing good, and wellbeing was an eventuality. That's what mattered, and nothing else.

The end justifies the means because, in her case, the final goal was good. Like all truths and other illusionary absolutes, good was relative, subjective, and she knew what benefited her. That's what ultimately mattered. Feeling no remorse, Mira Brennen carried a deep conviction that any action to advance the vision was entirely acceptable.

CHAPTER NINE

Manuel led me to a vast area behind the two warehouses where there were water tanks, large machines, and long concrete slabs. Men and women worked at different tasks.

I took out my notepad, caught my breath, and jotted a few notes. It was humiliating to be so out of breath after spending so many hours on treadmills at the gym. The workers on the farm scampered up and down the hills with no problem, and much of the time, they carried something weighty when I only held a computer bag with a super thin laptop. I couldn't let my huffing and puffing get in the way of my assignment. And, I needed to minimize the time spent thinking about Scott.

"We use a wet washing process," Manuel said, as he pointed to sizeable rectangular holding tanks. "The red cherries are put in the tanks where the bad ones float to the top and are skimmed off. The cherries stay in the tanks for up to thirty six hours where they become fermented and much of the pulp falls off."

The smell around the fermenting tanks was like rotten apples or pears that have been sitting for a long time in a garden.

Manuel continued, "Then, the beans go through an intensive washing machine where any remaining pulp is removed. After that, the beans are placed on the concrete slabs and sun-dried, being turned every six hours."

"It's unreal. I never realized that coffee beans required so much processing and hard work."

Manuel nodded. "There's more. Once the beans are dried, they go through a machine that removes a paper layer, and the machine sorts them by size. Then, they go through the final quality control where the women remove any bad beans. Finally they are put into jute bags and carried onto trucks."

On my note pad, I quickly wrote down impressions of lush mountains, carefully tended rows of coffee bushes, and of the back-breaking toil of selectively picking the beans, and washing, sorting, and loading them.

What coffee drinker understood all that went on behind a daily cup of coffee? I certainly didn't. And, what coffee drinker could keep up the intense effort of these farmworkers?

Manuel said, "If you have any questions on what you've seen, I am available. Please feel free to wander around."

"Thank you. I'm sure another look will help, but that's enough for now. What's next?"

"Follow me."

They walked back into the warehouse, where the workers had finished loading a truck.

Luke was closing the back door of the truck, his shirt soaked with sweat. He saw me and smiled. "How'd it go?"

"Very interesting. My main impression is that tremendous care is put into coffee, and it represents hard work. Your damp shirt is a good example."

"We'd like you to feature that in your articles. Not my shirt, but the care and labor," he laughed, "I want to show you something else important for the story."

"What's that?"

"After lunch, you need to see where these people live."

"Why is that important," I asked.

"You need to see the whole picture. It will put your life in perspective."

* * *

Luke went to clean up while I walked around the processing area to get more ideas. I again watched the men taking the coffee through the washing process. At the concrete slabs, three women labored with long rakes to turn over the drying coffee beans. The warm weather brought sweat to my forehead.

What did Luke mean by putting my life in perspective? Was that an attack, or was he being flippant? Or, most likely, I was being overly sensitive. The change of location from New York to Honduras and the news about Scott had deeply unsettled me.

My thoughts continually drifted back to him. I felt lost, knowing he was gone forever. The death of a person carries an inexplicable finality, an emptiness impossible to fill. The fact that I had anticipations about him only compounded my emotions.

One fundamental question kept going through my mind. What was he doing in Long Beach? I longed for another talk with Ernie, but it was doubtful he had additional information. I decided to wait until the end of the day to call him.

For some strange reason, my neighbor Stan Schultz came to my mind. Could he offer any advice? He was my mentor. Upon further reflection, I decided not to bring him into this. He would probably get carried away with another goofy conspiracy theory.

Then, I remembered that Stan had given me a flash drive containing information on his latest investigation. He said to keep it in a safe place, and I felt guilty that it was in my computer bag. I could at least copy the data to my cloud storage site. But, there was too much going on with this current assignment, combined with the shooting of Scott. I decided not to worry about Stan's affairs.

Luke returned. He had wet hair and wore a clean t-shirt.

We went to lunch, eating the same food as the previous meals, tortillas, beans, rice, and bananas, and I used that time to ask for clarifications on seasonality of the crops, working conditions, and how many people worked on the cooperative. I wrote on my notepad, all the time wondering how to spin this into something of interest.

After the meal, we drank coffee, and again I was struck by the exquisite flavors. I asked, "Why is this so different, that is, so much better than any coffee we pick off the supermarket shelf?"

"For many reasons," Luke replied. "First of all, it's the growing conditions, which I'm sure Manuel explained. It's also single origin, not a hodge-podge mix of coffees from unknown places."

"Isn't it more than that?" I asked.

"Yes. It's important to remember that the taste of roasted coffee beans deteriorates over time. Green coffee beans maintain their flavor over many months, but roasted coffee is another matter. If you look at the expiration date on bags of coffee in supermarkets, it can extend up to a year.. That's way too much time to sit on the shelf. Even though vacuum-sealed, coffee loses its flavor. It gets even worse if exposed to light for too long. The coffee in the cup you're holding came fresh off the farm, roasted in the last twenty-four hours."

I raised my cup and smelled the flavors, thinking about my high-end Ikawa roaster. "I suppose the roast profile is also important, whether light, medium or dark."

Luke smiled and said, "For sure, but it's more complex than that. It depends on temperatures applied during the roasting process. Do you start with low heat and gradually increase it, or quickly go high and keep it there, or use other combinations? Beans from different origins respond to different roasting profiles."

I understood this, for I had mastered this with the Ethiopian beans I roasted back home, but now I wished to experiment with beans from other origins. "How can I get beans from this farm?"

Luke grinned. "I'll give you a list of specialty coffee suppliers in the U.S. where you can get our green beans."

We talked more about coffee, and I took notes while wondering how Luke developed such a passion for this product.

Finally, Luke asked, "Are you ready to see where these people live?"

"For sure, but why is this so important?"

"You'll see."

Luke led me back to his Jeep. He twisted wires together to start the engine. Then we bumped along a dirt road, our bodies shifting back and forth as the Jeep rolled over the uneven surface.

"How far are we going?" I yelled, hoping it wouldn't be another two-hour trek.

"About a mile, to the village of La Fuerza. They named our coffee farm after the village." Luke answered with a loud voice.

"What does La Fuerza mean?"

"It means the force or power. Such as *la fuerza del destino*, meaning the force of destiny."

"So, nothing to do with the force of strong coffee."

Luke laughed. "I hadn't thought of that. Our coffee is subtle, but it can be strong if over-roasted."

Soon, we approached a village, a tiny rural community with houses of different construction materials.

We passed a field where children played, kicking a soccer ball. On one side of the area was a freshly painted building.

Luke pulled to the side of the road, turned off the Jeep's motor, and said. "That's a school we built. Around eighty percent of rural children in Honduras are illiterate, so we wanted to do something about that, at least in a small way."

"Why would your organization get involved in building a school?"

"Our association provided the funds. Our first objective is to make a profit to raise the salaries of workers on the farms, but we also raise funds for projects like schools and water systems. Besides learning to read, the teachers instruct the kids in hygiene and health."

"Health? Why is that?"

"Malaria, Hepatitis A, and diarrhea are prevalent, so we teach prevention. I'll show you around the village."

The idea of malaria was anything but nice, so I took the bottle of mosquito repellent out of my bag, and liberally applied the turpentine smelling liquid to my arms and neck.

We walked down the dirt road and passed houses, some made of bricks and blocks, with tile roofs, and some more like shacks made of wood panels and others with something like wood sticks.

"Those walls are sugar cane stalks," Luke commented. "If people can't afford tile roofs, we try and get tin roofing to keep the rain out, but it's not always easy to find."

Several women stood around a water pipe collecting water in plastic jugs, and they smiled and waved at Luke.

He said, "We found a spring up on the mountain, and then installed a pipe to bring in clean water. That greatly reduces waterborne diseases. The next step is to pipe water into their homes."

"So, you're not just running a coffee operation," I observed.

"Growing coffee is only one component of a solution for these people. One of the main problems in rural Honduras is malnutrition, where corn and beans are primary foods. Last year we cleared a field for vegetables beyond the village."

I reflected on this. Here you had people who struggled to exist while providing a product that many consumers in the Western World enjoy every day. A story was emerging and I felt excited.

Luke said, "It's like this all over the coffee-producing world where impoverished people are hardly able to feed and clothe their families. Millions of coffee-producing people live like this, but it's difficult to make an accurate count because of the rural nature of the farms. All one can say is that a lot of people work hard to survive while others benefit from their labor."

"We can't blame those who enjoy coffee," I remarked.

"That's correct, but maybe some structural changes could put a bit more into the production end."

"Are you suggesting to redistribute the wealth?"

"That sounds like a socialist ideology," Luke stated.

"That's what I thought you were implying."

"Not at all. Socialism rarely works. Just look at the history of some of these Central and South American countries. But, more could be done to give these poor farmers what they deserve."

"How would you do that?"

"One way is to reduce or even cut out some of the costs in the middle of the supply chain, thereby allowing more profits for the laborers. A more direct supply chain would also give a better coffee experience to the consumer."

"I'm not sure I fully understand."

"We'll get there," Luke said, showing the hint of a smile.

I felt a moment of doubt. How could my article adequately reflect these facts? I wrote about restaurants and didn't have a clue about complicated supply-chains. That had to do with business, and that was Scott's domain.

CHAPTER TEN

The growing complexity of this assignment was challenging and it would take time to package this into a set of articles. Open a new restaurant in New York City, and I was comfortable in my element. Now, the subject was entirely different, involving farmers and the processing and bagging of so-called cherries, and supply-chains. This was a fascinating new world and I decided not to be intimidated by it.

This is what journalism is all about, to explore the unknown and find the story.

The question was how to describe this in a way that readers find it interesting? And how to portray these hard-working people in a manner that was not overdramatic but still communicated the reality of their lives?

When we reached the edge of the village, Luke said, "I need to get back to the farm to help load another truck. Is there anything you'd like to explore further?"

I hesitated for a moment. "It would be interesting to find out more about the people in this village. It might help enhance the human interest aspect of my articles. Do you think I could wander around and talk to some of them?" To add the human aspect was a way to keep the articles from sounding like an economic textbook.

"Good idea, but you'll need someone to translate. Let me see if Manuel can join you."

Luke left me at a small clearing next to the road opposite the school, where three large logs were placed in a horseshoe shape, providing a place where people could sit and talk under the shade of the trees.

As Luke's noisy Jeep disappeared in the distance, the only sound left was from the children playing in the field. A bell rang, the children went to their classrooms, and silence filled the air. The contrast with New York City couldn't be more significant, and an uneasiness filled me, which I attributed to culture shock. It was just yesterday that I was jostling crowds on the subway.

I made a mental note of the surroundings, of the lush green jungle, the colors of the village, and shapes of the houses.

Then, my thoughts switched again to Scott, and I was still confused about what happened. My main question was why he started the research for this article in Long Beach? Wasn't it more logical to start from the beginning, where coffee was grown?

I had always admired his analytical approach. He was a business writer and understood balance sheets and cash flows and business management. Was there something from a business angle that led him to Long Beach, and did it have anything to do with my current assignment? That seemed implausible. Again, I fell back on Ernie's question of why shoot someone over coffee?

But, if his murder had something to do with these coffee articles, then where did that place me? It was stressful enough to step out of my usual routine and fly off to an unfamiliar location and write articles with little knowledge of the subject matter. His sudden, violent death, and the unknown reason for it, only added to the pressure. Was this assignment leading into something dark where I didn't belong? It seemed unbelievable even to assume this, but all options had to be on the table.

To make matters worse, I now sat on a log in the middle of nowhere. Was I in danger? I looked around and imagined several places where a sniper could hide and easily pick me off. Then, I thought of Stan Schultz. Was I becoming like him, suspicious, seeing conspiracies in everything?

I needed an update from Ernie, to hopefully obtain more information that would calm my mind. A discussion with Stan might be helpful, for, despite his paranoia, he had the instincts of an experienced journalist. I decided to call Stan when I got back to the coffee plantation, that is, if I got back? Oh boy, you are in a dark mood, I told myself. Get a grip on things.

* * *

Manuel's pickup truck bounced down the road, and I was relieved to see him. Hopefully, my anxiety would disappear, and I could focus on the immediate objective of interviewing a few villagers to strengthen my story.

Manuel parked his truck along the side of the road, got out, and walked over to me.

"Luke said you would like to talk with people in the village and that you needed a translator."

"Unless I used sign language. Thanks for coming."

Manuel smiled. "Let's go to the village. The children are in school, and many of the adults are working, so we may only find elderly people."

"That's fine. I want to get a better understanding of village life."

"I think I know of someone."

We went into the village and walked past small adobe houses. Instead of having front doors, some homes had canvas hanging in the door openings. When we got to one house, Manuel called out, "Hola, Maria."

After a minute of waiting, an older woman pulled back the curtain. She smiled, one tooth missing in the front. Her face was a maze of wrinkles, and wiry gray hair hung below her shoulders. She wore a simple cotton dress, stained, with the stitching unraveling on the bottom hem of the dress. Manuel said something to her in Spanish, and the woman nodded.

Manuel smiled and said, "This is Maria Lopez. She agrees to speak with you."

I said, "Thank you, ah, *gracias.*"

Maria raised a leathery, bony hand and pointed toward the interior of the house and said, "*Por Favor.*"

We entered the house where I saw a small wooden table with six wooden chairs around it, each chair a different shape and size. A door opened to a bedroom. Along one wall of the living room was a worn-out couch., and against the opposite wall was a simple kitchen with a wood-burning stove that had seen better days. Next to the couch was a desk, with photos hung above it. I assumed they were family members. On another wall, there was a small wooden crucifix and a page size image of the Virgin Mary. The smell of charcoal, cooked beans and coffee filled the air.

Maria directed us to the chairs around the table, and we sat down.

I said, "I'm not sure what Manuel told you, but I am writing an article about coffee farms, and it would be helpful to know more about the people in the villages."

Manuel translated.

Maria replied, and again Manuel translated. "Our people work in coffee. It's what keeps us alive, along with our faith in God."

"How long have you lived in this village?"

"All my life, eighty years. It has been a hard life, but many times of happiness. My husband is now with the Virgin and her Son in heaven."

"I'm sorry to hear that," I said, while quickly realizing my response might be taken wrongly, as though sorry Maria's husband was with the virgin. For a Jew, sometimes Catholicism was confusing. "I meant, I'm sorry for your loss." I quickly moved on. "Are you on your own?"

"No. My younger son lives next door with his wife and their son, my grandson." Maria's eyes brightened. "My son and his wife work on the coffee farm, and we also have a plot of our own where we grow coffee, raise chickens, and grow vegetables. Thanks to the cooperative, we now have a freshwater supply."

I pointed toward the wall. "Are those photos of your family?"

"Yes. Years ago, my oldest son moved to Tegucigalpa to seek work, and for his children to go to school. My oldest granddaughter finished university."

"What will she do now," I asked.

Maria dropped her head, her eyes fixing on her wrinkled hands. Her words started slowly, and she spoke as though talking to herself. Manuel waited until she finished talking, and then he translated.

"Maria says that her granddaughter Valentina was always a serious student, outstanding in math. In university, she studied accounting. She also learned English. When completing university studies, Valentina did not find work, just like so many people in our country. Out of desperation, she listened to coyotes. Coyotes are people smugglers, who make big promises about jobs in America. Four months ago, she left for the United States and the family has not heard from her. There is nothing we can do and we are worried."

Even though I didn't understand Spanish, the sound of Maria's voice and the movement of her hands expressed agony and desperation. Maria's emotions touched me. "I'm so sorry to hear that," I said.

As a trained journalist, I was supposed to first look for the facts, but in this story, there was something deeper, and somehow I connected with that. How many times throughout the centuries had my Jewish ancestors experienced desperation?

I needed more information about Valentina. "My understanding was that human traffickers charge money to take people to the United States. If she didn't have a job in Honduras, where did she get the funds?"

Manuel spoke without translating to Maria. "The coyotes don't always ask for money. Some hold the debt against you, and you have to pay it off when you get to the United States. The coyotes work with gangs that force people in low paying jobs. Smuggled immigrants work forever to pay off their debt. They receive threats of death if they try to run away and even threats against the person's family."

"Do you think that's what happened to Valentina?"

Manuel answered. "We can only assume it, and you know that jobs for young women are not always those promised. They put them in demeaning situations and violate them every day. And, many have terrible things done to them before they even get to the United States, especially the pretty ones, and Valentina is pretty."

I took a breath. It was a horrible thought that people would take such extreme risks because of lousy economics in their home countries.

"Can I do anything?" I asked, feeling powerless to bring any help.

Manuel translated, and Maria answered, "We feel great fear for Valentina. Please pray for us."

"I can do that," I said, aware I was stretching the truth. I was a secular Jew, and not always good at prayers, even those prescribed for holy days. Stan Schultz was observant, and he would know what to do in this situation. I carried an idea of a God, that is, the God of Abraham, Isaac and Jacob, for that was my culture, my ethos. Fundamentally, I believe there is a divine being out there, but sometimes he seemed so far away. Would he listen to me? But, I would say a prayer for Maria.

After more questions, I had enough information. More than that, I felt Maria's anguish and imagined that many others in Central America felt the same. So many had seen loved ones disappear on the road to the north. It was not an easy reality to capture in my articles adequately. To write about the colors of meals was one thing, but to touch the desperation of these people evoked an emotional level I reluctantly wanted to face.

Now, I was caught between two opposing concepts. On one side was production processes and supply chains, not my main topics of interest, but I could handle that. On the other was the agony of families ripped apart because of hopeless poverty. The second side was the most difficult to capture, for how do you effectively portray such pain? I related to it, for it was similar to the ache my Jewish people historically carried. Our families had been split apart for centuries.

Now, mixed in with this was my questions about Scott, and I felt a bit like a leaf shaken from a tree landing in an unfamiliar place. I didn't like this feeling and anger slowly crept into me. Come on, I said to myself. You are energetic and determined and you will pull this off.

As Luke had said, the visit to La Fuerza Village was to give perspective. The time spent with Maria Lopez opened an element of suffering I had to deal with.

CHAPTER ELEVEN

Valentina Lopez felt despair, for would she ever escape this terrible place? The coyotes had not told the truth, and she was foolish to have believed them.

It had been four months since she left Tegucigalpa, first taken out of the city in a nice car. Once in the countryside, the coyotes put her in the back of a pickup truck with six men, and another younger woman. Four of the men had paid a fortune for the trip, and one man and the other woman were like herself. They had no money and agreed to work off the debt once the coyotes placed them in jobs in Texas. The coyotes continually stared at her and the other woman with lusty eyes.

As an alternative to working off the debt, they stated that if she carried a backpack across the American border, then she would not owe any liabilities. She had studied accounting in University and understood that somehow costs needed to be covered.

Texas had sounded so inviting, ranches with cowboys, and big cities with restaurants and shopping centers. Texas has a sizeable Hispanic population so she could blend in. Her English was okay, school taught, but not fluent. She needed to hear it spoken and use it in everyday life.

The pickup truck took back roads to cross into Guatemala, and the driver was friendly, giving assurances that the travel conditions would improve once they were on a bus. Instead, somewhere in Guatemala, the pickup truck stopped, and a group of men carrying guns ordered the passengers to get into a larger open truck. All the passengers obediently got out of the pickup truck, went to the other vehicle, and squeezed in with others who were already in the back.

Valentina regretted not asking questions to the coyotes, but the guns were intimidating. Having lived in one of the world's most dangerous cities, she had learned to be cautious, for human life was cheap.

There were now fifteen people traveling together. Some talked, sharing their expectations of America and what they would do when they got there. Others were silent as though existing in a strange void, a group of desperate people now faced with the reality of leaving the certainty of their known world. The loss of the comfort and stability of family and friends was now a reality.

Valentina felt guilty that she hadn't talked with her family before leaving home. Instead, after writing a letter to explain her actions, she went to her parents' bedroom and placed the letter on her mother's pillow. Tears rolled down her cheeks while packing essential clothing into a bag. Then, she walked out of the house, feeling waves of sorrow, fear tightening her stomach.

Tears still came to her eyes when she thought of her mother finding and reading the letter. The emotions only intensified when she considered the anguish she brought to her grandmother at La Fuerza.

There were now a few more women travelers, and Valentina felt a bit better with strength in numbers. It was almost three thousand kilometers to reach the United States border.

They traveled for twenty-four hours, and then they stopped in a clearing near the border with Mexico. There had been occasional stops before arriving there, where they were allowed to relieve themselves, the men standing at the side of the road, and the women walking into forested areas.

At the clearing, Maria walked behind some trees with another woman, and she thought about running into the jungle to get away from the coyotes, to go back to her family. After some hesitation and feeling fear, she returned with the woman to the clearing. The coyotes had taken away her identity document. More than that, the coyotes repeatedly told the travelers not to run away, because if found by local police, they would be arrested and brutalized. When one of the young men complained, they beat him with clubs until he could barely get up. Blood streamed out of his nose for a long time, and one eye became swollen shut. The guns they carried were frightening.

At the clearing near the border, more people joined the group, and they followed a path crossing into Mexico. There were now over thirty people walking in a long line. They came to another clearing where a bus was parked, and one of the coyotes instructed them to go into it. Exhausted, Valentina found a place next to another young woman. They looked at each other and said nothing, and Valentina saw panic in her eyes, and also horrible suffering. The coyotes had violated the young woman.

Because of concern of the men, Valentina fought fatigue and tried to stay awake on the bus, but eventually, she fell asleep. Sometime after, a man shook her shoulder, and a bolt of fear caused her to jump in her seat. The man was only passing out bananas, handing two to each passenger. He also gave them bottles of water.

It took a week of constant travel to reach the north of Mexico, with the group changing buses several times. Sometimes the roads were smooth, and the Mexican police never stopped the bus. Eventually, they reached Mexican Highway 101, known as 'The Highway of Death.' It had been a place where drug cartels fought each other and left burned-out cars and bodies along the side of the road.

At one point, they veered off of Highway 101 and headed West on narrow roads until coming to a small town. The bus stopped inside a fenced area, and a man stepped onto the bus, and with a gun in his right hand, he commanded them to get off. Guards with terrifying machine guns corralled them into a smaller fenced area and told them to wait.

Groups of people sat in other fenced areas, and Maria estimated there were over one hundred people in total. As she waited, the men with the guns came by and pointed at her, and then directed her to a hut that contained five women about her age. Seeing a look of dread on the faces of the women, Valentina imagined that her greatest fear was about to be realized. Then, she heard one of the coyotes talking to another.

"Special shipment," he said.

The other coyote nodded and then told the women to get into a small van. A coyote drove them for an hour, and the van stopped in a remote place, where they walked out into the darkness of night. A man handed a backpack to each of them and told them to carry the packs to the other side.

"The other side of what?" Valentina asked.

"The other side of the river."

"Do we have to swim?" Valentina asked, knowing she wasn't a good swimmer, and the backpack would likely pull her under the water."

The coyote laughed. "If you get wet, it doesn't matter. What's in the bags must stay dry."

He told them to stay utterly quiet as they followed him down to a river where there was a small boat. The air was humid and carried a swampy odor. The women got into the boat, and a young man silently rowed them to the other side.

When they got out and stood on the bank of the river, the young man whispered, "*Bienvenido a los Estados Unidos.*"

Another man met them and led them along a trail where a dark cargo van waited. He instructed them to leave the backpacks behind some bushes and to get into the back of the vehicle. Once they were in the van, the doors shut, and it felt like a prison, and Valentina hoped there was adequate ventilation.

For the next week, they traveled and traveled, each day changing to a different vehicle. They spent the nights in rundown warehouses, sleeping on smelly old mattresses. This certainly wasn't the America she expected. Occasionally She saw city signs with names like Little Rock and Chicago. Sometimes the young women asked where they were going, but the drivers only told them to be quiet and not ask questions. The coyotes had lied. They were well beyond Texas.

Eventually, Valentina saw a sign that said New York City, and the van stopped inside a warehouse where the women were separated, and that was the last time she saw them.

Then, a heavyset man in black clothing instructed her to get into a car, and he drove her away.

"Where are we going? She asked in English.

"To your place of employment, to work off your debt."

"But I carried a bag across the border. The coyotes said there would be no debt if I did that."

"Can't believe everything you hear," he said.

"Where are the other women going?"

"To pay off their debt."

"Where?"

"Restaurant or factory work, or maybe personal services," he said with a smile."

"What is personal services?"

"You ask too many questions. Shut up," he commanded.

He drove her to a large house that someone called a brownstone, and she entered the most magnificent palace she had ever seen.

It was there she worked for three months, cleaning floors, washing clothing, and helping Jonas the cook prepare and clean up after meals. In the basement, she had a room connected to a bathroom. There were no windows.

The heavyset man's name was Ricco, and he warned her never to go outside the house because the New York police were cruel, and they would put her in prison for a long time. He also made threats, saying they would punish her family if she tried to leave. Every night, Ricco or one of his assistants locked her in her room. That was always a frightening moment because she never trusted the intentions of those men.

She was never paid for her work. When she questioned Ricco about that, he said the debt first had to be settled. Then, she asked how long that would be, and he said he would tell her when the time came. After three months of being confined in the house in a perpetual state of uncertainty, she realized she had stupidly placed herself in a hopeless prison.

But there was something more sinister.

When first seeing the owner of the house, the tall red haired woman with the penetrating snake-like green eyes, Valentina felt a deep sense of cold fear.

CHAPTER TWELVE

Manuel and I left La Fuerza village and returned to the cooperative, where we went to the dining area full of people. We joined Luke, and dinner was served, again, tortillas, rice, beans, and bananas.

As I took a bite of the tortilla, I knew I had the beginnings of an unusual story. In lush green mountains in a remote part of Central America, people struggled to make a living by providing a product enjoyed in other parts of the world.

The question was, how best to write the story? It was a human interest story with an economic component. But, a core question was, who would be reading these articles? When I wrote for food magazines, I had a reasonably good understanding of my audience.

The articles would end up in the cultural sections of Sunday editions of major newspapers, the parts talking about art and culture. They would also appear on the newspapers' websites. I was at home with that audience, but I was competing with pieces on movie stars, travel and books. Therefore, my material had to stand out. Besides being informative, they had to touch the readers' hearts. This challenge was motivating and I looked forward to the work.

Then, I thought of Scott. He was an economics guy. His pieces mostly went into finance publications and the business sections of newspapers. So, what was his interest in taking this on?

Luke interrupted my train of thought. "So, what is your impression so far?"

"A couple of things. First, consumers are oblivious to the hard manual work going into their cup of coffee. Second, it seems that coffee workers live in awful conditions, at least for someone living in New York City."

"Exactly."

I smiled. "And, from my interest, it looks like there are many coffee flavors to be explored."

"What's the personal interest," he asked.

"I'm an emerging coffee geek."

"How's that?"

"I visit many restaurants, and once met a top chef who introduced me to Ethiopian coffee. After that, I bought an Ikawa roaster."

Luke grinned. "Indeed, you are in a unique class. Nothing brings out the flavor like that machine."

"So, that's my interest." I needed more information for my article, so I shifted the topic and asked, "Do you live here?"

He laughed. "I come down every three or four months. We have several projects like this around the world. Manuel runs the operations around here, and sometimes he joins me on trips."

"So, where are you based?"

"New Jersey. Our headquarter is there, but I'm not there all that much."

"Why not?"

"Much of the time I'm out in the field."

"Can I ask how you got into this business?"

Luke glanced across the room. "An interest in coffee, and these people."

"How did that develop? And, may I ask about your background" It always helped the human interest side of stories when a bit of personal history was included and I was curious to know about him.

Luke glanced down at his hands and then rubbed his wrist as though he had injured it. Maybe he had strained it from lifting bags of coffee.

He said, "I've done this for a few years."

That was not a lot of detail. He would fit right in with Ernie, with vague replies when specifics were needed.

He looked across the room and said, "Excuse me just a minute." He stood up and carried his plate and silverware to the dishwashing area. Then he talked to the cook. It was evident he had evaded my questions, and it heightened my curiosity.

A few minutes later, he came back and said, "I need to go to the shipping area. Can we continue our discussion in the morning?"

"Ah, for sure."

"Then, I wish you a good night," he said. He walked quickly out of the room.

That was strange. I asked the guy a about his background, which wasn't offensive, and he quickly heads out. It seemed more like an evasion. Did he really leave the door open for further discussion? I grinned knowing there was no way he could escape my journalistic curiosity, thinking, I will find out what you are hiding.

I carried my used plates to the cleanup area and then walked over to the office and used the telephone. I called Ernie's number, and it rang five times and then went into his voice box.

"This is Ernie. Leave a message."

"Hello Ernie, this is Sarah. I guess you are out, so I'll head off to my super-duper cockroach infected living quarters that you wonderfully set up for me. Send me an email with the latest information on Scott. It's still too weird to believe. Bye."

I hung up the phone, lifted it again, and called Stan Schultz, and it went into his voice box. I said, "Stan, I need to talk with you, but my cell phone doesn't have a good phone connection here in Honduras. Something strange happened, and I'd like to get your take on it. Please send me an email to know if there's a good time to connect."

Frustrated that I couldn't get through to either Ernie or Stan, I walked back to my gloomy cabin, wrote notes on my laptop, and eventually tiredness took over. The dim light from a desk lamp only added to the suffocating emptiness I felt. It would be another night of buzzing insects, and I wondered if any of them had figured out how to work through the mosquito netting.

Again, I used a liberal slathering of the gluey stinky bug repellant.

* * *

I spent the following morning wandering around the farm, taking copious notes. It was a delight to see the contrast of green colors found in the coffee bushes and the surrounding jungle, and it took my mind away from shootings in hotel parking lots. This scenery was the opposite of my daily life of weaving between massive concrete buildings. I wished I had more time to get out into nature. Unfortunately, there was little opportunity to do so, other than the occasional walks in Central Park.

Once, Stan Schultz took me to upstate New York, where he has a cabin by a lake. It was a relaxing weekend, and after that experience, I was determined to get out of the city more often. But it never happened. Seeing this farm gave me a desire to change that, and a creative flash went through my mind. Maybe I should become a nature writer and get out of the restaurant writing business/

There was something I hadn't noticed the previous day, a garden with hundreds of coffee bushes, everything from a few inches high, to larger shrubs that looked ready for transplanting. The last time I had planted anything was in the fourth grade. It wasn't actually 'planting,' but instead soaking an avocado seed for a science project. After weeks of waiting, it sprouted roots and leaves, and it had given me an incredible feeling of satisfaction. I wondered if the farmers had pleasure from growing coffee bushes and from the rest of the work they did on the farm. Or, was it just a mundane and tedious task, a nine to five routine?

In a small building on the side of the warehouse, I joined in with Manual and another man standing next to a table with five bowl-like cups of coffee on it. Manuel explained that they were in the process of tasting different coffee samples of freshly brewed coffee. The beans came from various farms in the area. Manuel said this process was known as *cupping*, something performed throughout the coffee supply chain. Everyone from the growers, the coffee traders, and the final coffee roasters did cupping.

The process was to take small samples of green coffee beans and roast them in laboratory conditions. Then the ground beans were put in cups and infused in boiling water.

Manuel said, "Why don't you join us?" He handed me a round spoon, like a deep bowled soupspoon.

He broke the coffee grounds off the top of the coffee in one of the cups, put his nose close to the cup, and smelled the coffee. He said this was for sensing the aroma. I followed his example and sniffed the coffee in the first cup, and it was heavenly.

We did this smelling test from cup to cup, and when finished, Manuel scraped off white foam that had formed in each cup.

We waited a few minutes and then Manuel took his spoon, filled it with coffee, and raised it to his lips. This was followed by slurping the coffee into his mouth with a fast inhalation. He swigged it around in his mouth, and then spat it out into a plastic cup. Then he said something in Spanish, and the other man wrote on a piece of paper that looked like a score sheet.

Manuel went from cup to cup doing the same.

I laughed. "That's just the opposite of what any mother would teach her child. The spitting is disgusting."

Manuel smiled. "The goal is to evenly cover your taste buds with the coffee to pick up all the subtle flavors. Now, you try it."

I followed Manuel's example by slurping a spoon of coffee into my mouth and then swirling it around. I liked the taste. Feeling embarrassed, I spit the mouthful of coffee into a plastic cup.

Then I did the same thing with the remaining cups and sensed a slight difference in a couple of them.

Manuel grinned. "So now you are a professional cupper. What do you think?"

"Well, besides feeling foolish, I'm surprised to taste the change between the various samples. Are you giving a score?"

"Yes, and a description, which we send to our buyers. All these coffees are similar. The main difference is that some are grown in coffee fields, whereas two of the samples come from coffee plants in the jungle where the quality is better. The last two cups are jungle grown."

I reflected on what he said, and asked, "Did you say that others in the supply-chain do the cupping as you call it?" I was interested to know as much as possible, not only for the sake of the articles.

"It is standard in the industry. It's a way of ensuring quality, to confirm that sellers are not over-hyping their coffee. Of course, there is no need for our cooperative to do that." He laughed.

Manuel said that cupping took place at several steps in the coffee supply process. Had Scott done cupping in Long Beach, or somewhere else? It seemed a weird proposition that his death might be tied to this.

There were no answers because I didn't have enough information and that left me frustrated. I decided to be patient and pick away at this bit by bit as any investigative journalist would do.

But patience wasn't my strongest quality.

CHAPTER THIRTEEN

I sat in an uncomfortable metal chair next to a building with weathered wood siding and glanced through my handwritten notes. I had an uneasy feeling about this assignment, knowing what my heart told me. It was ridiculous to waste time on a coffee farm when instead, I should be helping to catch Scott's killers. But, it was unreasonable to believe the FBI would even ask for my support.

Combined with this was the frustration of knowing I had little choice in quitting the coffee assignment. The only option was to make the most of my situation, but there had to be something in this business that got him killed. Surely it wasn't in spitting coffee into plastic cups. I decided the only thing to do was to ask questions at every step. But, that had to be done in a way that Luke or anyone else would not become suspicious.

Anyway, I liked coffee and my time at La Fuerza Farm had given me a much deeper appreciation for this product.

One dilemma in any writing project is knowing when you have enough information to complete your story. The problem with the current assignment was the considerable amount of data to be learned, and I had a strange impression that I had only seen the tip of the iceberg.

At noon, I put my notes into my computer bag, went to the dining hall, and found a seat across from Luke.

He smiled at me and asked, "How's it going?"

"There's a lot to this, but I'm enjoying it."

"I'm glad. Are you ready for the next step?"

"I'm not sure because there seems more to learn on this farm. What's next?"

"We're taking two trucks to the port to unload coffee bags. I'd suggest you get all your things because we'll spend the night down there."

"How long is the drive?"

"About three and a half hours."

I lifted my hand and felt my hair still tangled from the ride from the airport. Riding inside the closed cab of a truck should be better, but a long trip was not a pleasant thought.

There was something else eating away at me. Luke rarely gave me any lead time on what was coming next. For sure, it would be useful to see the next step in the coffee supply chain, but he could have told me about the trip hours ago. That would have given time to prepare questions.

Irritated, I went back to my room and packed my things, glad to be leaving the bugs behind. At least there had been no bedbugs.

At the truck, Luke squeezed my carryon bag into an opening behind our seats, and we began the bumpy ride out to the main road. I placed my computer bag between my feet on the floor. Manuel drove, Luke sat by the right window and I was in the middle, while another truck led the way.

As we snaked through the mountains, I was again impressed by the lush green scenery. There were numerous banana and coffee plantations. Many villages had similarities to La Fuerza, where Maria Lopez lived.

I thought about the people, their work, and the economics of the country. What kept them poor? It's a fundamental question. Why are some nations wealthy and others are not?

That was an economic question, which was Scott's domain. Was there something going on at a government level that he had discovered?

Along the road, I noticed a group of twenty people or so walking together, mostly younger men with a few women and a couple of children.

"Where are they going?" I asked.

"North," Manuel answered.

"Why north?"

Luke said, "They are migrants attempting the long journey through Guatemala and Mexico, and then to the U.S."

"You mean, illegal immigrants?"

Luke smiled. "Illegal? Not yet, that is, until they sneak across the U.S. border. I suppose I'd attempt the same thing in the hope of a better future, but this is wreaking havoc in rural Honduras and other countries in Central America."

"How is that?"

"It's a complex equation. These people dream of a better life in the north, and human traffickers play on that hope. Some people make it through and end up finding work, thereby achieving unbelievable living standards at least for people here. But, when they leave the villages, the agricultural production goes down, and there is less revenue coming into the village, which only augments the poverty. Combined with that, corruption is a real issue, and this only increases bribery and exploitation. It breaks up families and destroys communities. As I said, it's wreaking havoc."

"But, you can understand why people desire a better life," I exclaimed.

Luke said. "Why not create a better life here? We can improve the standard of living in these villages and give people hope and dignity. They don't need to give in to corruption and see their families and values devastated."

I noticed how Luke spoke with passion, like communicating beyond me to a broader audience. I said, "It looks like you are giving hope to La Fuerza."

"We'd like to think so, but it happens too slowly. More funding is needed."

"How can that happen?" I asked.

"If the farmers received more from agricultural exports, it would make a huge difference. But, much of the supply chain works against them. There are a lot of players in the supply chain, and everyone rightfully needs to make a profit. Some at the end of the line make a lot of money, but the farmers here barely get by."

I had seen with my own eyes that coffee farmers were poor, but Luke also mentioned corruption, and that opened more questions about Scott. In his investigations, had he come across illegal activity in the coffee trade? It seemed remote, and most likely, the reason was something different, but all possibilities needed consideration.

I had to contact Ernie to discuss this.

The three-hour trip went by quickly. We stopped once for gas, where Manuel and Luke traded off driving.

Their destination was the Port of San Lorenzo. Luke explained that there were several ports on the Caribbean side of Honduras, the largest one being Puerto Cortés. San Lorenzo was smaller and on the Pacific side.

Coffee was the primary export of the country, with over three million coffee bags exported each year. In the trucks, we carried shade grown coffee beans, enough bags to fill a shipping container.

Late in the afternoon, we left the mountains and descended onto a road connecting with the Pan American highway, which stretched from Alaska to the lower reaches of South America.

After passing through the town of San Lorenzo, we took a road for several miles through mangrove swamps until we went through an unattended security gate and came to a warehouse. The first truck backed into the warehouse up to an empty shipping container. Local men went to the back of the truck and unloaded the coffee bags, stacking them in a shipping container.

Luke said, "A shipping container holds approximately two hundred and seventy-five bags of coffee. These will end up with a client in California."

He showed me the shipping documents, which had the name of the shipping company, Nyx Lines, and the name of the final destination. West Coast Specialty Coffee in Los Angeles.

The unloading from the trucks took time, so I used this to jot down notes about the port and the men at work.

As the men toiled to empty the truck, Luke said, "I wanted you to see this, because the hard work is not only done on the farm. We want you to cover this in your articles."

"I get the point," I said, not used to a client being directive. Most of the time, I had freedom in how I packaged my stories.

Luke said, "We'll stay at a hotel in town and can have dinner at a place along the water. It's the number one ranked hotel in San Lorenzo."

* * *

The hotel was anything but a hotel, a line of rooms on stilts over the water. Bats emerged from holes in the roof, with the outside walkway covered in bat excrement.

In the room, cockroaches scurried from place to place, the sheets looked like they hadn't been changed in years, and there were blackish-purple spots on the walls, the result of squashed mosquitos full of blood. In a couple of the blood spots were the dried out, spread-eagle carcasses of mosquitos. The netting over the bed had holes. I forgot to ask about malaria.

One could fill a library with descriptions about the state of the bathroom, or summarize it into one word . . . revolting. The guest-house shack back on La Fuerza Coffee Farm was a palace compared to this.

Manuel and the driver of the other truck had decided to drive back to the coffee farm, and I understood the reason. Why would anyone in their right mind want to stay in a place like this? After placing my bags on a table, I checked my phone and saw it had a signal, so I called Ernie.

"Ernie here," he answered.

"Never again," I said with a loud voice that bordered on a yell.

"What are you talking about?"

"I'm staying in places that are crawling with cockroaches, and floors covered with bat-crap. Don't you ever again assign me to anything like this."

"We need the money," he responded.

"You'd sell your soul and put your writers through hell to make a dime. You're despicable."

Ernie replied, "Calm down and don't overreact. A few bugs never hurt anyone, and anyway, this provides good color material for your article."

"Ugg," was all I could say. Words typically came easy, but I was speechless. Ernie didn't have an ounce of understanding. I screamed, "I've been in a cramped noisy truck for almost four hours, stuck between two sweaty guys, and there's nothing like being entombed in a stink-hole that claims to be the best hotel in town." Actually, leaning against Luke's muscular body hadn't been all that bad.

"Be thankful you're not in one of the other hotels."

"Is that your idea of looking on the bright side?"

"You'll live," he responded.

As he said that, I switched topics. "What about Scott? Any news?"

"Not much. I found out more details about the security camera that recorded the incident. A car pulled up not far from Scott, and two guys got out. They went up to him, stuck a gun in his face, and one of the guys tried to push Scott toward their car. He resisted, started a fight, and they shot him twice in the chest. When he was on the ground, the shooter put a bullet into his forehead. Then they carried him into the backseat of the car, the two guys jumped in, and the car drove off.,

"That's horrible," I said, feeling disgusted over the brutality of the murder. "Did the FBI or police identify the two men?"

"Not yet. The video is grainy, but they are working on it."

"Do you know what he was doing in Long Beach?" I asked.

"Earlier, he had visited some shipping company. It likely had to do with the coffee assignment.

"What's the shipping company?"

"Nyx Lines."

My heart dropped. Nyx Lines was the same company I had seen on the manifest at the port. My mind raced. What was this company, and was it connected in any way with his death? And what did 'Nyx' mean? Did it have to do with New York City?

The immediate worry was Luke Cotton. Could he, in some way, have anything to do with Scott's murder? In talking with Luke, he went on and on about the poor farmers and how they didn't get their share of profits from coffee sales. But, maybe that was a ruse. Was Luke involved in something sinister? He had mentioned corruption in Honduras. Was he part of that? I knew little about him. Who was he?

I found myself at a loss for answers, and that led to one vital decision, to remain extremely cautious.

"Sarah, are you there," Ernie asked.

"Yes. I was thinking."

"Do me a favor, will you?"

"Maybe."

"The FBI will figure this out, so focus on the writing assignment. Okay?"

"The quicker I get through this assignment, the better."

"I thought you took it because you liked coffee."

"That's the only redeeming thing."

"Get back to me," Ernie said, and he hung up.

I took a deep breath. I was stuck in a miserable hotel and needed to complete this assignment as quickly as possible and get back to writing about restaurants. Manuel and the other driver had taken off with the trucks, so how were we going to get back to the coffee farm? Luke was not forthcoming about anything.

I thought about Stan Shultz and knew he was the one person I could confide in, so I called his number. It rang five times and then went into his voice mail. I left a message. "Stan, this is Sarah again. There's some weird stuff going on, and I'm wondering if I could ask for your insight. Please call me on my cell phone."

I hung up and walked out of the hotel room onto the walkway covered with bat excrement and headed toward the hotel reception to meet Luke, to give him an earful about the living conditions.

CHAPTER FOURTEEN

When I saw Luke, I couldn't suppress my displeasure and blurted out, "Are you messing with me by saying this is the best hotel in town? It's absurd even to call it a hotel."

Luke smiled. "Believe me. I've stayed in worse."

"That's it? Do you have no shame in putting a New York culinary writer into a rat hole like this?"

He nodded. "I'm sorry. I never stayed here before and didn't know its condition. Honestly, on the travel sites, it's ranked as number one around here. I failed to look at the reviews, and I think the travel site miscategorized the place."

"And, how were the reviews?"

"Pretty terrible. But some were hilarious." He grinned.

"That's extremely comforting. I suggest we get a taxi and find a better hotel within a thousand-mile radius from here."

"No need. I had strong words with the hotel management, and they're taking action, starting with new sheets and pillows. They promised to scrub the rooms and put new mosquito nets over the beds.

And, they'll spray for bugs. Hopefully, it will be okay for our one night here."

There he was using that 'hopefully' word again. Was that the only word in his vocabulary besides *stuff*?

Still, there were the bats, although one should be thankful because they ate bugs. Did they carry rabies? Was there a hospital in this town?

With my computer bag hung over my shoulder, I walked with Luke to a restaurant not far from the hotel. There was no way I would leave my laptop in that room. The only positive thing about the place was the sunset, a magnificent orange streak on the horizon.

Even though he had apologized and did his best to fix things in our rooms, I was still angry. Did my feelings originate from the terrible state of the hotel room, or from the grief I carried because of Scott? Or, was Luke starting to wear on my nerves? In any case, I needed to know if Luke knew about Scott's shooting, or even worse, did he have something to do with it? The fact that he carried shipping documents with Nyx Lines was puzzling. I planned to question him over the meal.

We entered the restaurant's outside veranda overlooking the broad inlet from the sea. There were no houses or lights on the opposite side of the water, only thick mangroves catching the last reflection of sunlight. The evening was calm and warm until a small noisy boat broke the silence.

"Night fisherman," Luke commented. "When he gets to the fishing area, he switches on a large lamp that attracts the fish."

The server came with menus and handed one to Luke and one to me.

"What do you recommend?" I asked.

"They say that when you eat in a foreign land, you bake it, boil it, or peel it. I'd recommend the fish. It typically comes with rice and fried plantains."

I was tired of tortillas and beans but knew I had no right to complain. In this part of the world, people ate that almost every day. "Your recommendation sounds great," I said, while at the same time thinking of some of the meals I had in top restaurants in New York. If this trip kept going with contaminated cockroach hotels, I'd happily settle for being a New York restaurant journalist for the rest of my life.

We ordered our food, and with Scott still on my mind, I asked Luke how he found clients for his coffee. I planned to investigate this from several directions.

He answered, "It's not all that difficult. We've developed a network with small independent coffee roasters in the specialty coffee world. We also supply to coffee wholesalers selling green beans directly to the home roasting crowd."

"Why is that?"

"It's a long discussion, but many small coffee shops and independent roasting companies like to establish direct connections with farmers. By doing this, they cut out the costs of intermediaries. That means more profit going back to the farmers."

"Middlemen?" I asked. Is there something there that Scott discovered?

"There are a myriad of people in the middle, all the way from shipping companies to coffee shops, anyone sitting between the farmer and the consumer. As an example, let's take that five or six dollar cup of coffee you buy at a coffee shop. Only one or two percent goes back to the farmer. The owner of the shop needs to pay for rent and labor, so that's a significant component in that cup of coffee."

Rather than middlemen, perhaps Scott found something going on in coffee shops. The only thing I could think of was protection rackets because one time, I had come across that with a restaurant in New York.

Luke continued, "Now consider this. If people home-roasted, there is no need to include those costs in your cup of coffee, and by home roasting, you get a superior tasting coffee. Also, by doing that, you pay a lot less per cup for a far superior tasting product, and maybe our farmers can be paid more."

"I hadn't thought of that," I said, recalling the living conditions of the coffee farmers. "You said there are other examples."

"Examples of what?"

"Do you have more examples of middlemen?" My question was a bit dumb, realizing I was digging the bottom of the barrel for information. For sure, I was learning about the coffee business, which was necessary for the articles, but I was drawing blanks as to anything connecting to Scott.

"Think about the capsules people buy for their coffee machines," Luke stated. "They are expensive, and how much money goes back to the farmers?"

"Very little, I assume."

"More or less, although some of those capsule companies make a real effort to help farmers. Now, think of the roasted coffee bags you buy at a supermarket. The same measly profit distribution applies. I'm overdramatic here because there are many of the big coffee companies that care about the farmers and are trying to do something. They use the word, sustainability, which means ensuring production."

"I home-roast," I proudly said.

"And I bet you drink exceptional coffee."

I thought of my mornings, of the coffee brewing in the kitchen, and the pleasant smell that came into my bathroom. "Yes, my home coffee is better than anything." I felt a sudden pang of homesickness.

"Do you remember those migrants we saw today?" Luke asked.

"For sure."

"I've said it before, but if the coffee growers had a bit more money from their labor, they wouldn't have to leave their homes, and their families would not be devastated. The human traffickers are making a lot of money on this, and the U.S. government is paying billions at the border to handle the influx of refugees. Also, consider the huge social and health costs once immigrants make it into the U.S., as well as all the unnecessary political debates this creates. Shouldn't politicians be working on other things? It may sound simplistic, but if more people bought green coffee beans directly as possible from the farmers, some of this problem would go away. Not all, but some. Few people think about this as a solution."

"With what you're suggesting, the coffee companies and the coffee chains would go bankrupt." Was a bankrupt coffee company after Scott? That was absurd.

Luke laughed. "That's highly doubtful. Most people like the convenience of an off the shelf, ready-roasted bag of coffee, or a fresh cup from a coffee shop. I'm just suggesting to do a few things a bit differently."

Luke had a one-track mind getting to the same conclusion no matter the starting point. We had drifted away from talking about intermediaries. While all this was of interest, I needed to get back on target. Thinking of the name on Luke's shipping document, I asked, "How do you decide who transports your coffee?"

He gave me a quizzical look. "It depends on the shipping point. On the east side of Honduras, there are several ports, and therefore many shipping companies visit those ports. On the west, there is one main port, San Lorenzo. Because the port is small and the waterway not deep, we are limited to a couple of companies."

As Luke talked, a man walked into the restaurant and took a raised seat at the bar near the entrance of the restaurant. It was the same man at the port, with the checkered shirt and dark mustache, who had taken the shipping documents from Luke. He ordered a beer, and when the beer was served, he slightly turned and looked in our direction. His eyes fixed on mine for a moment and then his gaze quickly went to the beer in front of him. There was something unnatural in the movement, and it made me feel uneasy.

The presence of the man, as well as my discussion with Ernie triggered a question. "Today, on the papers you were holding, it mentioned Nyx Lines. What do you know about them?"

Luke paused for a moment and then answered, "They are not the biggest player, but have ships going all over the world. They carry a lot of containers with coffee, and that's important for us. Why do you ask?'

"The more I understand about the coffee business, the better it helps my writing. So, why is it important to choose a company that ships a lot of coffee?"

"Expertise. During shipping, coffee can pick up chemicals that destroys the taste. You don't want to put coffee bags in a container that previously carried paint. Also, the coffee bags should not be exposed to too much humidity, as the coffee beans would rot. Nyx Lines is dependable, and they have a low spoilage rate."

"Is that all?"

"They are also good at distribution. Once a container reaches the United States, they separate the bags, put them on trucks, where they arrive at final destinations."

"Do you know what Nyx means? Why was that name chosen for the company?" The man at the bar with the checkered shirt and thick black mustache kept glancing at Luke and me. It was like we were the main attraction in the restaurant.

"I don't have a clue in the world," Luke replied.

"Me neither," I said dryly.

I reflected on this. Why was Scott interested in Nyx Lines? They were a part of his investigation, but was there something more?

Our meal came, and it was surprisingly delicious. The potatoes and plantains delightfully complemented the fish. During the dinner, Luke asked me about my life as a restaurant journalist. We laughed when I shared experiences of visiting restaurants in New York.

Other than the guy at the bar who kept looking at me, our evening was enjoyable, and I couldn't remember the last time I felt so relaxed, especially when alone with a man.

There was one frustration. Whenever I tried to delve into Luke's background, he diverted the discussion to the subject of the plight of coffee farmers. It was impossible to get anything personal from the guy.

"What were you doing before getting into this coffee association?" I asked.

He glanced away at the dark water of the inlet and answered, "I've enjoyed coffee for a long time. The origins fascinate me. One of the best coffees comes from a large island in Lake Kivu, which is between the Democratic Republic of Congo and Rwanda. Have you been to Africa?"

"No. Maybe someday. So, what made you develop an interest in coffee?"

"I found out that it comes in many sublime flavors, not just the typical mixed bag you find in the supermarket where sometimes they combine Arabica and Robusta."

"Where did you grow up?" I asked, looking him straight in the eyes.

"Mostly in the middle part of the country, where you have a lot of traditional coffee drinkers. Robusta grows at lower elevations than Arabica, and the plant is a bit more bushy or robust, and therefore Robusta. The taste is not as subtle as Arabica, but a dark roasted Robusta carries a whopping dose of caffeine. Cameroon has some excellent Robustas."

My questioning was going nowhere. With every personal question, there was a deflection. It was frustrating to be with someone who wouldn't share the least little thing about himself, but that wasn't the primary objective. It was to find out if Luke knew about Scott's death, or even had a connection with it.

"May I ask you a question?

"Sure, but you've been asking many questions." He smiled.

"I'm curious to know if there is any criminal activity in the coffee trade?"

He paused a moment, frowned, and said, "Criminal activity? Why do you need to know that?"

"To do a good job, it requires as much information as possible. Is there any crime in and around coffee?"

He was still, his eyes drifting toward the table. He watched the movement of the waiter as he cleared the table. Then he said, "Unfortunately, there are many different kinds of crime. I already described the human traffickers who show up in coffee villages and decimate the population."

He paused, and I waited, and finally, I asked, "Anything else?"

"Farmers are robbed. In some African countries, the farmers hand-carry their coffee to markets in heavy bags, and there are cases where gangs rob them. Life is already hard enough for them, and it is devastating if someone takes away your only source of income." Luke's fingers tightened on the edge of the table.

"That would be tragic," I confirmed.

He said, "Recently, a large truck was hijacked in Tanzania while headed for the port in Dar-es-Salaam. It's not the first time."

"That's appalling." I exclaimed, then after a while added, "Is there anything more?"

"Bribes. All along the supply chain, there are instances of people taking under-the-table payments. For example, if there is a backlog at a port, there might be a payment to get your product to the front of the line. In the end, corruption hurts farmers, and it leaves them in poverty."

He hadn't mentioned the destination of coffee beans, so I went straight to the point. "Do you know of any crime associated with coffee in California, and particularly in Long Beach?"

A quizzical look came on his face. "Long Beach?"

"At the port in Long Beach."

"I've never encountered anything. A few times, we've had problems with shipping documents, but that was more of a computer hiccup."

"But nothing to do with crime?"

"Well, it's a huge port, one of the largest in the world where millions of dollars of products transit every day, mostly in containers. I'd assume some people try to avoid paying import duties, and with the huge influx of goods, there must be smuggling. But, I've never heard of anything specific to coffee."

It appeared he didn't know about Scott, but I couldn't be sure. "What about crimes after importation into a country?" I was pounding him with questions, but wouldn't let up.

The man at the bar was still staring at me and at that point I had enough. The thought was to walk over and confront him, but instead, I glared at him like a pit-bull ready for a fight. He quickly stood up, paid for his beer, and left, and it gave me a feeling of relief.

Luke noticed my menacing look and asked, "Is something wrong?"

"Just some guy at the bar who kept staring at me."

Luke turned. "Which one? Do you want me to go talk to him?"

"He just left." I didn't need Luke to talk to the guy on my behalf, and I would have done more than talk.

"Who knows? How can I put it politely? He may have gotten carried away with checking out an attractive woman.".

I grinned. Is that how Luke saw me with my tangled hair and the rumpled clothing? I shifted back to the previous topic. "You were talking about crimes after import."

"I guess there could be many things, but that's not something we encounter. As I said before, the coffee from our cooperative either goes to a known list of clients, or we sell directly to coffee aficionados who roast their coffee."

I smiled and said, "Like me."

He nodded. "Like you with your fancy roaster." He sat back in his chair and said, "I've been so busy that I forgot to tell you something."

"What's that?"

"My task in this project is to show you the entire coffee supply chain so that you can write your articles. Remember, we want to make coffee consumers more aware of where their coffee comes from and how it gets into their cup. Our next step is to see what happens once the coffee leaves the ports of origin."

"So then, what's the next step?" I smiled.

"Today, you saw the container loaded with bags of coffee beans. The container goes onto the ship. Then it takes a week or more to make its way up the coast. It may be longer if it stops in El Salvador or Mexico."

"Are we taking a cruise on the ship?" I laughed.

"I wish. We shipped a container a few weeks ago to Long Beach, and it just arrived. We want you to have a first-hand experience of the handling of coffee bags from there."

"Long Beach?" I gasped.

"Yes. Tomorrow we fly to Los Angeles. We need to leave the hotel at 6:00 a.m."

Again, this guy was unbelievable. Couldn't he give a little warning? In acting as a tour guide, he was doing a horrific job, and that infuriated me. And why Long Beach? That's where Scott was murdered.

CHAPTER FIFTEEN

My alarm went off at 5:30 a.m., and I was still fuming about Luke. Sure, someone attempted to clean the room, even wiping the dried blood spots with bleach, not exactly up to the standards of a cheap motel on the outskirts of Newark, but at least the sheets and pillows were new. The mattress was lumpy, but that didn't matter.

What mattered was the lack of communication in this assignment. From the very beginning, I'd been kept in the dark. First, it was Ernie who tossed this assignment at me, not having a clue what it was about. He should have done his homework. He had too many irons in the fire, and that didn't help anyone.

Then, I flew to Honduras without an inkling of who to meet or the parameters of the project. It was, "Go to Honduras for a day and write about coffee." Yeah. Thanks, Ernie.

That turned into a two-hour, cyclone ride in an open Jeep. Then, there was the shack with scampering cockroaches. I wasn't squeamish and could stand a bug or two, but one body blow after another added up, and it felt degrading. I had this crazy image of mosquitos with long straws sucking the willpower from my brain one drop at a time.

The most depressing thing was to hear about Scott. That shock disoriented me like nothing else, and it felt like I was flying a glider in a swirling cloud. More than that was the recurring anger. Was I taking it out on Luke?

I had to think of something positive to settle my emotions and get oriented. The tour of the coffee farm was fascinating, and I got my first lead on an article, poor coffee farmers who worked their butts off so that people in America could enjoy a good cup of coffee. Writing about that had redemptive qualities, much more than my recent cookie-cutter articles on food establishments. Maybe I finally had a chance to use my journalism skills to achieve something significant.

Meeting Maria Lopez and seeing the grief she felt for her granddaughter was sobering, and it left a deep impression.

Then unexpectedly, at lunch the previous day, I was informed we were taking a ride to a port. And, the last evening at dinner, Luke surprisingly announced the flight to Los Angeles. If this assignment were to continue, the unpredictability had to stop. Otherwise, I would walk away.

I concluded that Luke was worse than Ernie, and that was going pretty low. Luke had said, "If you have any questions, please ask me." His answers on some things were informative, even overly informative with the way he described aspects of the coffee trade. But, if this was a human interest story, then there had to be some humanness. The guy was a brick wall.

After packing my overnight bag, I walked out of my hotel room and carried it down the exterior walkway, not wanting to roll it over the bat excrement. I jumped when a small snake slithered across the walkway. It looked harmless, but weren't some of the tiny snakes the most poisonous? In any case, I was glad to get out of there.

When I got to the hotel lobby, Luke was waiting. He had two cups of coffee in paper cups and handed me one.

"Ready?" He asked.

"Nice one," I grumbled, showing teeth ready to bite.

"Was the room okay?"

"It's not the room."

"Not used to rising early?"

"I'm up early on weekdays."

"So, what is it?"

"From now on, I need a smidgen of warning. It's impossible to write a decent newspaper piece if you keep pulling unexpected events on me, also known as jerking me around. I need time to plan, to reflect, to prepare my questions, and to develop the storyline."

Luke grinned and picked up our carryon bags and said, "The taxi is waiting."

We got in the taxi and still seething, I asked, "How far is Tegucigalpa?"

"About two and a half hours."

"Is it a direct flight from there?"

"I have no idea," he responded.

"You mean you didn't look into the flight?"

"Not from Tegucigalpa."

"Well, how do you know if you didn't look into it?"

"We're not flying from Tegucigalpa."

"But, you said it was a two and a half-hour drive."

"I correctly answered your question, which was, how far is Tegucigalpa? Only, we're not going there. On the other side of San Lorenzo, there's an airport. We fly out in twenty minutes."

I groaned. Luke was beyond ridiculous. Unless he were more forthcoming, I would resign. Then, I had second thoughts, as I needed money to pay the rent. But, something had to change.

A light gray streak was on the eastern horizon. We traveled through San Lorenzo, some lights still on in the town. We left the city and quickly approached an airport. After Luke paid the taxi driver, we walked through a parking lot, and then passed through a chain-link gate, where a small Cessna airplane sat on the tarmac.

Luke pointed and said, "That's our plane."

"What?" I exclaimed. "Are we flying to Los Angeles in that? It will take a month to get there."

"Of course not. We are flying to San Salvador."

"Where's that?"

"San Salvador is in the country of El Salvador, just up the coast. You've got your passport, I assume."

"How do you think I got into Honduras?"

"Get on the plane. From San Salvador, we have a direct flight to Los Angeles."

"What did I say about advance notice?"

"I forgot," he shrugged.

* * *

The flight from San Salvador to Los Angeles was seven hours. We had two seats in the exit row in economy class, which gave extra legroom. That gave me the ability to stretch my legs and allowed room to work with my laptop. During the flight, I hunkered down and drafted an outline covering what I had learned about coffee thus far. Luke slept most of the way.

Occasionally I glanced at him, his eyes closed, head tilted to the side. He wore a gray t-shirt with the design of a steaming cup of coffee on it, and the words 'Coffee Trust' written above it. His muscular chest moved slowly up and down. He didn't wear a wedding ring, and I wondered if he was married or in a relationship.

I figured it must be challenging to maintain a relationship if he was always traveling around the world visiting coffee cooperatives. Despite his communication limitations, I found him attractive. He was soft-spoken and exhibited an extraordinary passion for his work. He strived to make the world better, to help redeem hurting people, and I wished I had the same enthusiasm for my job. He was the opposite of so many corporate-climbers I had dated.

Maybe it was human, but being single, I often evaluated men as I ticked the boxes. From dating different men, I understood that Mister Perfect didn't exist. The world is fallen, and everyone has cracks. Still, it would be nice to meet someone who met at least eighty percent of my criteria. My mother's standards were higher, several percentage points above perfection. Not too many men would meet her standards, I chuckled.

In thinking of Scott, he was what I was looking for, at least in my imagination, and I had put my hopes in finding out more about him. It was unsettling to know that would never occur. But then I had a chilling thought. Was there a dark side to him that caused the shooting in Long Beach?

The man in the seat next to me was fascinating. I liked his easygoing nature, and he seemed kind and considerate. While physically strong, it looked like he wouldn't harm a flea, but something had caught my attention. At the dinner table the previous evening, I noticed his tight fingers on the edge of the table when he described farmers being robbed. Was there a violent side to him? Because of his reluctance, or inability, to talk about his life, it felt mysterious and even unsettling.

I had a quick thought, which was more of a question. What would it be like to be in a relationship with Luke? That was a tough one because with many men, there was this ethnic, cultural, historical, religious thing that always got in the way. I was Jewish, and Luke worked for some Christian charity group that, for some strange reason, was helping coffee farmers. Honestly, that religious divide would propose a tricky riddle to solve, so it was best to leave it alone.

While it was tempting, I decided to avoid thinking of Luke in romantic terms, even as a fantasy. I had stupidly allowed myself to do that with Scott. And, at this point, to have thoughts about another man would seem like a dishonor to Scott. Or was I just overthinking it?

I made a decision. Just get on with the assignment, finish it, and move on to the next one. And, it would be unlikely that I would ever see Luke again once completing this assignment. My world was New York City restaurants. Luke's world was bug-infested remote farms and jungles.

Why make life complicated when it didn't need to be?

As the plane approached Los Angeles, I read through my first draft of the first article. It was respectable, but not yet up to my standards. What was needed was more of a human factor. For sure, I wouldn't get that from Luke, so it had to come from somewhere else.

Seeing Los Angeles spread out below us gave me an uneasy feeling, especially knowing we were going to Long Beach, the place where someone shot Scott. The circumstances surrounding his shooting were still unknown. As soon as possible, upon landing, I needed to call Ernie to get an update.

I wondered what Ernie would say about me being in Long Beach. Would he ask me to investigate Scott's death, or instruct me to back off? Knowing Ernie, I suspected he would ask me to get more information from the FBI. With his singular approach to the world, getting the story was primary, but maybe that was wrong. Taking anything that paid came first, even if it meant sending your journalists to snake and bat and cockroach-infested hotels. It took a minute to remember the FBI agent's name, Cortez.

At some point, I may need to tell Luke about Scott's death, but not yet. Luke had not given any advance warning about our travels, or any information on his personal life, so why should I tell him about Scott?

After landing, we went through customs, and the customs officer said, "Welcome home." I had only been outside the U.S. for three nights, yet it seemed like an eternity.

When we walked into the general public area, I turned to Luke and asked, "Where are we staying?"

"I don't know."

"You mean you didn't book a hotel?"

"I'm not a travel agent and I was thinking about other stuff."

I shook my head and asked. "How are we getting to Long Beach."

"I need to rent a car."

"Did you make a reservation?"

"No. There wasn't any time to do it. Let's go find a car."

I said, "You get the car, and I'll find a hotel."

While Luke joined a line of people at a car rental agency, I got out my phone and called Ernie.

"Ernie here," he answered.

"This is Sarah," I said.

"Zipper, I'm going into a meeting. How are things in Honduras."

"I'm in Los Angeles and headed to Long Beach."

"What?"

I quickly explained about following the coffee supply chain and wanting to see the shipment arrive at the Port of Long Beach. Then I asked, "Do you want me to meet with FBI Agent Cortez?"

The line went silent for a moment, and Ernie said, "That's interesting. There might be a story, so go for it." Ernie was so predictable.

"Okay, I'll see what I can do, but my priority is to write these coffee articles. By the way, what hotel did Scott stay at?"

"Just a second," he replied. The line was quiet for a moment, and then Ernie stated, "The Pacific Palm Hotel, which is near the port from what I understand."

"Okay, thanks."

"I've got to run," Ernie said. "Be safe and keep me up-to-date." He hung up.

I looked at my phone, realizing I had been so occupied over the past days that I failed to look at my text messages. There were a long string of them from my mother.

"Sarah, give me a call."

"Are you okay?"

"Where are you?"

"You should answer."

"Are you ignoring me?"

"Should I call the police?"

"I just disowned you!"

"Are you getting enough to eat?"

I felt guilty, knowing I communicated with my mother almost every day, and I had gone several days without doing so. I quickly typed a message and sent it.

"Sorry, mom, but I'm on an assignment, and my phone wasn't working. Will call soon."

It was a white lie but could be lived with. There hadn't been a phone signal at the farm in Honduras.

As Luke moved forward in the line, I thought about Ernie's go-ahead to meet with Agent Cortez. Should I go digging into Scott's death? With Ernie, his primary motivation was always *the story*. For me, it was different. It was personal. Someone had ripped away my hopes, and while those expectations may have been girlish and fanciful, it was more than desiring to solve a mystery. I wanted justice.

On my phone, I connected to the internet, found a hotel booking site, and reserved two rooms at the Pacific Palm Hotel in Long Beach.

CHAPTER SIXTEEN

Mira Brennen was coming to the end of her speech at the Women Business Leaders Conference, with over three hundred women attending. They were top managers from some of the largest corporations across America.

Mira gazed at the crowd and spoke of ethics, each word carefully paced, slowing at those critical points requiring emphasis and giving time gaps between words to augment drama, her deep rich voice mesmerizing the crowd.

The speech was a play on emotions, as a tactic to influence the audience to aspire to her ideals.

She worked toward the conclusion and said, "Each summer I would spend a week or two near the sea with my aunt and her family. She loved nature and enjoyed walking on the sand and looking for seashells. But, none of us knew that she would never get to see her child grow up to adulthood, the son she adored. A corporation took that away from her by exposing her to untenable, degrading working conditions. The saddest thing for me is that I never got to say goodbye."

She paused, her large green eyes slowly scanning the crowd to see if her magic was working. The story of her aunt was one she had used many times before, one that pulled on the heartstrings. She saw the drawn expectant faces of the women in the crowd and knew they were with her, so she continued, "You know, she, like thousands of other people working for corporations, never benefited from a fundamental human right, the right of wellbeing. At my company, Lyra-Dominion, we have taken this principle to heart. As a spiritual duty, we carefully consider the welfare of everyone working in our company, and this fundamental human right also applies to all others within our sphere, for we are connected. We may not always get it right, but we do our best to strive for this ideal. We make a concerted effort to examine every process and eliminate all negative forces hindering the achievement of this universal truth. It's holistic with the acknowledgment that we are all one.

"I believe that if every business in America worked to achieve this, we would have a better world, and wellbeing would become an actual reality.

"Thank you for allowing me to share my thoughts with you today."

As she concluded, loud applause rippled through the crowd. The women in the audience stood, and the noise became louder. The chairwoman of the conference walked up the steps of the stage carrying a huge bouquet and handed it to Mira, while the women attendees gazed at her with looks of intense admiration.

Mira made a slight bow, and her lips moved to communicate a soundless 'Thank You.' As she did this, she was aware that most of the women in the room worked for companies started by others. She was above them, having founded and built her company, and she was now a billionaire. None of the women there could claim that achievement, and it gave her a great sense of satisfaction.

Most rewarding was the power and influence she felt over these women. She recognized what this meant. Over the coming days, some would call her office, requesting her attendance at meetings to mingle with wealthy and influential people. Indeed, this was an immensely rewarding experience.

She held the flowers high above her, lowered them, made a small self-deprecating bow, and then confidently walked across the stage and exited behind the side curtain where an assistant rushed to take the flowers from her. The assistant handed over Mira's cell phone, and Mira pushed the button to call Sai.

"Where are you?" Mira asked.

"Still in New York," he answered.

"I'll see you there. I'm flying in tonight." She paused, knowing the caution on phrasing words. "Did you find the hindrance to our process?"

"The hindrance has been identified and is now being monitored. A cleaner will soon enter the dwelling, and when there is an opportunity, we will appropriately manage the hindrance."

Mira admired Sai's care over the phone. They were tracking an intelligent and dangerous old man, to take him away at an optimal moment without witnesses. This time it would be different than what happened in Long Beach. The old man's apartment would be searched, followed by the removal and destruction of any incriminating documentation."

"That's good," Mira said. "This is a blockage to the wellbeing of our ecosystem, and protecting that fundamental is the highest calling. Are there any others that might raise alarm?"

"Perhaps. It concerns the previous hindrance we removed and the media company he worked for in New York. The company replaced that previous hindrance with someone else."

"Do you know anything about the new subject, the replacement?"

Sai laughed. "The subject covers food and restaurants in New York."

"Should we be concerned?"

He laughed again. "The previous one was brilliant in numbers. This one is poetic when it comes to describing fried chicken and retro diners, but don't expect her to know anything about complex international finance. Currently, she's stuck on a dirty little farm south of Mexico. One of our reps saw her arrive at a port where she was with farmers in beat-up trucks. It seems she returned to the farm. It would be quite comical to see a spoiled New York City softie in the middle of squat-poor farmers. I don't think we need to worry."

"Get someone to keep an eye on the subject and try to find out what she's doing. We can't take any chances."

"Absolutely," Sai said.

Mira hung up and thought again about her speech. Indeed, it was extremely satisfying to have manipulated the women in the room, but Sai's work was more critical. Her plan was advancing. They must eliminate all obstacles to achieve the expansion of her company.

Indeed, wellbeing was the optimal word for effectively guiding people. It packaged the ideas of life, liberty, happiness, and social good, and the masses followed her when she dangled that promise in front of them.

But, for her, the term held an entirely different meaning, for all definitions were ultimately in the eye of the beholder. Her ultimate wellbeing was more than prosperity. It would be fully realized the day she achieved her rightful, elevated position in the world. She was the god of her destiny, and therefore any actions necessary to achieve that goal were justified, irrespective if others judged them as right or wrong.

CHAPTER SEVENTEEN

The Pacific Palm Hotel was more of a motel than a hotel, a long yellowish two-story building in an L-shape, consisting of fifty rooms. A reception office was at the front end of the building, and in the darkness of the evening, a giant neon sign illuminated the front part of the parking area.

After checking in, Luke and I agreed to skip a sit-down meal and instead, grab food at a nearby fast-food restaurant and eat alone in our rooms. We would restart our work in the morning.

I entered my simply furnished room, but compared to the previous three nights, it was one giant leap for womankind, at least to paraphrase from the first man on the moon. The furniture wasn't new, but at least no bugs crawled around the place. The Honduras trip had reset my standards. For sure that country had excellent hotels, but I hadn't been lucky.

The thought of Honduras and the condition of the farmers lingered in my mind and made me sad. I was grateful to live in a country where the economy worked. The United States had its share of poverty, but most people were able to feed their families and send their kids to school.

In looking around the room, I wondered why Scott Roberts had chosen this hotel? Was it just a place to stay, or was it a meeting point, or place of observation? Even more essential, why was he in Long Beach?

There was only one place to start. Removing my phone from my shoulder bag, I looked up the number of the FBI in Long Beach and called it.

"Federal Bureau of Investigation," a female voice answered.

"Hi, I'm Sarah Zipper, and I wonder if I could speak with Agent Cortez?"

"Just a moment. Let me see if he's still in."

I waited two minutes, and the woman came back on and said, "I'll transfer you through."

The phone rang once, and a deep voice answered. "This is Agent Cortez." He sounded tired.

"Hello, good evening. My name is Sarah Zipper, and I work with Real Media in New York. I'm wondering if I could ask some questions about the Scott Roberts case."

"Real Media? I already spoke with the manager there. What's his name again?"

"Ernie Finkel."

"Yes, with Ernie Finkel. There's not much more I can say. Anyway, this is an ongoing case, and what I can tell you is limited."

"I understand that," I replied, "but Ernie gave me Scott's assignment. Is there anything I need to know or be concerned about?"

"His assignment? You mean the one about coffee?"

"That's right. Now, I've taken it over. Should I be worried?"

"As far as our investigation, it's advancing. Yesterday we accessed Scott Robert's laptop. It was password-protected, and it took time for our techies to crack the code. Now, we're looking through the files. Other than that, it's an ongoing investigation, so I can't say much more."

"Why would anyone want to shoot Scott because of a coffee article?"

"Good question. Something more seems to have been going on, unless it was random, but the security video suggests otherwise. I told this to Ernie Finkel. Look, why don't you call me tomorrow afternoon after we have a time to go through the files on Scott Roberts' computer. We may have questions for you. For now, step back, be patient, and let us do our job."

Agent Cortez hung up, and I felt frustrated. I had gained nothing more than what I already knew. He said nothing substantial, other than what he had already told Ernie, that the killing seemed premeditated.

That made me angry. For my sake, and for Scott, I needed answers. There was no way I would step back and be patient. Patience wasn't part of my character. As far as Long Beach, I planned to make the most of my time, and not just look at the next step in the coffee supply chain. What good would that do?

Would the shipping world be of interest to Scott? It seemed nothing more than products transported from one place to another, a routine commercial act done hundreds of millions of times a day around the world, whether it was freighters moving across the seas, or small vans moving around in towns. Would looking at the Port of Long Beach help to get justice for Scott?

Then, I thought of Luke Cotton. At some point, he would find out what happened to Scott. Maybe I should tell him sooner rather than later because for some crazy unknown reason, our lives might be in danger.

At the same time, I was reluctant to tell him. Luke had been so ambiguous when informing me where we were going and what we were doing, only letting me know in the last second. And, I knew so little about him. He was evasive, more like an impenetrable wall, with a strange mystery on the other side.

A fast-food meal did not appeal to me, so I decided to skip dinner. Instead, I stretched my legs out on the bed, rested my back against cushions, and opened my laptop, expecting to advance on the coffee article. I was always good at creating text, but for some bizarre reason, words did not come. This project was beginning to feel like a depressing jumbled mess, especially with the unexplained death of Scott mixed in.

I considered my simple life of writing about food and chefs and restaurant owners. Sometimes it was fun and maybe not so bad after all. But, hadn't I had enough of that? Realistically, there were no other opportunities on the horizon.

The honest fact was, I did not know where to go from here, and didn't have a hint of what to do with the rest of my life.

* * *

The following morning the phone in my hotel room rang, jolting me out of a sound sleep. It took a minute to find the phone. I picked it up, held it to my ear, and answered, "Hello."

"It's seven-thirty. Are you coming?"

It was Luke. I looked at the hotel alarm clock next to my bed, and the red digital numbers blinked seven-thirty-three. "Ah, yeah, sorry. I was working late last night and must have slept in. Can you give me a few minutes?"

"I'll be in the car. And one more thing. I think we should get out of Long Beach today, and go on to our next place in the supply chain."

"Like where?"

"It's a coffee company on the other side of Los Angeles. Can you pack your stuff and check out?"

I exploded. "Well, thank's so much for advance notice. What did I tell you before? I need lead time. It helps with my writing process, and it's just downright disrespectful to do this to me."

"I forgot," he said. "Sorry. I'll be waiting in the car."

I hung up on him and then slowly rolled out of bed and headed for the bathroom and took a long shower. After drying off and getting dressed, I took time to pack my bag. I checked my phone for any messages, looked around the room to see if I had forgotten anything, and then walked out the door.

I went to the hotel office, turned in my key, and asked to pay the hotel bill, but Luke had already paid for it. Then I went into the parking lot.

Luke stood by the rental car, and I stormed past him, opened the back door of the vehicle, and flipped my carryon bag inside. I slammed the back door, took my computer bag with me to the front seat, and then slammed the front door.

Getting into the driver's side, Luke glanced at me. "I said, I'm sorry."

"Sorry, won't do. You've got to give me a little heads up. You haven't even told me what we are doing here today other than looking at the next step in the coffee chain. What does that mean?"

He glared at me. "You're the writer. Not me. You need to see how coffee moves from the world of the farmers to the world of the consumers, and then to contrast the two. That's about all I can tell you. Scott Roberts knew all about this."

I thought of Scott, and it seemed evident that Luke didn't know what happened. Should I tell him? He would find out at some point anyhow.

I asked, "Did you hear about Scott?"

"What do you mean?"

"Do you know what happened after I replaced him on this writing project?"

"No. I thought that the two of you were working on this together."

"After arriving in Honduras, my boss informed me that someone shot and killed Scott."

Luke stared at me, his mouth slightly open. After a long moment of silence with worry lines on his forehead, he exclaimed. "That's crazy. Is this some kind of joke?"

"That was my reaction when I first heard of it. Scott was here in Long Beach doing something. What it was, we aren't sure. He stayed in this hotel, walked out into this parking lot, and there was a scuffle with a couple of men. Scott resisted, and one of the men shot him, and then they pulled him into a car and drove away, and all evidence says he is dead."

"Right here, in this hotel, this parking lot?" Luke looked around.

"That's right."

His eyes glared at me. "You're a lunatic to have picked this place for us."

"Not really. I wanted to get an impression of the scene of the crime."

"It's seems unwise, no, more than that, insane," Luke said.

"I'm a reporter and journalist. We need first-hand impressions." As I said that, indeed, it didn't feel wise. What if I had been staying in the exact same hotel room as Scott? Wouldn't that be creepy?

"You mentioned that all evidence said Scott was dead? What does that mean?"

"The witnesses said he was shot twice in the chest and once in the head, and then he was dragged into a car. The hotel security camera confirms that."

"But, how do you know he is dead, and where is he?"

I hadn't thought about that. "Law enforcement is investigating."

"Now, I'd like to ask something," Luke said.

"Like what?"

"How long have you known about this?"

"Ernie Finkel informed me the evening I arrived in Honduras . . . so two . . . no, three days ago."

"And you didn't tell me?"

"I wasn't sure you needed to know." That wasn't exactly the truth, because I wasn't sure if Luke had anything to do with Scott's death, and I still wasn't sure.

Luke said, "You've been talking about transparency and sharing information. Don't you think the shooting is something I should be aware of? The word hypocrisy comes to mind. You're asking one thing from me, and I admit I'm not the world's best communicator, but you've been doing the same thing to me. Only, in your case, it's worse."

"Are you sure? There was only one thing I didn't tell you, but you have a whole string of failures, keeping me in the dark about where we were going and what we were doing."

"Are you kidding me. On my side, my lack of communication only had to do with logistics, a flexible day-by-day kind of thing. On your side, you didn't tell me about a homicide. That's a world of difference. "

"Flexible day-by-day? It's more like, oh, let's do this, and let's do that. Give me a plan and I'll do a better job."

"You put us in the same hotel as Scott. That's bizarre."

I took a breath. This wasn't the time to go to war with Luke. "Okay," I said. "Let's try and be reasonable." I wasn't ready to give apologies. And honestly, despite Luke's lack of a published travel itinerary, I had gathered enough material to write the articles.

Luke nodded. "One other thing. Why was Scott shot? And the follow-up question is whether our lives are in danger?"

"Two answers. I have no idea, and I have no idea."

"Then, isn't it a good thing that we get out of here today?"

"You mean to leave right now?"

"From what you just said, you don't know why someone attacked Scott. All you know is that he was working on this coffee assignment. Did he come across something in this job that got him in trouble, or was it caused by something entirely different?"

"We don't know."

"Exactly. And, I assume the police are working on it."

"That's correct. Only, it's the FBI working with the police, or something like that. I spoke with an Agent Cortez about it last night. He had already spoken with my boss in New York. Agent Cortez didn't have much to give me at this point."

"Of course not. It's an ongoing investigation, so any information given is few and far between, and why is the FBI in on this?"

"Same answer as before. I have no idea. Only one thing, I didn't tell Agent Cortez that I am in Long Beach."

"Nor, that you were staying at the same hotel as Scott Roberts," Luke stated. "This agent may have gone ballistic if he heard that. No detective likes it when outsiders meddle in a case. It's better that you let this FBI agent do his business. And why don't you stick to the job, the one we hired you to do?'

I reflected on that. Luke made sense. What did I know about criminal investigations? My expertise was in an entirely different sphere, mainly restaurant articles. "I agree. Let's stick with writing about coffee. Where do we go from here?"

"First, let's go get breakfast. Then we'll head to the port."

Was the task really to focus on coffee? I had given in to Luke too quickly because the criminal case still nagged in my mind. There was no way I would let it go.

CHAPTER EIGHTEEN

We ate breakfast at a diner in Long Beach, not far from the docks. The interior of the restaurant was an eclectic mix of 1950's furniture and every era since then. It was like the owner acquired whatever was available, with no consideration of color or style, the exact opposite of restaurants in New York, where interior decorators worked meticulously to harmonize and balance every visual, from forks to lampshades.

Luke and I sat on unmatching wooden chairs around a small round wooden table, and we both ordered the breakfast special. The restaurant was busy and noisy, and most of the clientele wore jeans, workboots, and hardhats.

The breakfast special came with three pancakes, two eggs, two small sausages, and two strips of bacon, a glass of orange juice, and all you could drink coffee. I was not a practicing Jew, but eating pork raised a sense of religious guilt, knowing Stan Schultz would not approve. I put butter on the pancakes along with a liberal dose of maple syrup.

As I cut into the pancakes, the homey smell of syrup and melted butter floated to my nostrils and attacked my brain. I took a bite and tasted mouthwatering fluffy, warm goodness. Did it really matter that the pancakes originated from a giant industrial size premix bag? Having skipped supper the previous evening, I was hungry.

Luke watched me eat as he dug into his plate of food. He smiled and said, "May I kindly suggest what we might potentially do today?"

"A suggestion?" I asked.

"Yeah, I want to avoid surprises."

I frowned. "Go ahead." At least he was making an effort.

"I propose that we only take a look at the port today. That will give you an idea of how coffee arrives into the United States. I had much more planned, such as the visit to the coffee wholesaler in Los Angeles. But, based on what you told me about Scott Roberts, it may not be wise to stick around Long Beach. We can cover those other things when we get home to the east coast."

"What other things?"

"It seems important that you visualize how coffee moves from the docks to the consumer. There are coffee wholesalers on the east coast. We might also visit a large brand name roaster to see how coffee is packaged and distributed to supermarkets and other points of sale. It would be helpful to contrast that with the flow of green coffee beans to specialty coffee places that do their roasting. And, of course, visiting a coffee shop doing its roasting gives another perspective."

"Were we going to do all that in the Long Beach area?" I sneered. He hadn't told me until now, and therefore he wasn't making an ounce of progress.

"Both Long Beach and Los Angeles, but, as I said, let's head home, and we can see the wholesaler and the roasting in New Jersey closer to my organization's headquarters, and of course closer to your base in New York. This news about Scott Roberts makes me nervous."

"Why is that?"

"I know a bit about detective work, and detectives always look for motivation. We know little about the motivation for this crime or even if it had anything to do with Scott's work on the coffee articles. So, my preference is to be cautious and get away from here."

I had a thought. Even though I had agreed to stay clear of the investigation, my reporter side was still curious. "Can we do one other thing besides visit the docks?"

"What's that?"

"To give more background to my articles, it would be helpful to visit the Nyx Lines distribution center, to see how they handle the containers full of coffee. You had mentioned that they specialized in that sort of thing." I wasn't fully transparent with him about my motivations.

Luke paused for a moment and said, "Okay, I can arrange it. In Long Beach, Nyx Lines has a staging area where they empty containers and separate the contents into smaller shipments. We can look at that."

Now, my imagination was racing. Scott Roberts had a document from Nyx Lines on his possession. By visiting their office, I would have a chance to peek into the operations.

The woman serving us came by, topped up our coffee cups, and I took a sip.

"What do you think of the coffee?" Luke asked.

I smiled. "Drinkable. It goes with the breakfast, but nothing like your coffee from Honduras. I give this coffee a two or a three. Your coffee is at the top, a ten."

"I agree," Luke said. "Are you ready to go?" The only thing left on our plates were smears of syrup.

"Let's do it," I said while feeling nervous we were covering the same territory where Scott had been. Was it wise to do this?

We traveled on a street parallel to the port, and the port seemed to stretch to infinity. As Luke drove, he explained that the Port of Long Beach was like the conjoined twin of the Port of Los Angeles, existing side by side, together becoming one of the largest shipping areas in the world. Those two ports generated billions of dollars of economic value each year.

Luke said, "We need a visitor's pass to drive into some areas of the port, where they handle the containers. Everything is highly automated, and if we went in there, we'd just be getting in the way."

He drove into a parking area where we had a view of what seemed to be tens of thousands of containers stacked in rows. He said, "Each day, an immense number of products come and go through here, everything from commodities to finished goods."

"Where's your coffee shipment?" I asked, seeing there was no way possible to distinguish the contents of one metal box from another. This also seemed like another dead-end in my endless questions about Scott. Was there anything in that mass of containers that would have been of interest to him?

"Our shipment is in there somewhere. Don't worry. A computer is tracking it. When a truck shows up at the front gate, the computer instructs cranes and loading machines to unstack containers, and find the appropriate one. The truck then goes to a loading spot, the container is quickly placed on the back, and the truck leaves."

"How do they control what's inside those containers?"

"Good question. There are electronic customs declarations completed at the points of origin. For instance, that took place in the port of San Lorenzo."

I remembered Luke handing the shipping documents to the man with the checkered shirt and dark mustache. And, I remembered the strange way the man kept looking at me when he sat at the bar in the restaurant.

Luke continued. "There's one last control for radioactive material when the container leaves the port. Still, I'm sure it's impossible to be sure of every single item entering the country."

I turned to Luke and asked, "May I ask why it's important for me to see this?"

"Let me ask you a question. What's different between this and our farm in Honduras?"

That was interesting. My eyes scanned the vast area and realized that it was almost impossible to do a comparison. "Just about everything is different."

Luke smiled. "That's right. Imagine the contrast between this and the coffee farms. The product originates from peaceful farms where backbreaking manual labor takes place. And then bingo, the coffee magically transitions into the industrialized, automated world. The farmers are now invisible, and we forget the human touch."

"It seems coffee would be more enjoyable if we knew about the origin, and even more so if we knew about the people who grew it." I thought again about my home-roasted coffee. I knew it came from Ethiopia but didn't have a clue about the people behind it, nor their living conditions.

Luke grinned. "Now you're getting it. In the future, that will be possible. Block-chain technologies will enable coffee drinkers to trace their coffee right back to the farm where it came from."

"What's block-chain?"

"It's the same technology used for controlling cryptocurrencies."

"That sounds complicated."

"Let's not get lost in that, but if it works, it will be a great step forward in what we want to achieve. For now, you must see the whole picture. Let's go visit the Nyx Lines distribution area."

A flash went through my mind. Did cryptocurrencies and coffee have something to do with Scott's death? This was way out of my league, but Scott would know these things.

Luke started the car, pulled out into the street, and then drove several miles to an industrial area in Long Beach. He steered the vehicle through an open gate and into a large parking lot full of trucks with containers. A massive warehouse stood at the end of the parking lot, and trucks backed up to openings on the side of the warehouse. The words, Nyx Lines, was written in big letters on the outside of the warehouse.

Luke said, "These trucks came directly from the port, and those containers hold coffee from many different countries. Much of that coffee goes to the large brand name companies you find in supermarkets."

"Is that where your coffee from Honduras ends up?"

"We try to avoid selling to large companies because they often push for big discounts, and they mix our beans with other origins. You can't blame them for asking for discounts, because that's a normal part of business. We prefer selling to smaller companies that package our coffee as single source, which gives consumers a unique tasting experience."

"Are you being hard on the large coffee brands?"

Luke smiled. "Probably, yes. If I'm honest, some of the large companies have a real concern for coffee producers. They use the word *sustainability*, which means they want the coffee supply to improve as worldwide demand increases. We are pleased when they invest at the farm level."

"Okay, I get it. Helping the farmers benefits all coffee lovers. And, drinking single-origin coffee enhances our experience."

Luke looked me, nodded, and grinned.

He was like a broken record replaying the same underlying theme. I understood it, but needed more. So, I will be a broken record and persist in my search, I told myself.

He parked in a visitors' parking spot, we exited the car and entered the warehouse through a side door. Inside the warehouse, machines and conveyer belts were running, and mountains of jute bags of coffee stood in the room.

Luke led the way to a walkway next to a wall. Behind a protective rail, he pointed and explained, "This is where they unload the containers."

Across the room, a machine with a gripper reached into a container and plucked a bag and placed it on a conveyer belt. It quickly went back for another.

"Everything is automatic," Luke stated. "Sensors on that gripper identify the bag, and then the gripper does its work. At the end of the belt, another robotic arm stacks the bags on pallets. Then forklifts move the pallets. From there, trucks deliver the bags to the next destination."

"There's little human effort," I remarked, remembering the sweaty, backbreaking work of Luke and the others when loading bags.

"And, less human injury," Luke said. "Think of the investment needed to buy and maintain all that sophisticated machinery. Why can't we have just a bit more of that investment on the front end?"

Again, he was replaying an old theme.

"Where is your coffee in all this?"

"It's in there somewhere, but for sure, the right bags get to our buyers."

As Luke spoke, three men exited an office and stood near us on the walkway. One of the men wore work boots, jeans and a blue shirt, and a white plastic hardhat. The other two wore dark suits, white shirts, and dark ties. I noticed a holster with a gun inside the suit jacket of one man.

The man in the hardhat glanced over and nodded at Luke, and Luke waved back.

I overheard their conversation. The man with the hardhat said, "I'll be glad to help if I can think of anything."

One man reached into his inner jacket pocket, pulled out a business card, and handed it to the man in the hardhat. He said, "Call me on that number."

The man with the hardhat took the card and looked at it. "For sure, Agent Cortez."

A flash of horror went through me when I heard that. Was this the Agent Cortez I had spoken with on the phone? I hadn't told him I was in Long Beach. Why was he here? But, that was logical. Scott had a document with Nyx Lines on it, so of course, the detective would follow up on that.

I leaned toward Luke and whispered, "I need to talk to that man."
"Who?"
"The one on the right in the dark suit. He's investigating the case."
"What are you talking about?"
"The case of Scott Roberts."

CHAPTER NINETEEN

Agent Cortez and his FBI partner left the building, and I said, "Let's go. I need to speak with them."

Luke said, "You agreed not to get involved."

"Yes. I mean no, but this is a chance to gather information. Maybe now the FBI guy has more material." I searched for an argument to persuade Luke. "Maybe he knows if we're in danger."

I moved quickly toward the exit door, and Luke followed. I saw the men heading for a dark sedan car and I yelled out, "FBI agents, can I speak with you?"

They turned around, saw me, and waited as I walked toward them.

I asked, "Excuse me, but are you the Agent Cortez working on the Scott Roberts case?"

"That's correct, one of them answered. Why do you ask?"

"My name is Sarah Zipper. I spoke with you last night."

"I remember, but what are you doing here?"

"As I told you, I'm taking over Scott Roberts assignment. This is Luke Cotton, one of the parties that hired me to write articles on coffee."

Luke shifted his weight, as though uneasy to be there.

I continued, "Can I ask if you've made any progress?"

The second detective stood back and stared at Luke. Agent Cortez frowned and said, "I'm not sure why you are here at this distribution center, but I thought I asked you to back off from this case?"

"We weren't doing anything about your case. We were only looking into the coffee supply chain. Luke's company ships coffee with Nyx Lines, so we were looking at the physical flows."

"That seems an unusual coincidence."

"It is what it is," I stated. "Is there anything you can tell us?"

Agent Cortez's eyebrows narrowed. "It's an ongoing investigation and there's nothing I can share.".

"So, you don't know who committed this crime, or why?"

He looked at me with a cold stare. "We are exploring different scenarios." He waited a moment, and said, "I asked you to let us do our work."

"Like what scenarios," I asked.

"I told you to back off. Stick with your writing project, and quit trying to play detective

"Are we in danger?"

Agent Cortez abruptly turned to Luke and asked, "What involvement does your company have in this?"

Luke hesitated, then answered, "I don't have a company. My not-for-profit organization, Coffee Trust, works with poor coffee farmers."

"Why are you here?" Cortez asked with a forceful voice.

"As Sarah mentioned, we're following the coffee supply chain to gather information so she can write a series of articles for important coffee organizations."

"And what is your interest in this warehouse?"

"Our coffee transits through here," Luke replied.

"Interesting," Cortez remarked. "Does Coffee Trust, have any activity in Colombia or Venezuela?"

"Not yet. For now, we only operate in a couple of the Central American countries, like Honduras and El Salvador. Why do you ask?"

"Does coffee coming from South America transit through Honduras?" Cortez sharply asked.

"I'm not sure what you mean."

"Exactly what I said. Do these jute bags of coffee from South America ever stop off in Honduras? Do they get restacked in containers along the way?" His questions were like an interrogation.

Luke held his ground. "I suppose it could happen, although that's not what my organization does. We work with farmers who grow coffee to improve their crops and their lives. We also handle the sales and distribution of their coffee in North America."

Agent Cortez looked at his partner, who nodded back at him. Cortez said, "That's all for now. We'll get back to you if we have questions. If you think of anything that might be helpful, call this number, otherwise, stay away from this case." He handed his business card to me."

I asked, "Can't you give us any information? Are we in danger?"

Cortez glanced at Luke, and then back to me. "We need to do our research without public interference, and I keep telling you that this is an active investigation. My recommendation is that you return to New York, and be careful who you talk with when writing your article. There are unknowns."

* * *

We got back in the car, and Luke said, "Let's get out of here."

I asked, "What did he mean by that?"

"By what?"

"To be careful who I talk with." The image of the second detective staring at Luke stayed in my mind.

"It means what they said that there are unknowns, and fundamentally, they don't have a clue in the world what's going on, and he's fishing for evidence."

"But why be careful? Am I in danger? Have I done anything to warrant what happened to Scott?"

"He's just trying to keep you from dirtying up his investigation."

"I'm not so sure. It sounded like Agent Cortez gave me a specific warning."

"They're probably working on different hypothesis, that's all. Maybe in Scott's files, there was something about Nyx Lines. Their job is to follow up on all leads."

"Do you think we are safe here?"

"That's exactly what I was getting at earlier, that we should return to the east coast. We can accomplish everything there. Can you check to see if any flights are available?"

Luke was right, and I didn't see how I could add anything to the FBI investigation. I took out my phone and, in a few minutes, found a possibility. "There is a two ten flight out of Los Angeles this afternoon that gets into Newark at ten-twenty this evening."

"If the traffic isn't bad, I think we can make it. Can you book it for us?" Luke reached into his back pocket, took out his wallet, and handed me his credit card.

He broke the speed limit driving to the airport, and after a long run through the airport terminal, we caught the flight. Once in the air, I again asked personal questions to Luke, but got the same old diversions. Eventually, he put earphones in his ears and listened to something on his phone, and from time to time, nodded off to sleep.

It was frustrating to be with him. When sleeping, this attractive man appeared gentle as a baby who would have nothing to hide. Yet, he was as open as a clam and it was driving me nuts. This made me even more determined. I would open him up, just wait and see. I smiled.

I had a couple of takeaways from our time in Long Beach. Concerning the coffee article, I was astonished to see the contrast between rural coffee farms where all tasks were done with back-breaking manual labor, versus the sudden modernization and automation once the coffee entered the United States. At the farm level, there was a human touch, from picking to washing to separation of green beans. Then, starting with the boat, it became depersonalized, first with transport in soulless shipping containers, and then going to a warehouse where robots manipulated bags along a conveyer belt. Subsequently, coffee became like any other mass-produced merchandise on a production line.

My second takeaway was troubling. To stay at the same hotel as Scott was probably foolish. Rather than giving insights, it unsettled me. Even more unnerving was to meet Agent Cortez. He gave no new information, and he seemed hostile. That only left me with questions. What was the motivation for the crime? What did the detective mean by being careful with who you talked with? His warning was sobering, even frightening. And, why did Luke appear to be on his guard and nervous when we were with the two detectives?

I peered over at Luke. Indeed, he was an interesting man who seemed to have a big heart for his poor farmers. He was also a handsome man, and the blue eyes were killers. Yet, he was unapproachable. Was there a mystery here that posed danger?

As the airplane approached Newark Airport, I turned to Luke and asked, "Do you think those two FBI agents knew more than they were telling us?"

"Of course," Luke replied.

"Why do you say that?"

"It's just a hunch, but why would they be asking about shipments from South America? There's something behind that."

"What could it be?"

"Just the fact that the FBI is taking the lead means there's something more to this. If the murder of Scott were a random act or even premediated, the Long Beach Police would take the lead. The FBI steps in if there's something more like terrorism or organized crime."

When Luke said this, he seemed sure of himself, and I wondered how he would have these insights. What would a guy with a focus on coffee farms know about the workings of police departments and the FBI? Did Luke have a criminal background where he learned these things? Is that why he didn't share about himself? Is that why he seemed nervous around the two FBI agents?

I stated, "Scott was working on the same assignment that I am. Correct?"

"That's right."

"In all that we've done over the last days, have you identified anything criminal?"

Luke paused a moment and said, "Human traffickers. I dislike them to the core."

"I know, but is there anything else?"

"Don't you think it's criminal not to pay workers adequately for their labor?"

Was he deflecting my question? "None of that seems likely to lead to Scott's death unless I'm overlooking something. How much do you know about Nyx Lines? We see that Nyx Lines is of interest to the FBI, but would it have been of interest to Scott?"

"It's part of the coffee supply chain, and he must have been researching this for the articles."

I thought of Scott and his business perspective. What was he investigating? "How big is Nyx Lines?" I asked.

"What do you mean?"

"Are they a big player in international shipping?"

"I'd say they are small to medium. As stated before, their specialty is shipping commodities like coffee and cocoa beans."

"Is Nyx Lines a publicly-traded company, that is, can you buy their shares on the stock market?"

"I'm not sure. We use them to transport our coffee, and they've always done a good job at a fair price."

I wasn't sure company ownership was a relevant question, but it is one Scott probably would ask. I needed to do some research.

As the plane descended toward the airport, Luke turned to me and asked, "I'm wondering if this is a distraction."

"What do you mean?"

"Aren't all these questions about Scott Roberts sidetracking us? I keep telling you our objective is to make consumers more aware of where their coffee comes from and how it arrives in their coffee mug. It's not to do a criminal investigation. Why don't we focus on the writing assignment? I understand that Scott's death is unsettling, but getting these articles is also important, at least to the International Coffee Organization and the Specialty Coffee Association. And it's important to me. Can you do that? If you're intent on investigating this crime, then perhaps we need to consider assigning this to another media company."

I thought of Ernie and the grief he would bring on me if Real Media lost this project. But it was more than that. There was a story here. The coffee articles had to be written, because coffee drinkers needed to know about the farmers who produced their daily cup of coffee. "I understand. Let's complete this writing assignment."

As I said that, my thoughts immediately shifted to Nyx Lines. I needed more information on this company.

My second thought was about myself. What was I doing getting mixed up in this, a lowly restaurant writer taking on a homicide and whatever was behind it? I took a breath, realizing that what I had been in the past wasn't that important. Now, what mattered the most was to get answers.

Someone had taken Scott away from me, or at least my idealized version of him. My feelings of self-pity were real, but there was another sobering reality. Someone had brutally taken away his life and they had to pay.

CHAPTER TWENTY

Valentina tried to stay unnoticed, but it wasn't possible. During the day, Mira Brennen, the owner of the house, had been coming and going. The woman's icy demeanor frightened Valentina. Ricco's threats only made it worse, warning that the American police would put her in jail for years if they found her in New York without a visa. She was determined to find a way out of this desperate predicament, but how?

When Mira was somewhere in the house, Valentina purposely went to other places to dust and clean. She was allowed in all rooms but one, Señora Brennen's office. Ricco locked it when Señora Brennen left the house. Valentina cleaned the office once a week, always under Ricco's direct supervision. Ricco gave a stern warning never to set foot into that room without his presence.

Valentina stayed incognito during the day, but she was unable to remain in hiding forever.

Several hours before dinner, Jonas, the cook, called Valentina into the kitchen to help prepare food. He was cooking a feast, and he explained each dish from starter to dessert, consisting of golden Ossetra caviar, king crab salad with honey crisp apple, and mosaic of *poularde* with foie gras, and roasted lamb. The dessert was caramelized flan with pistachio pastry cream. Valentina marveled at the colors and smells, too shy to ask Jonas for a taste.

Valentina's job was to serve the meal. Señora Brennen insisted on a specific dress code, so Valentina wore a white trimmed black dress that came just below her knees. She also wore a white half apron, along with a lace headpiece.

At the dinner table sat Señora Brennen and a man named Sai, who worked with her. Ricco was also there, and Valentina guessed that Ricco handled Señora Brennen's security.

Every time Valentina entered the dining room to serve food or take something away, their voices lowered, and occasionally conversation stopped until she walked away. They ate less than a third of the served food, and Jonas threw the leftovers into the trash.

At the end of the dinner, Señora Brennen said to Valentina, "Bring us Cognac, the Louis the thirteenth, Remy Martin. Serve it in the living room."

That was the first time Señora Brennen had ever spoken to Valentina, although she had glared at Valentina numerous times. That stare chilled her to the bones.

Valentina went into the kitchen and told Jonas what Señora Brennen ordered.

Jonas asked, "Do you know how to serve Cognac?"

"Of course, in a glass" She felt it was a ridiculous question.

"Not just any." He reached into a cupboard with beautiful glasses and took out three large round ones. "These are crystal glasses from Bohemia and costly. You pour two fingers at the bottom."

"Two fingers?"

"Horizontal, not vertical." He laughed while positioning one finger on top of the other and holding them next to the bottom of a glass.

Jonas reached into another cupboard and removed a bottle. "This is very expensive cognac, over three thousand dollars per bottle. Whatever you do, don't drop it or spill it. Move slow when you serve it. Don't smile and don't stare at anyone."

He put the glasses and bottle of Cognac on a tray and handed it to Valentina. "Don't be nervous and good luck."

Valentina carefully carried the tray through the dining area and out into the living room and placed it on a coffee table. Señora Brennen, Sai, and Ricco sat leaning back on the soft couches with silk upholstery.

Valentina slowly lifted the bottle of Cognac, her hand trembling. It would take farmers in Honduras several years to make three thousand dollars. She removed the cap from the bottle and poured the golden liquid into the three glasses, and then put the cap back on the bottle and placed the bottle on the tray.

Then Valentina stood at attention, staring across the room.

Señora Brennen said, "Go," while flipping the back of her hand like shooing away a fly.

Valentina left the living room but stopped when she entered the dining area, leaning sideways just out of view of the three people, to hear the conversation. Their voices became elevated, and she understood every word.

"What happened to the old man? What was his name again?" Mira asked.

Sai answered. "Ricco is handling the detail here in New York."

Valentina remarked that Sai spoke with a different accent than the *Norte Americanos*. He was not Latino but came from somewhere else.

Ricco spoke. "The old man's name is Stan Schultz. I hired a team to go through his apartment. He has several bedrooms, and one is his office, and it's an unimaginable mess, with stacks of books and papers, and thousands of newspaper clippings going back fifty years. A normal person would go insane in a place like that. The team found one file related to Lyra-Dominion, but it only contained public information like annual reports and some articles. There was one article about a speech you gave to investors a few months back. But, there's nothing there to hang the guy."

Mira said, "Yet, we know he used to be one of the best investigative reporters in New York. He won the Pulitzer Prize for work he did in the financial industry."

"He's retired," Sai said. "People in the publishing industry still treat him with respect, but during the last few years, he's gained a reputation of being a looney conspiracy theorist."

"Tell me again how he got on our radar," Mira said.

Sai answered, "A couple of months ago, he started calling our accounting department, not the public one, but the one here in New York. How he got the number, we don't know. They tried to put him off, but he ceaselessly called day after day. And he asked penetrating questions. Those that spoke with him said he was intense, almost deranged, like a bulldog that didn't let go."

With a deep, dominating voice, Mira growled, "It's best to remove people like that quietly. It needs to be done differently than what happened in Long Beach. Where do we stand with the FBI investigation? It's disconcerting they are involved."

Sai answered, "To the best of our knowledge, it's leading nowhere. We're working to deflect their investigation into a rat's maze where others will be blamed."

"That's good. Going back to Stan Schultz, where exactly do we stand?"

Ricco spoke. "We had a tail on him, but he disappeared. He's a slippery old coot. Our team put out a notice to their network in the city, and everyone is looking for him."

There was a pause, and Mira said, "Would he go outside the city?"

"We are looking into that," Ricco replied.

"Well, you used the right word."

"What's that?"

"Disappeared. This man is a hindrance and needs to disappear for good. Sai mentioned someone else who replaced Roberts."

"Her name is Sarah Zipper," Sai stated.

"Zipper?"

"I know. It's a weird name. We tracked her to a primitive farm in Honduras."

"What's she doing there?"

"Looking into how coffee is grown. She normally writes about restaurants and food. As far as understanding business and financials, she's nowhere at the same level as Roberts or Schultz. I read a couple of her food articles. They were poetic, with little about the business side of things."

When Ricco mentioned Honduras, it caught Valentina's attention. It made her nostalgic to hear someone pronounce the name of her country. She thought of her family and wondered what they were doing. They must be worried about her because she had not communicated since leaving Honduras. She wanted so much to be back with them.

Mira spoke. "We must purge Schultz. He is a detriment to the wellbeing of Lyra-Dominion. Make sure no one finds him. Sai, concerning Long Beach, are you sure there isn't any way to track that back to us?"

"I used an intermediary who will never open his mouth."

"What happened to Scott Roberts, to his body?"

"Buried in the hills."

"Good. Let's consider this concluded, an excellent removal of a threat to our company. And from what you say, the investigation will take other avenues. Still, let's keep an eye on it." Mira paused for a moment and continued. "To be absolutely safe, make sure someone tracks the movement of Zipper, the food writer."

"I'll make sure that happens," Ricco said.

They quit talking, and Valentina heard movement noises on the couches. She quickly turned from her listening position and went to the dining table and reached for a dish just as Mira came around the corner.

Mira stopped and stared at Valentina and demanded, "How long have you been here?"

Her heart rapidly beating, Valentina replied, "*No entiendo mucho inglés, Señora.* No, understand much English. Speak slow, please."

"What are you doing here?" Mira asked.

"Table to be *limpiar.*"

"Do you mean to clean?"

"*Si, debo limpiar los platos.* To must clean *deeshes.*"

Valentina picked up a few dirty plates from the table and carried them into the kitchen. Her head felt dizzy. She didn't know what scared her most, what she had heard during the conversation in the living room or Señora Brennen's glaring, never blinking eyes.

CHAPTER TWENTY-ONE

I caught the transit train from Newark Airport to Penn Station, and then took the subway home, arriving at my apartment a few minutes before midnight. I agreed to meet Luke at his office the following afternoon, where we would visit a coffee shop and then see the headquarters of his organization, Coffee Trust.

When I entered my apartment, it took a few minutes to adjust. The place seemed empty and even strange. It felt like I had been away for weeks, when, in fact, it was only a few days. During those days, I had traveled from the jungles of Honduras to the busy Port of Long Beach, from discoveries of coffee to a murder investigation.

The contrasts stood out in my mind, especially for the coffee part. It's a no-brainer to differentiate a street food truck versus a Michelin starred restaurant. The complexity of the coffee trade was a different ballgame, which I found to be an interesting challenge.

Luke demanded that I focus on the writing assignment rather than what happened to Scott. I understood this. He was the client, and he needed the articles. I had agreed, and knew they were important, but it was impossible not to think about Scott.

I wasn't tired, because my body clock was still on West Coast Time, and I had slept a bit on the airplane. So, I turned on my laptop. For the first time in days, I had a decent internet connection.

First, I checked my email. There were over a hundred messages, many from contacts in media companies, but nothing from Ernie. I would call him in the morning.

I left my email account and searched for the Nyx Lines website. After going through it, nothing jumped out as being of interest. I saw that the majority owner of Nyx Lines was a company called Lyra-Dominion.

I went to the Lyra-Dominion website, and then remembered that it was an investment company started by Mira Brennen, a young entrepreneur. Mira had appeared in numerous journal and newspaper articles. I had never taken a direct interest in this, as my focus had always been on restaurants.

Lyra-Dominion's website gave an overview of its investments. Most of the company's holdings were in high tech companies in the Silicon Valley, companies specializing in telecommunications, internet search, marketing, and social media. Lyra-Dominion held significant shareholdings in the shipping company Nyx Lines and a trucking company. It also held positions in a restaurant chain and some clothing manufacturing companies. It seemed odd to focus on the internet high tech world of social media, and at the same time to mix in industrial processes like shipping, trucking, restaurants, and clothing. How and why did the company get so stretched out into these different sectors?

It was a long shot, but I wondered if I could learn anything about Nyx Lines if I spoke with someone at Lyra-Dominion. Stan Schultz said that journalism was the process of following every thread available to build your story. Then, I thought again about the flash drive Stan had given to me and questioned what I should do with it. What was on it? Was it wise to keep it with me everywhere I went?

I wished I could talk to Scott, but that would never happen. Then I thought again of Stan. He was a top financial reporter. He might give some insights, and I decided to stop at his apartment in the morning.

Switching back to Lyra-Dominion, an idea came to me. Would it be possible to speak with someone in the company, maybe even Mira Brennen? Stan often said that at some point, you need to go to the top, that is, interview the person with the most power. If I went to Lyra-Dominion, it would be a fishing expedition, but I had done that before.

On the internet, I researched Mira Brennen to find out more about her. Mira was the darling of the financial world and was also rubbing shoulders with politicians in Washington, D.C. Mira's parents had worked for different government agencies, and that gave her access to government leaders. Some retired politicians even served on the board of directors of Lyra-Dominion.

In all the articles, it seemed that Mira's main goal was to better the condition of the world. She packaged that in the word, *wellbeing*. It was nebulous what she meant by it, but it seemed to mean improving economies and living conditions. Her motivation was not to become wealthy. While that unexpectedly happened, according to Mira, she had a higher calling, to make the world better.

Seeing that Mira split her time between California and New York, I decided to make a cold call to the Lyra-Dominion office in the morning. If I could not speak with Myra, there had to be someone else who could answer my questions.

I eventually turned off my laptop and went into my kitchen, where I took out a bag of Ethiopian green coffee beans and poured them into my Ikawa roaster. I set the roasting profile and pushed the start button. Seven minutes later, I put the roasted beans into my coffee machine and set the time to brew for the following morning, and then I went off to bed.

It took a while to get to sleep as my mind skipped from one topic to another. The past days had been an overload of images and experiences, one particularly troubling, the death of Scott. The image of that hotel parking lot in Long Beach stuck in my mind.

Then, I thought of Luke Cotton and was still not sure about him. He was an alluring man, to say the least, soft-spoken and driven by a mission. But, his lack of transparency disturbed me. I remembered how he shifted his weight when we talked to Agent Cortez and his partner. What was Luke hiding? After several days of being with the guy, I still couldn't read him and that bothered me. Was he up to something? I was determined to find out more about him.

* * *

The following morning, as I sipped a cup of my superb home-roasted coffee, I again looked at the Lyra-Dominion website and found the telephone number for their offices in New York City. I had a moment of hesitation, remembering what Luke had asked of me, but my question about Nyx Lines and its parent company were too compelling. So, I picked up my telephone and called the number.

A friendly voice answered, "Lyra-Dominion. How may I direct your call?"

"My name is Sarah Zipper, and I'm a journalist from Real Media. Would it be possible to arrange an interview with Mira Brennen? We want to feature her in an article." I knew that Mira liked being on the cover of magazines, so I played on that.

After being put on hold, three minutes later, the same voice was back and said, "Ms. Brennen is extremely busy, but she agreed to meet shortly with you this morning at eleven o'clock. Is that okay for you?"

"Yes, that would be perfect," I replied, astonished at how easy it was to get an appointment with the person at the top. I typically had to wait days or weeks before interviewing someone with the business stature of Mira Brennen.

Fifteen minutes before eleven o'clock, I stood in front of a tall building in the middle of the financial district in Manhattan. It was a glass-fronted building that reached to the heavens.

I walked inside and took the elevator to the thirtieth floor, where Lyra-Dominion had its offices. I didn't know what to expect and wasn't even sure what questions to ask, but I had enough journalistic experience to handle a simple interview. And, as Stan Schultz always said, "Good journalists know how to wing it."

Exiting the elevator, I walked across a hallway where a receptionist sat behind a shiny desk.

I said, "My name is Sarah Zipper from Real Media, and I have an appointment with Mira Brennen."

The young woman smiled, stood up, and said, "Yes, Ms. Brennen is expecting you. Please follow me."

The receptionist walked past a dividing wall and headed down an aisle. I walked along with her. The offices were similar to hundreds of others in New York City, an open space with desks separated by partitions, and people hunkered in front of computer monitors, only in this case, the office wasn't that large. I counted three people in the room, far less than I had expected for a multibillion dollar company.

We came to a closed-off area at one corner of the room and the receptionist knocked on a door and waited. A minute later, there was a buzzing noise and the door automatically opened.

On the opposite side of the room, Mira Brennen sat in a chair behind her desk, and the receptionist said, "Ms. Brennen, this is Sarah Zipper to see you."

Mira Brennen stood up and moved to the side of the desk. She wore a dark green turtleneck top, black slacks, and black low-heel shoes. Her alluring full lips coated in bright red lipstick contrasted with her copper red hair, pale complexion, and large green eyes.

It was as though I had entered the presence of a divine creature, and I felt shoddy to be there in my sneakers, jeans, and unruly thick hair, a lowly peasant meeting royalty. With Mira, everything was perfect, but what caught my attention was the thin eyeliner around her eyes. It somehow amplified her stunning eyes, like making them the focal point in a magnificent painting.

Mira walked toward me, smiled, and stuck out her hand. I shook it. Mira was tall, equal in height to me, and her handshake was firm. The only word that came to my mind was, *commanding.*

"It's a pleasure to meet you," Mira said, her cheeks tightening, pulling her lips upward into what seemed like a spurious smile.

I noticed that Mira's green eyes seemed like round expressionless saucers, exhibiting little emotion. I said, "It's nice to meet you too, and thank you for agreeing to see me on such short notice."

"I'm always happy to meet journalists," Mira said. "Please take a seat."

I sat down in a chair while Mira took her seat on the other side of the desk. After Mira sat down, she reached to the underside of her desk and pushed something, and the door to the office automatically closed. Once shut, something on the door made a metallic sound, like a bolting lock. In all my years of working in New York, I had never seen an automatic door to someone's office. It gave a strange sensation, as though trapped behind a jail door.

Mira said, "Unfortunately, I only have a few minutes, as I need to go to a meeting, but please let me know how I can help you."

The locked door unsettled me, and I suddenly found myself at a loss for words. "I, ah, was wondering if you could help me with an article I'm writing."

"An article?" Mira asked

"I'm, ah, am a food writer and am working on an assignment about the flow of coffee from farms to drinkers." Drinkers was the wrong word, and I questioned why I had used it. "I meant, from coffee farms to consumers."

"Oh," Mira replied. "What does that have to do with me?"

"I was reading that Lyra-Dominion has holdings in companies dealing with coffee."

"I'm not sure what you mean?"

"You have an ownership position in a large national restaurant chain. They serve coffee." I realized this was a stupid thing to say. All restaurants served coffee. "And, your company owns a shipping company and a trucking company that move coffee."

"Our restaurants serve meals if that's what you are asking."

"Well, I guess I'm more interested in the flow of coffee. Can you tell me about Nyx Lines?"

"It's uncertain how I can help you. Lyra-Dominion invests in numerous companies. Nyx Lines is just one of them, and if you want more information on specifics of cargo, others can be more helpful than me."

"What I'm wondering is why Lyra-Dominion would even want to own a shipping line? Most of your investments are in high-tech companies in Silicon Valley. Shipping, trucking, and restaurants seem to be out of place when looking at your portfolio of holdings."

Mira smiled, again transmitting a feeling of insincerity. "Diversification is fundamental to investing. Just ask any financial advisor here on Wall Street." She waved her hand toward the window and the buildings beyond it. "And in any case, shipping and restaurants fit into our overall philosophy of wellbeing."

"Wellbeing? How is that?"

"Society benefits from the goods and services we provide. This is an important element in the concept of how to achieve a better world. Happiness, welfare, safety, and security are not only noble goals. They are fundamentally integrated with prosperity. You can't see any of these independent from each other. At an early age, the death of my aunt taught this lesson to me."

I was confused. It sounded like Mira was giving one of her canned speeches. I dealt in the world of cooks and pans and ingredients that created meals, not in ethereal concepts.

I asked, "But why coffee?" It was the only question I could think of, and I wasn't even sure what I meant by it.

Mira paused for a moment, as though the question was utterly foreign, or meaningless and irrelevant. "Please be aware that Nyx Lines ships many commodities, and as already stated, our restaurants serve more than coffee." She paused again, and coldly asked, "Are you sure you know what you are researching for your coffee article? If you want more information for the article, then why not go back to the people who are using the product. I'm uncertain how I can help you."

"I guess I was just curious to know why a holding company that focuses on high tech would also own a shipping company and restaurants. Something doesn't seem to fit."

"That was answered. It is for diversification, and those operations perfectly conform with our objective of wellbeing."

"I understand," I said, but I didn't. It still seemed odd.

"If it is coffee you are interested in, then why waste your time looking into restaurants and shipping companies? If I might say so, it sounds like a waste of time." Mira paused and stared for a moment into my eyes. It was a condescending look with a hint of intimidation. "What are you really after?"

I froze. The entire situation was offsetting. "Just as I said, I'm writing articles about coffee."

There was a long moment of silence, and Mira said, "Now if you will excuse me, I need to get to a meeting." Mira reached behind her desk and pushed a button, and there was a metallic unbolting sound, and the office door slowly opened. It was a definitive signal that the meeting had ended.

"May I ask one other thing, just out of curiosity?"

Mira took a noticeable breath and said, "What is it?"

"In knowing the size of Lyra-Dominion, I somehow expected more people to be working in your offices."

Mira smiled. "The majority of our employees are on the West Coast. The people here perform administrative tasks."

"Administrative tasks?"

"Just the consolidation of financials. As you observed, our company is quite diversified. Our people here perform control functions."

"What does that mean?" I asked.

Mira looked at her watch and stated, "I'm sorry, but I need to go to my meeting."

That was the second signal, so I figured it was an excellent time to escape. I stood up, reached out my hand toward Mira, and said, "Thank you for your time. This has been very informative and helpful." In reality, it wasn't all that enlightening and would take time to understand what just happened.

Mira took my hand in a firm, almost menacing grip.

I could have squeezed back, but that would have been silly, although, for some girlish reason, I felt like crunching Mira's fingers. While I'd be happy to go one on one in a female version of macho-man, this wasn't the time or place. Instead, I turned and walked out of the office and took the elevator downstairs. As I got out onto the street, my legs felt wobbly, and I took a breath of the outside air. It was uncertain what I had accomplished, but I left with a realization not to take Mira Brennen lightly.

Then, I felt confused. What did this have to do with the connection between Scott Roberts and Nyx Lines, if anything? Had it been a stupid wild goose chase that, in the end, made me look foolish? Probably yes. Luke was right. Stick to the writing assignment.

CHAPTER TWENTY-TWO

Valentina carefully swept the hallway of the upper floor of the house, something done three times a week. She vacuumed two times a week. It was on the schedule of the housecleaning tasks given to her by Ricco. Her days were long, and in the beginning, she had been exhausted, but she had learned to pace herself and to skip tasks if possible.

This work was significantly different than anything she had imagined while working her way through the Catholic University of Honduras at their campus in Tegucigalpa. It had taken four years of intense study to obtain a Bachelor of Science Degree in Finance, where the school's objective was to give students "the knowledge and ability to manage the money of an individual, company or State." When choices of classes were available, she took accounting, knowing this subject would be more likely to lead to a job. Economically distressed circumstances forced one to be pragmatic.

The university had given her a scholarship because she finished at the top of her class in high school. Living at home helped cut costs. So, at the end of her studies, and with high expectations, she applied for the few jobs available. Most were filled by internal applicants within the companies or by people coming from the right families or having the right friends.

Facing a poverty rate of close to sixty-five percent in the country, out of desperation, she had joined the coyotes and headed north, leaving her father, mother, and younger brother. What broke her heart was not being able to see her beloved grandmother, who lived in La Fuerza village. Would she ever see them again?

As she slowly swept the hallway, Valentina considered her options. She had tried many times to leave the house, but it was secure with thick locked doors and unopenable windows.

Ricco controlled whoever entered the house. Jonas, the cook, came whenever Señora Brennen was in town, and once Valentina tried to discuss her situation with him. His only reply was, "My family is in danger if I get involved. Just do your job and try to find a solution. If I can help, I will do so, but like you, my options are limited."

So, she found herself in hopelessness, but each day she considered how she might leave the house. The other problem was what to do if she made it outside. In New York City, there were many people from Central and South America. Perhaps she could find someone to help, but she needed to be wise.

As she pushed the broom down the hallway, she noticed that something was different. Señora Brennen's office was on this floor, and it was always locked. Once a week, Ricco opened the door and Valentina went inside and vacuumed and dusted the room, with Ricco watching her every move. During those times, she had tried to memorize every detail in the place.

Today, the door to the room was open. Señora Brennen was in town and had been using the office. Valentina looked inside and saw Señora Brennen's laptop on the desk. She looked down the hallway, knowing that Ricco was with Señora Brennen at her company office in New York, and Sai might also be with them. Jonas, the cook, was downstairs.

Holding the broom in her hand, she slipped inside the room and went directly to the laptop. During her four years at university, she had learned her way around computers. The computer was on. She moved the mouse, and a login screen popped up. Seeing that it was password-protected, her heart sunk. It would be impossible to find a password, but she tried.

First, she typed 'mirabrennen' in one long word. That didn't work. Then she typed 'lyradominion,' and that also didn't work, so she sat for a moment and considered the word that Mira Brennen used time and again, and she typed it onto the screen, 'wellbeing.'

It was an insidious word because Valentina often wondered who the term applied to, certainly not to herself.

She tapped the enter button, and a moment later, she was into the system. She did not waste time, and went straight to a browser, opened her email system, and typed a quick message to her brother.

Once finished, she went to the 'Documents' folder on the laptop. She clicked on it and it was full of sub-folders, one titled 'Financials' and another 'Personal.' Not risking the time to look at them and not knowing if there was anything of interest, Valentina quickly opened her cloud account where she had many gigabytes of spare space.

She clicked on the Documents folder and copied it to her cloud account, setting the cloud account to log off Mira's laptop once the files were copied. She clicked back to the desktop screen, knowing the data would continue to be copied in the background. Valentina prayed it would not take much time before the screen timed out. Otherwise, she would be in big trouble.

She wasn't sure why she copied the files, but if ever there were an opportunity, she would look through them.

Feeling uncomfortable, she stood up from the desk chair and took her broom that was leaning against the desk.

Then, she heard someone walking down the hallway, and a moment later, Sai Bashir walked into the office.

He stopped, and with a tight face and raised voice, asked, "What are you doing here?"

In a sweeping motion, she moved the broom on the floor beside the desk. "It is cleaning day," she replied.

"You don't belong in here."

"The door is open, and it is to *limpiar* because Señor Ricco say I must always clean here on this day."

"Even so, you don't belong in here. Get out."

"Si Señor," Valentina said, as she submissively lowered her head and walked past Sai, her heart pounding like horses' hoofs on racetracks.

She felt relief when he followed her out of the room and then shut the door, thankful he didn't see the illuminated screen on the laptop. Then, she was nervous, wondering if she had left any kind of trace.

CHAPTER TWENTY-THREE

At a convenience store, I bought a large coffee to go, and then walked to the 33rd street station to catch a subway to Hoboken Station in New Jersey, where I had agreed to meet Luke at one o'clock in the afternoon. We planned to spend the day visiting a coffee shop that did their own roasting, and then the office of his humanitarian organization.

It was a twenty-five-minute ride, and as I sipped my coffee, I wondered about its origin. Did the person serving it even know where the beans had been grown?

I also thought of my so-called interview with Mira Brennen. It still rattled my nerves, and I wasn't sure why, other than my idiocy in asking for the meeting. Was it Mira's imposing personality? It seemed there was more than that. It felt like Mira was vetting me, and there was an element of bullying. I had been around Chief Executive Officers of large corporations, and many had imposing personalities. With Mira, it went beyond that. Underneath the expressionless pale face, was something raw and dangerous.

I had learned nothing significant from the interview, and I felt foolish to have even asked for it. It seemed that Mira Brennen knew little about Nyx Lines or the restaurants in which her company held shares. In fact, Lyra-Dominion wasn't even the majority shareholder in some of these operations. I still wondered why Nyx Lines and the restaurant chain were part of Lyra-Dominions holdings.

I also questioned if I should feel guilty for interviewing Mira, having agreed with Luke not to pursue the Scott Roberts mystery? Not really. I was going on my instincts, and what he didn't know wouldn't hurt him.

Then I thought of Luke and was again perplexed with who he was. I needed to know more about him, and where do you go to find out about people? You go to the internet.

Until now, I didn't have a good connection or the time to surf the internet. So, I got out my phone, went to a browser, and searched 'Luke Cotton.' Surprisingly, there were quite a few hits on that name.

I found a small bio about Luke Cotton on the Coffee Trust website. It said nothing more than he was a graduate of Georgetown University and was the President of Coffee Trust. Georgetown was a terrific school. What was his major?

I dug deeper into the internet, and an article popped up, 'Police Detective in Shootout With Crime Boss.' There was a photo of a man standing in front of an ambulance with a uniformed police officer on one side, and a medic on the other.

The man in the middle was a younger Luke. He stood slightly hunched over while supporting his left arm, his left elbow cradled in his right hand. There was a large dark spot on his left shoulder and a dark stain running down the front of his shirt. The article said that a crime boss shot him. The pain in his face was evident, but there was something else disturbing about the photo. It looked like Luke was in a trance, his eyes round, staring at the ground, almost as though oblivious to what was going on around him.

There were several related articles, and I pieced the story together. In Baltimore, a policeman had pulled over a car for speeding. Riding with the policeman was a rooky law enforcement officer. When the speeding vehicle stopped, the driver and his passenger got out and opened fire on the police car, and in the ensuing battle, the two men that opened fire were shot and killed by the police officer.

It turned out that the driver of the speeding car was the son of a local crime boss. The crime-boss was angry, and in wanting revenge, he and two of his thugs went to the policeman's home and shot him dead. Then, to add to the payback, the crime-boss went to Luke's apartment, and there was a gun battle. Using a shotgun to defend his home, Luke shot and killed the crime-boss and his two goons. During the shooting, a bullet killed Luke's wife, and he was wounded.

After reading the articles, I was stunned. This couldn't be the same Luke I had been traveling with over the past days. I could not imagine him in a gun battle. Even worse was the thought that Luke had lost his wife. Was this why he was so reluctant to reveal anything about himself?

He probably still carried psychological hurt from that terrible experience. Then I remembered the scar close to his left shoulder.

Questions filled my mind. How did Luke go from Georgetown University to working for the police department in Baltimore? And, how had he ended up in New Jersey working for Coffee Trust?

As the train pulled into Hoboken Station, I felt emptiness. The interview with Mira Brennen had been a disaster. It was a stupid, frantic act to have even asked for it, and it led nowhere. Going to see Mira was the complete opposite of what Luke had asked me to do.

Then, finding out about Luke only added to that painful emptiness. I felt foolish to think of him as impenetrable, unwilling to share about himself. Now, I understood why.

That obsession had caused me to fail on two other fronts. I had not checked-in with Ernie, and I had neglected Stan Schultz. When I had time, I would call both of them.

Now was time to get focused, to stay on track, and write the best articles possible for the International Coffee Organization and the Specialty Coffee Association, and especially for Luke.

I ordered myself to stop being sidetracked with murder mysteries and start doing my job.

* * *

I walked off the train and made my way to the Hoboken terminal, a magnificent structure built in the early 1900's, with high ceilings and a stained-glass skylight. The Hoboken train station was said to be the most beautiful train station in America. I had been to Hoboken several times, to write about restaurants and once to attend an event with Stan Schultz. The Jewish synagogue celebrated Jews being in Hoboken for over one hundred and thirty-five years.

People briskly walked through the main hall of the station. I scanned across the vast area and saw Luke waving at me, smiling. He wore jeans, tennis shoes, and a black t-shirt that said Coffee Trust on the front.

We approached each other, and I felt a rush of warmth. I wanted to hug him, but we awkwardly stopped a couple of feet away from each other.

My reaction was surprising. Luke was nothing more than a client, although, in honesty, I felt an attraction for the guy. After several days together, there was a puzzling chemistry between us. Added to that, having discovered his dreadful experience as a young police officer, I felt compassion for him. Jews are overcomers, and while we may suppress our anguish, in our soul there is a deep-seated understanding of heartache.

"So, you found Hoboken," Luke stated.

"I've been here before. I love this terminal."

"Indeed, it's quite a structure. And busy. Thousands of people come through here every day."

"What's the plan?" I asked.

"It's to visit a coffee shop not far from here. I'll tell you more about it when we get there. Then, I'll show you the Coffee Trust offices. And, if you want, we could review where you stand with the articles and what further information you require."

"Sounds good."

We left the terminal building and walked down a street named Hudson Place, which ran alongside the railway station. The coffee shop was on this street, and Luke described how the shop benefited from the thousands of passengers passing by each day. Many stopped in to take away an exquisite cup of coffee.

As we made our way down the street, I wondered if I should mention what happened earlier, with my visit to the Lyra-Dominion office, but I refrained from doing so. Luke had asked me to stick to the writing assignment, and he probably would be upset if he learned about the meeting with Mira Brennen.

After walking three minutes down Hudson Place, Luke stopped in front of a brick building built in the early 1900's. Above the door of the building was a sign, Hudson Place Coffee.

"The name fits," I remarked.

Luke laughed. "Finding names isn't easy. So, we went with the name of the street."

"We?" I asked.

"Oh, I forgot to tell you. Our organization, Coffee Trust, owns the place. We could have visited thousands of coffee shops across the country, but this one was easy to arrange."

I did a quick think. Several times I had written articles about coffee shops in Manhattan, but I had never considered the origin of the coffees sold, or if the coffee shops were doing their own roasting.

Luke led me inside, where there were approximately fifteen tables, all occupied with people hunkered over cups of coffee, plates of bagels and pastries. Three people working in the shop warmly greeted Luke. He made a quick introduction to me.

I looked around and suddenly had a realization. While coffee shops came in all shapes and sizes, from drive-in booths at the edge of parking lots, to spaces with elegant interiors similar to gourmet restaurants, they provided more than a product. They were places where people went to relax or carry on conversations from politics, to religion, to planning their next holiday. Business transactions were completed in coffee shops. They were places where poetry and term papers were written, books read, and romantic relationships kindled. Coffee shops served an extremely valuable multifunction service unlike any other place in society.

In addition, the baristas and servers in coffee shops give something greater than just handing over a plastic container with hot liquid. In a world where we are glued to our cell phones, the people running coffee shops offer a point of real human contact As they proudly serve a simple cup of black coffee, or an artistic coffee topped with a creamy heart design, their friendly smiles convey something profound, for our identity comes from contact with others.

In watching the workers at the Hudson Place Coffee Shop, I had a glimpse of what was taking place all over the country, and it somehow gave me a sense of reassurance. Coffee shop workers deliver products and services that on the surface may seem simple, but they deeply benefit others, and that work is a noble calling.

Luke led me into a large back room. In it were burlap bags of coffee with signs on them, Ethiopia, Tanzania, Rwanda, Colombia, and Honduras. On a table, a large roasting machine spun around. Exhaust pipes came out of the back of it and connected to a tube going into the ceiling. The smell of fresh roasted coffee filled the air. A coffee grinder sat at the end of the table. I closed my eyes and enjoyed the aroma.

He said, "Obviously, this is where the roasting takes place. You'll see something like this in many other coffee shops. By roasting their coffee, it ensures the best flavor possible. There's both science and art to this, and every barista has opinions on the best methods for roasting and brewing."

"What is the best technique?"

Luke had a grin. "You're not asking the right person. All I can tell you is that each origin requires a different roasting profile to get the best taste from the beans. For a mild coffee, they heat the coffee until it cracks. It sounds something like popcorn. With two cracks, you get a dark roast.

"I like it mild to medium," I said.

"Me too. The unique flavors can be tasted in a medium roast, whereas with a very dark roast, the taste can sometimes be bitter and charred. But many people like it like that."

I saw an Ikawa roaster on the bench. I pointed at it and asked, "What makes that roaster different?"

"Most roasters cook the beans at around five hundred and fifty degrees Fahrenheit. When the beans get around four hundred degrees, they begin to turn brown. That's when the oil in the beans begins to emerge, and technically, it's called *pyrolysis*, where the flavor is created. But, as I said, not all beans are the same, and the Ikawa roaster finetunes the process, to get the best from each origin."

I looked at the burlap bags of coffee on the floor, and I thought of La Fuerza, and the hard work and love gone into growing those beans. With all the questions I was asking, with all the information gathered, I still didn't have an answer to Ernie's question of why shoot someone over coffee?

"Do baristas know about the origins of those green beans and the care put into them?"

"More and more so."

"And, why is that?" I asked.

"You ask a lot of questions," he smiled.

"That's what you pay me for."

"Many baristas now visit places of origin, getting to know farmers. But, please remember that the target market for your articles is the average coffee drinker and not baristas."

"I'm aware of that, so don't worry. I'm accustomed to writing for everyone from foodies to the broad populace."

"That's good. You'll achieve success when consumers change their buying patterns and they begin to purchase coffee from companies that look out for farmers."

That last bit was something entirely new. I was hired to write articles and not change peoples' habits, unless that was in the contract? And, how would you measure that?

This was a classic example of definition creep, where a client kept adding specifications to the project, by saying, "Oh, can you do this, and this, and this?" The assignment starts small, like one or two days in Honduras to write about coffee, until it becomes this gigantic, wishful mountain that can never be delivered, and is only bound for failure.

I said, "There's no way I will take responsibility for changing the buying practices of coffee lovers."

"What do you mean?"

"I write first class articles and that's it, and you and your coffee organizations will be proud of them. Hopefully, readers will be enlightened."

"Hopefully?"

There I was using his word. "Behavioral modification is not part of my mandate."

Luke raised the palms of his hands, smiled and said, "Well, it was more of a wish than a requirement, and let's hope for the best, hopefully. And, it never hurts to ask."

We laughed. At least I let him know the limits of my services, but then again, I had seen the farmers and knew they needed help.

I turned and looked at the burlap bags. They carried a story. Was I missing something?

CHAPTER TWENTY-FOUR

Sai Bashir entered the Lyra-Dominion headquarters in New York City, went to Mira Brennen's office, and took a seat across from her. She pushed the button on the side of her desk, and the door automatically closed, followed by the metallic clicking sound of the lock. They needed privacy.

Mira said, "It was so strange, the sudden appearance of Sarah Zipper, the journalist."

"Tell me about it," Sai stated.

"This morning, she called our office, and I was surprised she was in New York and not in Honduras. That caught my attention. I agreed to an appointment at eleven o'clock. She was on time. The interview was short, but I sensed she was nervous, and it was anything but organized. It seemed she didn't know where she was going."

"What do you mean?"

"I asked her about the reason for the interview, and she drifted off into her study of the coffee supply chain. Then she jumped over to our holdings in restaurants and how we serve coffee. Then she talked about Nyx Lines. It was like she was fishing for information, but had forgotten her fishing pole."

"We have to be careful with her," Sai stated.

"I agree."

"It just seems odd that she sits between the two journalists who didn't know each other."

"You mean Scott Roberts and Stan Schultz?" Mira did not need to use vague terms, like when communicating, over the telephone.

"Yes. Those two men didn't know each other, each working from different angles, and suddenly along comes Sarah Zipper."

"We need to look into her background, but it's obvious she doesn't have the bandwidth to understand anything except the colors of desserts," Mira stated with a small grin.

Sai shook his head. "Still, I have an uneasy feeling about her asking questions about our restaurants and shipping operations. It shows unusual curiosity despite her limitations."

"Do you have any suggestions?" Mira asked.

"Here's where we stand. The screw-up with Scott Roberts was unfortunate, to shoot him in the parking lot. They should have done it out of sight, and we are lucky there is no way to trace it back to us. To be safe, we have given the FBI a red herring to redirect their inquiry."

"Are you sure they won't implicate Nyx Lines?"

"Of course not," Sai asserted. "Nyx Lines ships containers, and that's it. They can't be responsible for every item inside every container, especially when you are dealing with millions of bags of coffee filled on remote coffee farms across central and south America."

"It's imperative that Nyx Lines stays out of it. Where do you stand with Stan Schultz?"

"He's still missing, and Ricco's investigators are working on leads."

"So, what's the plan of action?"

"We will find him, and then make sure he disappears."

"And, what about Sarah Zipper?"

"Once finding her, we will monitor every movement she makes. Currently, we believe she is traveling with someone named Luke Cotton, who works for a do-gooder operation called Coffee Trust."

"Remove her," Mira dryly demanded.

"Maybe eventually, but that would only raise more curiosity. I suggest we take our time with a different tactic. Why don't you have our lawyers call Sarah Zipper's boss at Real Media and complain about the interview this morning? More than that, it seems Real Media is struggling financially. Can you figure out a way to work behind the scenes to cut off their cash flow? Then Sarah Zipper would end up with a small-town newspaper in Kansas writing about local hamburger joints, which would serve our purpose."

Mira smiled. "I like your strategy. It's also imperative to find Stan Schultz. His digging into our financials must stop."

"As I said, Ricco is working on it."

Mira paused for a moment. "That interview with Sarah Zipper this morning was upsetting. Who does she think she is to walk into my office and ask questions? My instincts tell me she is a potential fly in the ointment, and you know what we do with flies. Besides putting pressure on Real Media, I think there's something more we can do. Have Ricco tighten the noose and make her feel uneasy, so she goes back to writing about dirty dishes in restaurants."

Sai smiled and said, "I sense you dislike the lady."

"That's a reasonable conclusion."

"I'll see if we can give her a scare. I'll talk with Ricco."

"Agreed. That will ensure our wellbeing."

Sai left the office, and Mira sat in quietness, reflecting on where they stood. She trusted Sai, and Ricco was a steady hand in these situations when force was needed.

At the same time, she was nervous, but that wasn't anything new. From the very beginning, her business ventures had been on shaky ground, and they only survived through shrewd dealings with wealthy people. All this bother with Scott Roberts, Stan Schultz and Sarah Zipper was only a bump in the road. She would make it through this.

She thought of the future. She now influenced business leaders, financiers, and politicians. Her network was remarkable. Power is what she craved. Once eliminating those pest journalists, Lyra-Dominion would sail smoothly. After that, she envisaged another conquest. Political office.

The country needed someone like her at the highest level, and she had all the skills and cunning to get there. She could sweet talk baby-boomers, and she knew the language to manipulate millennials. Wealthy donors would line up behind her campaign. The country begged for more female leaders, for men had run it into the gutter.

By making that move, she would no longer require the associates from Mexico. But for now, the cash flow was helpful.

Indeed, once through this current challenge, the future was bright.

She picked up the phone to instruct her lawyer to call Sarah Zipper's boss at Real Media. Legal threats would rain down like fire from heaven.

CHAPTER TWENTY-FIVE

Leaving the coffee shop, Luke and I went out a back door and entered an alley.

Luke said, "I'll show you around our offices, but maybe we could chat better over at my place a few blocks away. It's more comfortable than sitting around a desk, and we can talk uninterrupted."

"That's fine with me," I said, feeling this might be an opportunity. Luke had never given details on where he lived, and going to his place might reveal more information about him.

Luke led the way up metal steps going to the next floor above the coffee shop, and we entered an office. There was a large room with four desks. A woman sat behind one, and the other three were empty. The woman had slightly graying hair and seemed to be in her late forties or early fifties.

Luke said, "Rosie, let me introduce you to Sarah Zipper, who is our journalist writing the articles."

Rosie moved her fingers away from the keyboard, smiled, put out her hand, shook my hand, and said, "Thank you so much for doing this. I look forward to read your articles."

I smiled back and replied. "They are in progress. The visit to the coffee farm and the rest of our travels have been very enlightening." Except for the visit to Lyra-Dominion, I thought to myself.

Luke waved his hand around the room and said, "Well, this is it. We only have a few people working full time for Coffee Trust and a variable number of volunteers that mainly come from church groups. Rosie runs the office. Manuel Espinosa and another staff member operate from field cooperatives. Then we have one agronomy expert that trains farmers in agricultural methods, and an architect that manages the construction of warehouses, washing stations, schools, houses, and wells."

"You forgot to mention yourself," Rosie said. She turned to me and said, "Luke is the incorrigible hard-driven boss who runs this place."

Luke laughed. "Incorrigible is the right word, meaning I'm just like all the other misfits around this place."

I grinned. "For sure, I've seen him hard at work at the farm," I looked at the empty desks and thought of a question. I said. "I hope I'm not being too straight forward, but I've wondered about the finances of not-for-profit organizations. May I ask about your funding? How is Coffee Trust supported?"

Luke answered, "It's okay to ask. Our funding mainly comes from donations, with a little coming in from the coffee shop downstairs. To some extent, most of our full-timers have other incomes, so that keep costs down. For us, it's a passion, and each person sets their work hours, which usually averages sixteen hours a day." Luke laughed."

"What do you mean by other incomes?"

"Several members of our staff are financially independent. Coffee Trust pays travel expenses. Church groups support the organization and donate for projects in the field."

I was reluctant to get into the religious aspect of this, but I noticed a poster on a wall that said, "This is true religion, to look out for the needs of widows and orphans." It was a quote from the Book of James in the New Testament, of which I knew little. But it was a profound statement.

Another poster said, "Grace is a gift of God."

Curiosity got the best of me, and I asked, "You mentioned that church groups support Coffee Trust. What does coffee have to do with religion."

Rosie replied. "We like coffee, but there's something more important. On those farms and villages, people need help, and many are hurting. God is in the business of redemption, and assisting poor farmers and their families is a part of doing that. We are Christians and want to share what God has done for us."

I let it go at that. I had grown up with Christians in my school, and I met them at work, but as a Jew, it always seemed a strange culture. My views were secular and my identity came from a different source, although I had to admit that it was a Jew who started their faith system. My philosophy was to let them have their beliefs, and I had mine, even if sometimes I wasn't sure what I believed in, other than the traditions followed by my people through the centuries.

I learned there were other church-led organizations involved in coffee. Switching to other topics, we got into the running of the office. This part was more comfortable than getting into redemptive religious motivations. It was familiar ground, for I had a list of memorized questions to ask managers of restaurants.

After an hour of questions, Luke led me back down the steps, and we headed for his apartment.

The visit to the Coffee Trust offices opened up an entirely new line of thought needing incorporation in my articles. There was a humanitarian side to be covered. I hadn't realized it, but this concern for farmers was a goal at many levels, from coffee companies working toward sustainability to coffeeshops making connections with individual farmers, to independent organizations, both secular and religious. It was a recognition that something must be done for poor people, for widows and orphans, as the poster said.

The importance of my articles was becoming daunting, as I needed to create that same awareness with average coffee consumers.

* * *

Making our way on a sidewalk running next to the Hudson River, Luke pointed to the busy street and said, "That's Sinatra Drive. Frank Sinatra was born in Hoboken, and he is one of many famous personalities associated with this city."

It was a pleasant afternoon, and I felt comfortable walking alongside Luke. We came to a tall brick faced building and took an elevator to the top on the twelfth floor.

Luke opened the door and said, "Welcome to my place."

We entered, and I was surprised to find a large living room with almost floor to ceiling windows looking out at the Hudson River. On the opposite side of the river was the skyline of New York City. I recognized many of the buildings, for I looked at them from a different perspective whenever I entered the Real Media offices.

"That's quite a view," I said.

Luke smiled. "I'd prefer to be on a rural coffee farm, but if you have to live in the city, this is the way to do it."

I knew the cost of apartments in New York and New Jersey. Having a penthouse apartment with a view like this must have cost a bundle, or was he renting it? Owning a penthouse apartment didn't fit my notion of a struggling humanitarian worker living out of a basement room.

Modestly furnished, the apartment had an open kitchen on the opposite side of the large bay windows. In looking down a hallway, it appeared there were at least three bedrooms if not four.

"Would you like something to drink?" Luke asked. "Coffee, tea, or something else."

I laughed. "Because of the nature of the assignment, we better stick with coffee."

I stood on one side of the kitchen island while Luke prepared the coffee. Against one wall was a narrow desk with several photos of people in frames. One was a large family photo with what looked like grandparents sitting on two chairs in the front, with adults and children grouped to the side. Behind the grandparents, Luke stood with the adults.

In another frame was a single photo of an attractive young woman with bright eyes and a captivating smile. Then, I remembered the article about Luke's wife and how criminals shot her.

Luke handed me a cup of black coffee and led me to couches in the living room where we sat facing each other across a coffee table.

He said, "Well, in a few short days, you've seen a lot. How do you feel at this point about the articles?"

I hesitated. "I have enough material, for sure, yet it seems there is always something more jumping out of the woodwork. There will be no problem to write the articles, although, I have one concern. It's not that difficult to inform readers but to write in a way that changes behaviors is entirely more challenging. To do this, one needs to touch logic and emotions. I'll need time to get it exactly right."

"Is there anything else you need?"

"For now, I don't think so, unless you have something else to throw at me unexpectedly."

Luke chuckled. "In coffee, there's always something new to learn. I've purposely kept you away from coffee traders. That's a crazy, confusing world. A journalist might spend a lifetime in this industry and still find things of interest."

"Tell me a little bit about coffee traders. Who are they?" It sounded like a business side of the coffee industry. Why had Luke kept me away from it?

"Traders facilitate the movement of coffee around the world, and the coffee business wouldn't function without them. They buy coffee from producers and then find markets for those products, and they arrange the shipments. Most coffee bought and sold goes through them."

It sounded like an additional level of complexity. "Maybe, for now, I'll focus on the farmers." I decided to come back to coffee trading at a later point, for every avenue needed exploration. "Is it okay if I ask you a few questions."

Luke paused for a moment. "Sure, that's what we hired you for, as you stated." His eyes were mischievous.

"Tell me how you got involved in this coffee business, and please don't sidetrack into technical things."

Luke stared at the coffee cup in his hand and his demeanor changed. He said, "My background in university was not agriculture. It was law, with a bit of business. After graduating from university, I got a job, and then something happened where I was injured. It took more than two years of intense training before I regained full movement and strength in my body."

Full strength indeed, I thought, as I remembered Luke's power in manhandling heavy burlap bags of coffee."

Luke continued. "I was mentally lost for a while. Because of the nature of my injury, I received a pension and a settlement, but felt empty. Then, after meeting some people, I found faith in God, and that gave me hope. One of those persons had started Coffee Trust and he asked me to go out as a volunteer. Maybe it was divine guidance, but five years later, here I am. It's been good for me, to move past some grief."

I understood Luke had brushed over details, but it was the first time he had spoken about himself. I wondered how painful it was to do so? He skipped the shooting of his wife. While it seemed he healed physically, I wondered how this impacted his ability to function socially, or to be in a relationship. Was he really over the grief?

I said, Thank you for sharing that and I'm sorry to hear about your injury. It gives context, and I'm happy to learn more about you."

Luke's face softened. "I'm not sure how that helps, but maybe you can tell me more about you sometime."

That made me feel guilty. All my efforts had been to break through this guy's defenses, and I had not told him much about myself, other than some of my restaurant stories. Was I being a hypocrite?

I smiled. "There's nothing much to tell. I grew up outside Chicago, where my father was a history professor. I went to Northwestern University School of Journalism."

"That explains why you don't have a New York City accent." He grinned.

"That's right. After university, I got a job with Real Media, and that's where I've been for six years, the first year assigned to a big food company, and five years covering restaurants."

"Are you one of those food critics?"

I laughed. "Not really. They are in a class of their own, either loved or despised by chefs. I mainly write about restaurants for travel and food magazines, and sometimes for newspapers. People have an insatiable need to discover places to eat."

"You mentioned your father. Did he retire?"

"He died from a heart attack three years ago."

"I'm sorry to hear that."

"Thank you. It's okay," I said, but it wasn't, for one can never really get over a death. "My father spent too much time in books, with no time for exercise, and he had a bad heart, so there you go."

Luke said, "I'm sorry for your loss. It's so easy to say that death is natural, but that's almost impossible to accept. Death is unnatural, not how humans were created."

I paused, considering what he meant by that. In the Jewish world, the spirit and soul are eternal, depending on the rabbi, and death was the result of a screw-up in the Garden of Eden, a couple of people arrogantly thinking they could be God. I continued, "I have an older sister with two kids and another on the way. Her husband is a rabbi in training in Brooklyn. They moved there from Chicago shortly after my father's death. My mother sold our family home and bought a place a block away from my sister. She couldn't see herself in Chicago, far away from her two daughters living in New York City."

"So, do you see her?"

"Often. Do you know the stereotype about Jewish mothers?"

"Not really."

"It's that they are in the kitchen making matza ball soup, and overbearing, steamrolling over everything. My mom is some of that, but more. She's warm and not afraid to express her love, and at her place, you never go hungry. She often has advice, and most of the time, it's pretty good. She encouraged my sister and I to be independent and ask questions, and I suppose that led me into journalism. She loves her grandkids, and the great thing is that she laughs at herself."

"Sounds like a wonderful mother."

"She is." I felt my eyes becoming moist. The past few days had shaken my emotions. Indeed, it was a great feeling to know I could always depend on my mother. I needed to call her to hear her voice. There was something else that touched my fragile emotions. To have Luke take a personal interest was moving, and I liked how he intently listened.

Luke's phone rang, and that saved me from breaking down into a teary spectacle.

He answered, "Luke Cotton."

He held the phone to his ear. "Hello Manuel," he said. Then he listened for what seemed like several minutes, and he said, "Send it to me, and I'll see what I can do."

He clicked his phone, put it on the table, and said, "That was strange. I'm sorry to break up our conversation, but could you please come with me."

We got up, walked down the hallway, and turned right into the first room. It was an office. A bookshelf was along one wall, full of thick books on law and some on religion. The law books were probably holdovers from Luke's university days. Rather than a desk, there was a long wooden table. Around it were six office chairs.

Luke said, "Sometimes we have our Coffee Trust team meetings here.

Luke went to a chair positioned in front of a laptop. He pulled another chair next to his, motioned to me, and I sat down. Then he opened his computer, went to his email system, and clicked on a message from Manuel.

Luke said, "This is the English translation of a message originally written in Spanish. Valentina, the granddaughter of Maria Lopez, sent it to her younger brother, and then her brother contacted Manuel."

We read through the message.

To My Beloved Brother Pedro

I have little time to write this because the people where I am staying do not let me use the computer. It was a difficult trip to the United States, and then I was taken against my will to a home where I am being held as a servant, not allowed to go outside the house. It is the home of Señora Mira Brennen in New York City. I don't know what to do. Can you call Manuel Espinosa at the La Fuerza farm and see if he can help, as he knows people in the United States? I may not have another opportunity to use the computer.

Please give my love to Mother, Father, and our precious grandmother.

Sending much love,

Valentina

I took a deep breath, my head spinning. Was it real or a prank? "It's crazy," I said.

"I agree," Luke stated.

My mind began to race. I said, "Valentina seems to be in a dreadful situation and is asking for help. Is there anything we can do?"

"For sure, but isn't Mira Brennen the businesswoman who runs that successful company?"

"It's called Lyra-Dominion. What's incredible is, I was with her this morning."

"You what?"

"Lyra-Dominion owns Nyx Lines. I went to their offices in New York and interviewed Myra Brennen."

Luke's eyes narrowed. "I thought I asked you to focus on the articles. What are you thinking? And, who isn't being transparent?"

I felt like a fool. I couldn't let up on investigating what happened to Scott Roberts. Even worse, I had lost Luke's trust.

"The interview didn't go well," I confessed. "It was done on a silly whim." But how else does a journalist get great articles without once in a while taking some risk?

Luke tightened his fists and raised them to his head, his knuckles resting against his forehead. "I talked with Valentina a few times when she came to La Fuerza to visit her grandmother. She's a bright and beautiful young woman. Who knows what they have done to her?"

"The email doesn't mention anything like that, but maybe she's trying to protect her family from grief."

"Every time I go to Central America, I see the results of economic hardship and the desperation forcing people to seek new lives. They make the tortuous journey north and then get abused. It's like modern-day slavery is happening on our doorstep. It deeply angers me."

I realized this was personal for Luke. I felt the same when remembering the agony expressed by Maria Lopez. It was mind-boggling to think of Valentina as a hostage servant, and even more unbelievable to know I was with Mira Brennen. It seemed implausible that Mira was somehow involved in human trafficking. Or was it?

Then I recalled the end of the interview and Mira's cold, emotionless stare, and it left questions. Women have intuitions about other women. I perceived that Mira carried a grandiose sense of self. She was wealthy and powerful, but was Mira missing normal human emotions? How did she justify holding Valentina in forced labor? Did she carry any feelings of guilt or remorse?

Luke's imploring question was right. We must do something, but what and how?

CHAPTER TWENTY-SIX

I felt lost, like walking a path through an unknown forest. Could we believe Valentina or was it just the fanciful imagination of a young woman? It didn't seem right that Mira Brennen would treat someone like this, because Mira spoke so often about the wellbeing of people. "Do you think Valentina's email is the truth?" I asked.

"She didn't appear to be someone that fabricates stories," Luke replied. "Her family lives in hard reality and not in a world of fables."

"Where in New York does Mira Brennen live?"

"I've no idea. Does she even live there?"

I took my small laptop from my shoulder bag. "Let's find out. Can I connect to your Wi-Fi signal?"

He gave me the Wi-Fi code, and I connected to the internet.

We both began to research Mira Brennen's address. We found out that she had moved to New York three years ago when setting up the Lyra-Dominion office in Manhattan. There was nothing about her purchasing a home. After fifteen minutes, neither of us found anything.

"What about New York City property records?" I asked.

"Good idea. Go for it." Luke rolled his chair next to me and watched as I accessed the website of the New York City Department of Finance, Office of the City Register.

I typed in Mira Brennen, but nothing came up.

"Maybe it's in a company name," Luke said.

I typed in 'Lyra-Dominion,' and again, nothing appeared. I said, "It makes sense that she wouldn't put her personal property in Lyra-Dominion's name because the company's shareholders would all own a piece of her house."

For ten minutes, we went through online articles on our laptops until Luke said, "I found something. An old article from several years ago mentioned that Mira bought a house in Silicon Valley under the name of Wellbeing Properties LLC. Try that."

I typed the name into the city register website, and a record popped up for Wellbeing Properties LLC. It showed the borough, the lot, and other information. "It was purchased three years ago," I said.

"Where is it?"

I clicked on a button, and the address popped up. "It's on the Upper West Side near Central Park. We should check it out." The Upper West Side was not far from my apartment, so it wouldn't be much of a detour in going home.

"Do you mean now?"

"Yes," I answered.

Luke hesitated for a moment, and with grim determination in his eyes, he said, "I agree. Let's go."

I felt uneasy seeing the look on his face and stated, "I said, check it out. Let's not do anything radical. Is there any way to verify if she's there against her will?"

"Who said anything radical. We can start by looking at the place and then decide a course of action." Luke's fist tightened.

I was surprised to see a change in Luke, like a flame rising in a furnace. "Okay, let's do it," I said while questioning what was behind his tight fist.

* * *

We retraced my journey from earlier in the day and took a subway to the Upper West Side, and then walked down the street of Mira Brennen's house.

"Do you know this area?" Luke asked.

I answered, "A bit. It's trendy and upscale, with many excellent restaurants. Between Central Park and the Hudson River, there are hundreds of beautiful old brownstones, some divided into apartments, and others are complete homes. The apartments are pricy, whereas single townhouses would put a gigantic hole in your bank account."

When saying that I thought of Luke's apartment facing the Hudson River, which would equal the price of any similar-sized apartment on the Upper West Side. A thought came to me again. How did he get the funding for his place, considering his attire was t-shirts and jeans?

"Why do they call this the Upper West Side?" Luke asked.

"Simple logic I suppose. The Upper East Side of New York is on the east side of Central Park. The Upper West Side is to the west of the park. There might be another reason, but at least that's my logic."

Luke smiled. "Easy to remember."

We walked halfway down a block and found Mira's house, a modernized six-story brownstone. Steps led up to the front door, and large windows faced out to the street. The windows were mirror-like, making them impossible to see through from the outside."

We walked slowly on the opposite side of the street.

"Don't be too obvious in looking at the place," Luke said. "I'm sure there are surveillance cameras everywhere."

"Whatever we do, let's not act like a SWAT team," I stated.

"Of course not." Luke glanced at the front door. "I wonder if that's the only way into the place. It's early evening, so Mira Brennen is likely there, and maybe others. Do you think we should go up and knock on the door?"

"Definitely not when Mira is in the house." I remembered Mira's menacing stare.

At that moment my phone rang. It was Ernie.

"Zipper, where are you?" Ernie asked.

"Working on my story."

"Are you sure?"

"What do you mean?"

"This has been a day of absolute hell."

"I'm not sure I follow you."

"Two clients called in and canceled their contracts. They said they can't be associated with a media organization that uses aggressive fake-journalism tactics."

"We've never done that." I knew that Real Media prided itself on ethical journalism.

"Are you sure you didn't do that?" Ernie demanded.

"Why do you ask?"

"In addition to the two companies that canceled their contracts, I got a call from a lawyer."

"So?"

"What were you doing at Lyra-Dominion's offices today and barging in on Mira Brennen."

What could I tell him? "I was working the coffee story."

"What does Mira Brennen have to do with coffee?"

"Just following a hunch."

"That doesn't make sense, and it puts you out on a limb. The lawyer is threatening to sue you and Real Media for harassment."

"Harassment? It was just an interview." One that didn't go very well.

"I want you to back off. If not, Real Media will go bust, and you'll be living on bread and water. Just stay away from Mira Brennen."

"What if she's central to my coffee story?"

"Stay away, and that's final. Don't go running around like a loose cannon, like you sometimes do."

I felt anger. I wasn't anything like a loose cannon, at least most of the time. "You don't appreciate what I do for you."

"I certainly won't if we lose all our clients."

"Tough. I'll do what I always do and write a good article." I refused to apologize or make firm commitments. How could I, having just walked past Mira Brennen's house.

"Don't mess up," Ernie commanded. He hung up.

I pushed my phone into my bag, turned to Luke, and said, "I think you were talking about knocking on the door before my phone rang. Tell me more about that." I had a quick image of the bankruptcy of Real Media, and then living on bread and water.

CHAPTER TWENTY-SEVEN

The phone call from Ernie rattled me, and I wondered if I had stirred up a hornets' nest and if something was going on beyond my level of understanding. Why would Mira accuse me of harassment?

When I thought back to the morning's interview, I couldn't identify anything even close to harassment. Perhaps Mira was simply trying to protect her image, and she may have suspected that I was there to do a hit-piece. Was she doing some odd form of damage control?

But, none of that made sense.

I turned to Luke and explained the phone call from Ernie.

He reflected on this and said, "It looks like you struck something sensitive."

"I guess. Now tell me how we should approach that house."

"This is going back to something I read in the past that police officers sometimes need to pick the best time to serve a warrant. It might be when there are a lot of people around, or when the suspect is on their own."

"You mean from your police training?" I asked. This was the time for the opaque to become transparent.

Luke stayed still for a moment, then looked me in the eyes and stated, "I take it that you know."

"Yes."

"How did you find out?"

I raised my eyebrows. "In an internet world, one can unearth a lot of information. I'm sorry for what happened to you."

"It was seven years ago, and there are times when it feels like it happened yesterday."

"You lost someone. I'm sorry."

"The loss of my wife was a thousand times more painful than a bullet to the shoulder."

"I apologize for opening this up."

"It's okay. We should be honest with each other. Maybe you can do the same, knowing I didn't do a deep-dive on you on the internet."

A rush of guilt flooded me. I said, "I apologize if it seemed I was prying into your personal life, but I'm a journalist, always looking for background. I understand how hard it would be to get through something like that."

"More than you know."

Not knowing what to say, I waited, and then asked, "What now?"

"Without digging deeper into each other's souls, we need a plan on how to get through the front door of that house. My gut feeling is to go there when Mira Brennen is away. Based on what you told me about your boss and the harassment charges, we should stay clear of her. If we come back in the morning after she goes to work, then potentially, we might only need to deal with one of her staff. That person may let us know if Valentina is there or not."

"And if she's there?"

"Then we go in and get her."

CHAPTER TWENTY-EIGHT

What did Luke imply by, go in and get her? Since being with him, I sensed a hard determination deep in his character, and I wondered if there was something more. It was there when he talked about poor farmers, and now it reappeared when discussing Valentina. Was Luke like a comic book action hero, mild-mannered most of the time, but once triggered, becoming an angry beast? After all, he had used a shotgun to blast several men into the next world. An inner voice told me to be cautious around him.

We walked toward the subway station, and I asked, "Rather than going all the way back to New Jersey, why don't you save time and stay at my place?"

Luke showed hesitation, then asked, "Is that okay? It means we could get an early start."

"I have a one-bedroom place and a comfortable couch for you."

He laughed. "It might be slightly better than our guest house on the La Fuerza farm."

I smiled. "I forgot all about that, but now that you remind me, I can guarantee that my place doesn't have cockroaches."

We rode the subway back to my stop at 96th Street Station when my phone rang. I answered. It was Stan Schultz.

He said, "Sarah, I can't talk much, but I need to warn you."

"What's going on?" There were so many things happening I had forgotten all about him.

"I'm in grave danger, and you too."

"What do you mean?"

"Some bad people are looking for us. Where are you?"

"I just left our subway stop and am now walking home."

"That's terrible. Don't go there." His voice was high and insistent.

"Where?"

"Don't go home."

"Why?" I considered this was like asking the basic journalistic questions, what, where, why, and how. It appeared Stan was being paranoid again.

"Despicable people are watching our apartments?"

"How do you know that?"

"I just know. Promise me you won't go home. Hide in a hotel somewhere. Pay cash so no one can track your credit card payments."

That was typical Stan, where the forces of the world were out to destroy you. Was he losing his mind with the advancement of age? Yet, with all the freaky stuff going on, it might be reasonable to consider his warning.

"Okay, Stan, I'll do what you say, but we need to meet to talk about this."

"We will. I'll call you tomorrow. Just be careful." He hung up.

I turned to Luke and said, "That was the second strange phone call I received today, the first one from my boss."

"Why was it strange?"

"I have a neighbor, an elderly man who is a friend. He's been a mentor to me. He was a successful journalist and is now retired, but he still works stories, and he's bit of a conspiracy theorist. He didn't tell me about his latest work, but he talked about dangerous people wanting to control the world. Now, he says there are people out to get him, and me. He said they are watching our apartments. He lives down the hall from me."

Luke stopped walking and said, "This is getting weird. How do you want to play it?"

"I need to know if someone is actually watching our apartments."

Luke took a step and said, "Let's go see, but we should do this carefully. Are there any shops down your street?"

"There's a convenience store on the far corner."

"Okay. When we get to your street, let me peek around the corner, and you describe your apartment building. Then, I'll continue down your street, and you turn around and go back to the subway entrance. If someone is watching your place, they probably won't know me."

"What will you do?"

"I'll walk down to the convenience store, buy something, and then head back. I doubt that people would be waiting in the hallway of your apartment building. Most likely, they'd be out on the street somewhere."

"Okay," I said.

We walked one block, and just before the corner of a building, I stopped and said, "That's my street. Look down there. Do you see a gray building, number one thirty-two?"

He glanced around the building. "I see a gray building, but not the number."

"You'll see it when you get down there."

He said, "I'll meet you back at the subway." He walked away from me, holding a slow and steady pace.

I turned around and went back to the entrance of the subway and waited. Things were moving too fast, and I didn't like the way this was evolving. It had started as a short adventure to a rural coffee farm in Honduras and had morphed into the murder of a colleague, meeting an unpleasant woman running an investment company, a young woman held captive as an unpaid servant, and Stan's strange conspiracy. And, on top of that were the articles to write.

This started because of my love of coffee and it was just too crazy. What on earth had I gotten myself into?

Hopefully, no one was watching my apartment. Then I could at least put Stan's conspiracy theory to rest.

Suddenly, I thought of Stan's flash drive in an interior pocket in my computer bag. When I had time, I needed to take a look at it.

CHAPTER TWENTY-NINE

It took almost fifteen minutes of waiting until I saw Luke turn the corner and head in my direction. He walked briskly and carried a brown paper bag.

He walked up to me and said, "Let's go."

"Was Stan correct?"

"I'd say yes. There was a guy in a dark Chevrolet. When I walked by it, food wrappers and bottles of soda were next to him on the front seat. I didn't see it, but he probably had a pee-bottle in there with him. It seems he's there for the long haul. When a woman entered your building, his eyes were fixed on her like glue, without even glancing at me."

I turned and headed for the subway station's stairs, and Luke followed. There would be time to talk, but we needed to get out of there. That cranky old Stan was right. If that man was staking out the place with an intent to cause harm, was it only for Stan, or also for me? Either way, it was disturbing.

In the ticketing area, Luke pointed at the subway map and asked, "Do you have any idea where we should go?"

"The easiest would be to go to your place in Hoboken, but we don't know who that man was and if he's working for someone."

"Nor do we know the resources he has at his disposal," Luke added.

"What do you mean?"

"Can he track us electronically?"

"Stan said I should get a hotel and not pay by credit card. That implies that someone can track credit card payments. Perhaps we should follow his instruction. Where should we go?"

"Your friend sounds like a smart man. Let's find an ATM, but not close to where we stay. If someone can track credit card payments, they may also trace cash withdrawals."

"Got it," I said.

Luke reached into the paper bag he carried and took out two blue baseball hats with NY on the front, the logo of the New York Yankees. "We better wear these to hide from any security cameras."

I took one from him and put it on. "You're scaring me," I said.

"Just being cautious. Remember that I worked for law enforcement. They use technology, and bad guys can use it just as easy as the good guys. The hats may give us a slight advantage, and then again, maybe they won't."

"Stan Schultz will kill me."

"Why's that?"

"He's a Mets fan."

Luke laughed.

We discussed several options and then took a subway toward the Upper West End, stopping once, where Luke took out cash from an ATM. While riding in the subway, I caught a reflection of Luke and I seated together wearing the matching baseball caps. I had a quick impression that we made a cute couple.

After arriving in the Upper East End, I took out my phone and searched for a hotel. I didn't make a reservation online, not wanting to leave an electronic trace of our movements. The idea was to walk into a lower-priced hotel that might take cash payments from clients, especially in cases where discretion was needed.

We walked several blocks until we came to a hotel.

"What do you think?" I asked.

"It's better than nothing. Why don't you wait here and let me go in to try and get rooms?"

Luke disappeared into the hotel, and a few minutes later, he came back and handed me a plastic keycard. He said, "They took cash and didn't even ask for my name. It seemed the desk clerk was used to doing that sort of thing. Shall we get something to eat?"

Having skipped lunch, I was starving, but there was something important to do. I needed to look at Stan's flash drive. I said, "We passed a sandwich place down the block. Can we get some food to go? Then, I'd like to eat in my room. I'm tired."

"Sure. That sounds good."

We walked to the shop, and ordered sandwiches and drinks, then headed back to the hotel.

* * *

The hotel room was basic, minimally furnished with a small TV hanging on one wall, a table, a wooden chair, and a bed. The bathroom was old and smelled of bleach, giving a notion of cleanliness.

While eating a sandwich, I turned on my laptop. Then I plugged Stan's flash drive into my USB port. Only one file popped up, a spreadsheet, which I opened. It contained massive columns of numbers.

What is this? I thought to myself.

Upon a closer look, it seemed to be an enormous profit and loss statement, or was it a balance sheet? I never understood the difference between the two.

The spreadsheet was a list of industries with a lot of numbers. These were mostly high tech with such headings as telecommunications, computers, and software, but there were also a few in shipping and restaurants. Then there were comments. One comment said,

Gross anomalies in several of these. Business volumes don't add up to revenues. Revenues way higher than industry norms. Results inflated? MONEY LAUNDERING? What is origin of additional income?

Stan had discovered something. What company was this? Was someone trying to stop his research? And was it connected with the guy watching the apartment building?

Then I had another question. Why would I also be in danger? I had nothing to do with his investigations, and while I was Stan's friend, there was no way to know about me carrying the flash drive. Nothing made sense

I needed to speak with Stan and wished he would call me back.

* * *

The following morning, Luke and I walked to the nearby store where we ate muffins and coffee. Luke got into a discussion with the store manager and asked where the coffee came from, and the manager had to get the bag showing its origin. It was a mix of Arabica and Robusta beans from Central and South America, Africa, and Viet Nam, meaning it came from everywhere.

Luke told the manager that they should get another supplier. I didn't find the coffee to be that bad, but it certainly wasn't at the level of La Fuerza farm.

We walked several blocks to the street with Mira Brennen's house. Before we got to the house, I asked, "What now?" I noticed Luke's fist tighten.

"If Valentina is in there, I'm bringing her out, and then we go to the police, although on second thought, that may not be the best thing."

"I thought the same thing. Valentina is an undocumented person in this country. What will happen to her?"

"We're on the same wavelength," Luke commented.

"And, Mira Brennen probably has powerful lawyers representing her, and you know how they can bend facts. Who knows where Valentina would end up?"

"What are you suggesting?" Luke asked.

"We need to take time because there's something deeper here than we understand. Valentina is one problem, but there's something else. What about the connection of Scott Roberts to Nyx Lines, to Lyra-Dominion, to Mira Brennen?"

Luke shook his head. "I thought you agreed to focus on the writing assignment and not on Scott Roberts?"

"Look who's talking. Instead of working on the coffee articles, someone is playing liberator to Valentina."

"This is different," Luke said. "We know who's holding Valentina. Scott Roberts is a case being worked on by law enforcement."

"I don't see it that way. I'm just suggesting to give it some time before deciding how to proceed with Valentina, at least before immediately going to the police."

"Okay," Luke said.

"What's the plan?" I asked.

"I'm going in there to get Valentina."

"If she's not there, what happens?"

"I guess I'll look like a fool."

"That's right. So go up to the front door and knock. If someone answers, then ask questions."

"What kind of questions?"

"I'm not sure. Stan said that journalists need to learn to wing it."

"Then, why don't you do the questioning?"

"I can't."

"And why's that?"

"Mira Brennen's lawyers threatened my boss at Real Media, warning to charge me of harassment."

"Harassment? That's insane."

"I know. It means you have to do this one on your own."

"That I can do," Luke said. He turned and walked toward Mira Brennen's house.

I stood behind a tree, peering around it, watching Luke go up the steps. There was a security camera hanging on the wall, several feet above the front door.

When Luke arrived at the front door, he pushed the doorbell button, waited, and a few minutes later, it opened. A large man moved into the door frame and stood in front of Luke. He was about Luke's height, but broader in the shoulders, and bulky. His shirt, pants, and shoes were black. His black hair was combed straight back, accentuating his broad face.

Somehow the conversation between Luke and the man became animated. The man pointed his finger at Luke and then poked Luke in the chest. Luke raised his hand, as though to calm the man, but then the man pushed Luke.

The man dropped his hand to his waist, reaching for something inside his jacket.

Luke quickly stepped back, and then his right fist tightened, and his legs shifted to a boxer's position, and he swung, and with all the force that comes from lifting heavy burlap coffee bags, his fist solidly connected with the man's chin. The man's legs wobbled, and he fell backward and his head bounced against the door jam and his body collapsed to the ground.

Luke stepped over the man and disappeared inside the open door.

Oh no, I said to myself. The mild-mannered comic book character has just morphed into the beast.

I hesitated behind the tree for a moment, positioned the baseball hat low on my head, and then sprinted to the house, adrenalin driving me up the stairs.

I hopped over the motionless man on the ground and went inside the house and proceeded into a large entrance area. Down a hallway, I saw Luke coming in my direction. A young woman trailed behind him, holding his hand. She wore a t-shirt, jeans, and house slippers. I recognized her from a photo at Maria Lopez's house.

"Let's go," Luke commanded, as he and Valentina ran past me.

I followed. The man on the ground was on his knees, and he reached out and attempted to grab my leg as I zoomed past him. He fell back to the ground on his side, and I noticed a gun in a leather holster inside his jacket.

We sprinted down the street, and my heart pulsated like a high-speed drumbeat.

CHAPTER THIRTY

Three blocks later, we crossed the street, entered Central Park, and found a bench where we caught our breaths. Valentina and I sat on the bench, our chests heaving up and down. Luke stood, bent over, his hand resting on his hips.

Breathing heavily, Luke introduced me to Valentina, and then I exclaimed, "Are you crazy? What were you thinking?"

"What do you mean?"

"Hitting that man like that and barging into the house like the Incredible Hulk, without knowing if Valentina was in there. That's what I mean."

"I knew she was there. He gave it away when we were talking at the front door."

I grinned. "He had a glass chin. That was quite a shot."

Luke smiled. "It was lucky. He was reaching for his gun."

I wondered about that. The power and precision of the swing seemed more than luck.

"He is a bad man," Valentina stated. "His name is Ricco."

"Who is he," I asked.

"He works for Señora Brennen. When I arrived in New York, he took me to the house and locked me up. He is mean. Much of the time, I am very scared. It made me miss my family so much, and I felt stupid to have left them."

"I totally understand your feelings," Luke said.

Valentina said, "I learned that Ricco has bad men working for him, and they could soon be looking for me. Are we safe in this park?"

I looked around. "She's right. We can get more information later on, but first, we should find a safe place to talk."

"Why would Ricco be so interested in looking for you?" Luke asked.

"I may know things," Valentina stated.

I felt uneasy. Ricco and his men would be looking for us. "We should go," I said.

"It may not be safe to go to my place," Luke stated.

Luke was right, and then I thought of a possibility. "If I can contact Stan, he may have ideas, but first, let's get Valentina some clothing. Look what's on her feet."

Luke looked down. "Slippers?"

"She needs comfortable shoes, and let's get her a jacket."

We caught a taxi to a clothing store in East Harlem where we bought Valentina, a pair of tennis shoes and a light jacket.

Valentina spoke Spanish with the workers in the shop, and then with a big smile on Valentina's face, I led them to a Latin American café. Luke ordered three coffees and *Semita de yema*, Honduran egg yolk cookies. The coffee came from a cooperative in El Salvador.

When our order arrived, Valentina took one of the small round cookies, dipped it in the coffee, and took a bite. Tears came to her eyes. "This is just like home," she said.

"You needed that," Luke affirmed.

Luke and I followed Valentina's example, and Luke said, "There's more than one way to drink coffee."

I put the coffee-soaked cookie into my mouth and made a mental note of this for my articles. It was sweet, somewhere between a cookie, cake, with a hint of sweet-bread.

While enjoying the cookie, a different reality set in. How relevant were the articles at this point? First, we had to find a safe place. Valentina mentioned that she might have information that would cause Ricco to come after her. What was it? And, the big question was whether the security camera above the front door of Mira's house had captured an image of Luke and me? We had worn baseball hats, and I had done my best to hide my face from the camera when I ran up the steps, but had I been careful enough? And what about Luke? When Luke swung his fist at Ricco, did he reveal his face? It depended on the angle of the camera.

"Where do we go from here?" I asked.

Luke said, "My initial thought was to go to the police, but your earlier advice was right. We don't have enough information. And Valentina doesn't have a visa to be in this country, so we need to figure out how to handle that. Both of you can stay at my place. I still have some friends in law enforcement who might give insights. Let me talk with them."

Luke's phone rang, he answered it, and then got up and walked away from the table. For four minutes, he carried on a conversation out of hearing distance from Valentina and me. He eventually put the phone in his pocket, came back to the table, and with a gloomy look on his face, he said, "I have a problem."

"What's that?"

"I just spoke with Rosie, who called me from our Hudson Street Coffee Shop. She used a client's phone. The FBI showed up at the Coffee Trust office, and they are looking for me. They had a warrant and are now removing all the files from our office."

"What for?" I asked.

"The FBI opened a shipping container holding coffee from our La Fuerza farm. Two of the bags were full of drugs rather than coffee. Someone informed them that I am behind it."

"That's unbelievable," I exclaimed.

"Do you remember Agent Cortez and his partner? I suspect they were looking into shipments when they visited the Nyx Line offices in Long Beach. And, there's something else."

"Like what?"

"Rosie heard something crazy. It seems the informant said I was responsible for the death of Scott Roberts. The story is that Scott became suspicious of drug smuggling, and that's the reason they shot him."

A quick thought went through my mind. Was that accusation plausible? The illegal drug trade generated a lot of money. Luke worked for a small not-for-profit organization that seemed to be financially stressed. Where did he get the funds to purchase such an expensive apartment? It was undoubtedly several grades above my accommodations.

I looked up at the sign of the coffeeshop. Latin American Café. Was there a connection between La Fuerza Farm and South America? All I had observed was men and women working their tails off from sunrise to sunset. I had seen their homes, where they lived on little. It seemed farfetched to implicate them in drug trafficking.

As far as Luke, would someone involved in smuggling trafficking spend his days helping farmers by loading trucks with heavy bags of coffee? Would he have such an intense dislike for human traffickers?

There were too many contradictions, and I didn't know what to believe. If Luke had the funds to buy a penthouse apartment, everything I had learned about the guy told me that his money didn't come from illegal sources.

CHAPTER THIRTY-ONE

Across the table from Mira Brennen sat one of the most prominent investors in America. She had just given him a pitch on partnering with Lyra-Dominion where they would take a controlling position in a large company. It was a hostile takeover, and the investor agreed to her plan.

The company to take-over was high tech, and while the financial return of the deal was sizeable, what convinced the investor was Mira's self-confidence. She had boasted on her exceptional management abilities, her superior intelligence, and how she had used these qualities to create her successful financial company.

That's what she liked about New York City. In a day it was possible to arrange meetings with the most influential business leaders in the world. With women, she manipulated their feminist egos. With men, she used her cunning, superior intelligence, and beauty to sway their thinking.

Her core skills were manipulation and persuasion, and nothing could stop her ambitious plans.

She shook hands with the investor and promised to meet for drinks and dinner in a few days, which would provide further opportunities to sway the man. It's a known rule in business that the purpose of a meeting is another meeting. For her, the underlying objective of every interaction was to gain an advantage.

Wellbeing was working in her favor.

She left the conference room, and Sai waited for her. He had a look of concern. "How is it going?" Mira asked.

"Something happened at your house."

"What do you mean?"

"Ricco went to the front door when the doorbell rang, and some thug blindsided him and knocked him out. When he woke up, the maid was gone."

"That's absurd. Who could knock out Ricco?"

"That's not the point. The girl is missing."

"What was her name?"

"I think it was Valentina."

"How long was she with us?"

"Two or three months."

"It was getting time to replace her anyway, to send her to a factory, or restaurant, or put her into the trade," Mira said.

"I don't like it that's she's free in the wind. If she says anything about her conditions over the past months, our sleazy fake news media will put this on their front pages, and investors will back away. People won't like it that you hired an illegal domestic worker."

"What's the problem? Everybody does it," Mira stated.

"I know, but you have to be careful."

"What's your opinion on this?"

"We should find her and then make sure she keeps quiet."

"Isn't it more important to find Stan Schultz and that crazy journalist, Sarah Zipper?"

"We will find them all," Sai stated.

"I'm curious about the thug that hit Ricco. Who was he? Did my security camera get an image?"

"Ricco is looking into it, and he'll let me know when he has something."

"Let's not get too worried about this. In the grand scheme, these events are of little significance. We can manage. We have funding and lawyers and connections. Just remember that we have power."

Sai nodded and said, "On another front, we deflected the FBI investigation in Long Beach. It seems a coffee farm in Honduras has been working with a do-gooder organization in New Jersey to smuggle drugs. They also murdered a journalist in Long Beach." He laughed.

Mira smiled without expression in her eyes. "Well done. Indeed, we have power."

CHAPTER THIRTY-TWO

We sat in silence at our outside table at the Latin America Café. What Luke shared seemed unbelievable, and my mind spun as I considered our situation and the options. The FBI blamed Luke for drug trafficking and Scott's murder. Some strange people were after Stan and me, and according to Valentina, Ricco would be searching for her.

Added to this, Mira Brennen was putting pressure on Real Media, and who knows the consequences coming from Luke's attack on Ricco and forcefully entering Mira's house? Probably little would happen because Mira wouldn't want people to know she had forcibly kept an unpaid domestic worker in her home.

There was another mystery, Stan's spreadsheet, with masses of numbers. It must have taken him months to compile all that data. I wished I could speak with him. I took out my phone and called Stan, and it went into his voicemail. "Stan, I need to speak with you urgently." Then I hung up.

When Luke went inside the café to pay the check, I turned to Valentina and asked, "When you were in Mira's house, did you ever speak with her?"

"Only one time."

"Only once in three months?"

"She was often gone, and when at home, she treated me as though I wasn't there. It was always Ricco who gave instructions, and he never said my name."

"Who is this, Ricco?"

"He is like a security man or something like that, but I think he does more."

"What do you mean?"

"Mira once called him their New York fixer. If something has to happen, even bad things, then Ricco does it. Mira and Sai instruct Ricco on what to do. Mira called Sai their California fixer."

"Sai Bashir?" On the Lyra-Dominion website, I had seen that Sai Bashir was the company's, Chief Operations Officer. "What kind of fixing does Sai do?"

"I'm not sure, because it was not easy to listen to their conversations, but something happened in California."

"In California? Was it Long Beach?"

"Yes, I heard the name of that place. It sounded strange to name a town after a long beach."

"What else can you tell me about Myra?"

"I was afraid of her. Most of the time, she ignored me, but every once in a while, it was like she was looking through me. It made me scared."

I had a similar impression, for indeed, Mira's stare imposed fear.

We sat waiting for Luke and were startled when there was a brisk movement behind us, and two men in black suits ran past our table. Two policemen followed. A black car screeched to a stop directly in front of us, and then three police cars arrived, their police lights blinking. The men in suits and the two policemen ran into the café while clients sat staring. A couple of clients got up and quickly moved down the sidewalk.

After three or four minutes of waiting, the two policemen walked out of the café, and Luke was between them, with his hands handcuffed behind his back. The two men in dark suits followed behind.

Luke's eyes glanced at me, and he slightly shook his head and then moved it to one side as though telling me to leave.

Then, I saw that one of the men following Luke was FBI Agent Cortez. Agent Cortez focused on Luke, and he didn't look in my direction. I wore the blue baseball hat, so that gave me a small element of concealment, and the fact that I was sitting with Valentina may also have provided a diversion.

Luke entered the back of one of the police cars, and it sped away. The FBI agents and the remaining police officers got into their vehicles, and a moment later, the street was back to normal, except for the customers nervously talking between themselves.

I leaned across to Valentina and said, "Let's get out of here."

* * *

After leaving the café, while tempted to run, we kept a slow and steady pace, two women out for a relaxing stroll that was anything but tranquil.

The arrest of Luke was a shock, and I felt lost without Luke's support. The arrest had happened so fast. How did they know Luke was there?

Then, I remembered the phone conversation with Rosie. The FBI must have been tracking Luke's phone. Were they doing the same with me? I felt the bag on my shoulder and considered getting rid of the phone in it. But I needed it to call Stan and Ernie, that is if Ernie was still talking to me?

"Where are we going?" Valentina asked.

I had run out of ideas. "Honestly, I don't know."

"Why did the police arrest, Señor Luke?"

"It's a long story." I described it to Valentina, trying to condense it, explaining how the police thought that La Fuerza farm and Luke were suspected of drug trafficking and even killing someone.

Valentina's eyes became large. "The workers at La Fuerza would never do that, and Señor Luke is a good man."

"I know that. The question now is, what shall we do?"

I thought of Stan, and my best guess was that he was at his cabin by the lake in upstate New York. It was more than a three-hour drive. Where could I find a car, and what if he wasn't there?

Stan claimed that every Jew should have an escape plan. He said this is the primary lesson learned from history. Was Stan implementing his plan?

When we got to the intersection, my phone rang. It was from a number I didn't know.

"Hello," I said.

"Sarah, this is Stan."

I blurted out, "Where are you and why all this concealment, and who was the guy watching our apartment, and a whole bunch of other questions?"

"Go to Mort's store."

"What are you talking about?"

"Mort's store. Go there, but first, ditch your phone."

Stan hung up.

I exhaled a breath of desperation. Why all the mystery?

"Who was that?" Valentina asked, her eyes full of worry.

"A friend. We need to talk to him. It's only a few blocks away."

CHAPTER THIRTY-THREE

We walked three blocks out of the heavily Latin neighborhoods of East Harlem, circled past the street where I lived, went another block, and came to Mort's store. The name on the front was 'Mort's Kosher Fine Wines and Spirits.' It was where I went to buy a good bottle of French Bordeaux or California Chardonnay.

We entered the store, and Mort was behind the counter. He came around to me and, with a soft voice, asked, "Were you followed?"

"No. We were careful."

"Come with me," he said.

Mort led us into a storage area at the back of the store, stacked with boxes full of wine. Many had Hebrew characters. I could read some of the words, but my Hebrew was minimal. One summer, my parents had sent me to a language school on a kibbutz in Israel, but learning Hebrew was secondary to the Tel Aviv nightlife.

Mort led us out through a back door and then up some steps. Mort owned the building. He lived on the top floor and rented out several apartments.

We went up the steps, entered a hallway, and passed a couple of doors. At the end of the hall, Mort knocked on a door.

It opened just a crack.

Mort whispered, "It's me, and Sarah, and someone else."

A whisper came back. "Who is the someone else?"

I commanded, "Stan, open the door." I pushed on it, and Stan moved back.

"Who is she?" Stan pointed at Valentina.

"A friend. Now, what's going on?"

We entered the room, which turned out to be a small apartment. Mort went back to the store, and Stan invited us to sit on wooden chairs around a table.

I said, "This has been the craziest twenty-four hours of my life, starting with your freaky phone call yesterday with the warning about the people watching our apartments. Then a whole bunch of other things have happened, and the spreadsheet on your flash drive is bewildering."

Stan's back went stiff, and he raised his hands in the air. "I told you not to look at it. Your very existence is in danger just by having it."

"So, what are all those confusing masses of numbers?"

Stan shook his head back and forth. "They are going to take over the world."

I heard that so many times from Stan that it had become like a broken record. "What is it this time?"

"The numbers are proof."

"Proof of what?"

"There is something extraordinary going on with a company I researched. Money is coming from somewhere, and it doesn't make sense. I don't know from where, but I have theories that need proving."

"Explain it to me."

"It's a holding company that owns quite a few companies." He looked at me and asked, "Does that make sense."

"Stan, my business knowledge isn't that bad."

"Well, I just had to check," he said.

"Please continue."

"So, all these individual companies are in different industries, and all of them are doing well, but several of them perform exceptionally. Compare their assets to cash flow, and they are making a ton of money."

"I don't follow."

"See. I knew your financial knowledge is pitiful. Your ancestors would be ashamed."

"Come on, Stan. That's racist. And, assets to cash flow is not that difficult to understand. I was just asking for more information."

"But it's true. You need to take some business courses."

"Get off it. Everyone's not a numbers guru like you. What's going on?"

Stan took a breath. "If you compare those companies with similar companies in their respective industries, their earnings are way out of whack."

"So?"

"Don't you get it? Money is coming in from unknown places. It's called money laundering, and those profits support the entire holding company, which makes that company and its management look like heroes, and outside investors don't know it. The holding company is cooking the books."

"Why hasn't anyone discovered this?" I asked.

"Because the investors and the media and the politicians and the tax authorities are all hoodwinked. They are imbeciles, but I have the facts."

"Then why are you in danger, and why am I in danger?"

"I'm in danger because they know that I know. And you, Sarah Zipper, are in danger because you know me. Simple as that."

"What kind of danger?"

"Bad."

"What's the name of this company?" I asked.

Stan looked in both directions, waited several seconds, and then whispered, "Lyra-Dominion."

* * *

When Stan stated the name of the company, I gasped. Something was obvious. He said bad people ran it. Evil was a better term.

Valentina remained silent during the discussion, but now she was squirming in her chair.

"Are you okay," I asked.

"Lyra-Dominion. That is the company of Señora Brennen."

Stan's head jerked toward Valentina, and he asked, "How do you know that?"

I replied, "It's a crazy story, but Valentina has been working in Mira Brennen's home."

Stan had a quizzical look on his face and asked, "In her home?"

"That's correct."

"Then, how do we know that this young lady is not working with them. This is a disaster."

"Stan, she is the victim, so just listen to her."

Stan took a deep breath and nodded his head.

Valentina said, "I think Señor Stan is correct. Money can come from hidden places."

"Like from where?" I asked.

"My study in university was accounting. We know that all the numbers must balance."

"But what do you know about Lyra-Dominion?" Stan asked.

"Sometimes, I hear them talking?"

"Who is *them*?" Stan asked.

"Señora Brennen and Sai and Ricco work together. I heard them talk about cargo on their shipping company."

"Nyx Lines?" I asked.

"Yes, Nyx Lines. And, they were happy when the shipments made it through. Then several times men came to visit Señora Brennen, and Sai, and Ricco. The men spoke English, but when they were away from Mira, they spoke Spanish with a Mexican accent. I knew they were cartel men, and they talked with Señora Brennen about bank accounts."

Stan said, "Did they mention the bank where they have an account? This is important to fill in missing details in my research."

"I don't know the bank, but I may have a way to get that information."

"How is that?" I asked.

"Only once I was alone in Señora Brennen's office at her home, and I used her laptop to send a message to my brother. I found many files on her computer. Maybe in them, there is the information you need."

"If the information is on her computer, is there a way to get into her office?" I asked.

"It is not only on her computer."

"Where is it?"

"It is on the cloud. I made a copy of everything."

CHAPTER THIRTY-FOUR

Stan pointed a slightly trembling finger at Valentina, and said, "This young lady is brilliant. She might hold the unaccounted for pieces. Can you show me the files?"

"Yes," Valentina said. "Is your computer connected to the internet?"

Stan took his laptop from a shelf, brought it to the table, and turned it on. Valentina and I sat on either side of Stan, and in a few minutes, we were into Valentina's cloud account looking through the files.

One folder was labeled *Financials,* and another labeled *Personal.*

Stan zeroed in on the financials folder, and I suspected I'd be of little help in the analysis of the numbers. I reached into my bag, took out my laptop, turned to Valentina, and asked, "Can you log me into your account?"

Valentina nodded, and in a few minutes, I copied the 'personal' folder onto my laptop.

I found dozens of different sub-folders covering a host of various topics, everything from property contracts, newspaper articles, and prepared speeches. Mira was organized, and I wished I had those skills. One file that caught my attention was 'calendar.'

I tried to open it, but it was unreadable, so I looked at the file extension and then found a calendar program that could open the file. Ten minutes later, I was looking at Mira Brennen's calendar.

Mira was a busy person, and with great detail, she logged every tiny event in her life, from meetings to phone calls to lunches. There were copious notes like, 'need to call Sai,' 'convince bank to advance loan,' 'day successful, persuaded investor over dinner,' and, 'the crowd loved me, can you blame them?" The notes made it look more like a diary than a calendar."

I looked at the previous day and found a note about the disastrous interview with Mira. The note said, 'Disturbing meeting with Sarah Zipper. Is she unhinged? Need to monitor.'

Just as suspected, the meeting was a flop. The word, unhinged, had several synonyms, such as deranged, crazy, and confused. Which one of those descriptions was Mira referring to? For sure the meeting was a failure. Why was there a need to monitor?

I went back through previous days and weeks of notes and meetings. Some entries were condensed, as though written in code. Some were expressions of emotions or incomprehensible entries with single words like 'horrible' and 'enemy.' What did that mean?

Many entries were given categories for easy classification of events, such as *Speaking Engagements*, and *Investors*.

I clicked on the investors category and a long list of meetings and dates popped up, so I went through them. Some were with managers of mutual funds and with well-known independent investors. Then, one investor caught my eye. Carlos Ortega. There were three years of quarterly meetings, and they all took place in Mexico City.

There was only one Carlos Ortega that I knew of, and he was the head of the Zapteros Cartel. Inevitably there were many people named Carlos Ortega. But, why would Mira be going to Mexico City so often?

The notes associated with the meetings were clear. 'Carlos is pleased with the investment.' 'He wants to provide more funds.' 'Transportation network functioning without problems.' 'Redirect Nyx Lines to Honduras for repackaging of shipments from further south.'

From what I read of Mira, she was prudent, someone who exercised great self-control. Every action seemed calculated, and every word carefully delivered. To slip up by documenting the name and meetings with a questionable person appeared to be out of character. Yet, did Mira have a character flaw? In the interview that morning, she was arrogant. Did that get the best of her? Did she haughtily believe no one could hack her personal records? Anyone can slip up and do stupid things, even Mira Brennen.

I sat back in my chair and closed my eyes. Pieces of the puzzle were falling into place, yet I had more questions. The FBI had charged Luke with drug smuggling. Instead, could it be that Mira Brennen was the one doing this? There was nothing conclusive at this point, with only a set of assumptions.

I turned to Stan and asked, "Are you finding anything?"

"Lyra-Dominion has holdings in over sixty companies, in most cases as a minority shareholder. But there's something strange. In all the companies where Lyra-Dominion is the majority shareholder, those companies show spectacular results. And, while Lyra-Dominion promotes itself as a high-tech investor, it has more cash coming from its low-tech companies than the high tech."

"What do you mean?"

"The restaurant, and the trucking and shipping companies are owned one hundred percent, as well as a car-wash chain. Those companies are rolling in cash, and that's what provides dividends to shareholders. I could never figure out the origin of the cash."

"I bet that's the piece of the puzzle Scott Robert's found, unless he suspected drug shipments in Nyx Lines."

"Who is Scott Roberts?" Stan asked.

I explained what happened in Long Beach.

Stan shook his head. "See, I was right. These people are wicked and dangerous. And, they are trying to take over the world."

I wasn't sure about the taking over the world part but agreed that Mira and whoever was working with her were evil. Someone had to stop them.

I looked again at the calendar to find out what meetings Mira scheduled during the day. In the afternoon, she was speaking at an investment seminar in the financial district of Manhattan. That might be a place to learn more about her.

I turned to Stan and asked, "Can you identify exactly where this cash is coming from?"

"It will take time to get through these files. Hopefully, there are records of bank accounts."

Stan and Valentina hunkered down in front of Stan's laptop and began discussing numbers, and I needed a break to think. I excused myself, went downstairs, and headed for a coffee shop down the street.

As I walked, I considered all that was going on, with one shock after another. That morning I had seen Luke arrested, and now he was facing charges of drug trafficking and homicide. And, I learned that Stan had already been investigating Lyra-Dominion, and had gathered incriminating evidence.

Things were coming together in my mind. Before getting to the coffee shop, I called Ernie.

He answered, "Ernie here."

"This is Sarah. What's happening?"

"It seems the FBI has a person of interest in Scott's shooting."

"They've got the wrong person."

"How do you know that?"

"I'm working the story. It has to do with Lyra-Dominion."

Ernie's voice elevated. "I thought I told you to stay clear of that company. They are about to ruin us."

"There's a story here, potentially massive." I knew how to play on his susceptibilities.

"I don't understand."

"Just trust me, for once."

"Why should I trust you?"

That was an insult. Every article I ever wrote was factually correct, well, maybe with a few embellishments. "Have I ever let you down? I'm on to something exceptional, and it's not just the description of restaurant kitchens."

Ernie was quiet for a moment, and then he asked, "Are you sure about this?"

"Pretty sure."

"That's not very comforting."

"I know, but let me work it, and then I'll get back to you."

"Zipper, you've always been solid. I'll wait, and at the same time, I'll try and stop our client exodus. If you need help, let me know. Getting the story is the highest priority."

"Thanks, Ernie."

We hung up, and I felt grateful. Ernie had my back. I slipped the phone into the front pocket of my jeans.

Nearing the coffee shop, I wondered about Luke. Where was he, and what kind of interrogation was he going through? Did he get a lawyer? Was there any way to contact him?

After entering the coffee shop, I was surprised to see that they listed the origins of their coffees, so I ordered a cup of Ethiopian Yirgacheffe. The description was 'medium roast, mellow with a wide-body and distinctive floral notes, containing hints of berries, nuts, chocolate, lemon, wine.' That was quite a sales proposition. Coffees from other origins had different descriptions.

When drinking it, I could taste a hint of chocolate, and indeed, floral notes hit my pallet. It was excellent, but still not as good as the Ethiopian beans I roasted at home.

I took a chair by a table and considered my next move when I saw a black Chevrolet pass by on the street. It reminded me of the car Luke had described, the one with the guy who was watching my apartment.

Then, the car slowed, and in the front on the rider's side was a face I recognized, a broad face, with black hair, combed straight back. It was Ricco, the man that Luke hit. In the rear seat sat two other men, and one was looking at an open laptop.

The car stopped and backed into an empty parking place just beyond the coffee shop.

I quickly stood up and went to the barista and asked, "Is there another way out of here?"

He pointed toward an opening to a room behind the counter, and I sprinted toward it.

* * *

Panicked, I ran out of the backdoor of the coffee shop and turned into an alley. To see Ricco was unreal. It wasn't by chance that his car stopped in front of the coffee shop. He now had a team, and that only made things worse.

I wondered how he had found me, and then remembered Stan telling me to get rid of my phone. I failed to do so. And, what had Luke said? Both the good guys and the bad guys had technology. Ricco had somehow tracked me to the coffee shop.

The thought of throwing away my high-end phone was against my frugal nature. That stupid decision, or lack of it, now worked against me. I had to get rid of the phone. Halfway down the alley was a loading dock and next to it was a small pile of wooden boards that looked like they were there for a long time. I quickly turned off the phone and placed it between two boards, unseen.

I ran to the end of the alley and looked both ways down a main street, and then darted to the sidewalk on the other side. A car had to slow, and the driver gave me a New York welcome, with a flip of a finger and a loud, long honk. Did Ricco hear it?

At the next corner, I turned down a street, passed a couple of shops, and then went into a used bookstore. A young woman stacked books on a shelf. She smiled at me.

I said, "Excuse me, but I've got a problem. Could I please ask your help?"

The young woman's smile disappeared, and her eyes opened wide. "What do you need?"

"This might sound like a crazy story, but I'm a journalist and have gotten myself in a fix. Some men are following me, and I need to make a call."

"For sure. Use the phone on the desk."

I went to the phone, wanting to call Stan to warn him and then realized that his phone number was in my phone. Even that wouldn't help, for Stan had called me from an unknown number. "Could you look up a number for me?"

"The shopkeeper came over to the desk and asked, "What do you need?"

"Can you give me the number of Mort's Kosher Wines and Spirits?"

The young woman went to a computer, and quickly, Mort's number appeared.

I called it, and Mort answered.

I said, "Mort, this is Sarah. Please get an urgent message to Stan. Tell him that Ricco almost found me, but I'm okay for now. Tell him that he and Valentina must be cautious. If there's a better place to hide, he should go now."

That was all I had to say, for Stan would understand. We hung up.

I put the phone back on the cradle, turned to the shopkeeper, and said, "Thank you."

The young shopkeeper said, "Your welcome, but why didn't you call the police?"

It was a good question, the only logical question, and I didn't have a straight answer. "It's complicated."

"Why?"

The bookseller would make a good journalist. "At this point, my team is working to compile information, and going to the police would be premature." I wished I would have used the word *evidence* rather than *information*. Did they have enough evidence?

As far as teams, the men in Ricco's car looked intimidating. My crew consisted of a nearly eighty-year-old man and a young Honduran who had worked as an unpaid domestic for the past three months. The other member of the team was sitting in a jail cell somewhere.

I felt stuck. I couldn't go back to Mort's place. And I didn't have enough information to go to the police or the FBI. Would anyone believe someone who is making allegations against an up and coming businesswoman who is the darling of the business management world? Politicians wanted to have their photos taken with Mira. Her lawyers were nasty and had already threatened me with harassment charges. Mira had all the dominant players on her side.

I needed a moment to think. I considered calling a taxi but didn't know the technological capabilities of anyone working with Ricco. Someone might be tracking calls to taxi companies in my area. Maybe I was becoming paranoid. Perhaps I had become like Stan! The subway was half a block away. If I could make it there, then I could disappear.

I thanked the storekeeper again, went to the front door, and looked out into the street. When I felt it was safe, I left the shop and walked briskly toward the subway entrance thinking that Central Station might be an okay destination, at least until I put together a plan. I knew that area because the Real Media office was close by. But, maybe Central Station was the last place I should go, for it might be a prime surveillance target for Ricco?

Then, I wondered if anyone had the technology to track the call from the bookstore to Mort's place. Had I put the seller in danger?

CHAPTER THIRTY-FIVE

Once outside Central Station, I went to a shop and bought a green New York Jets cap. The blue New York Yankees hat went into my bag. Would a disguise change actually work? Probably not.

I walked out of Central Station, found a busy coffee shop, and bought a sandwich and a soda. After finding an empty table, I ate my sandwich while opening my laptop. The place had a free Wi-Fi connection. With my phone now squeezed between two planks of wood in a back alley, I had lost my ability to connect to the internet anytime and anywhere.

I logged into my email and saw the most recent message. It was from Stan.

Call me from a safe phone.

That was it, and it was unlike Stan. He usually went on and on, whereas this was short and cryptic. What did he mean? Obviously, my phone wasn't safe, for it seemed that Ricco was able to find me through some kind of GPS tracking. But, was Ricco also able to listen in on my calls?

Luke had said that both the good guys and the bad guys possessed technology. Then, I thought of Lyra-Dominion. It owned some leading high-tech companies. That implied that Mira had access to incredible capabilities.

I closed my laptop, left the restaurant, and walked a couple of blocks where there was a store selling telephones. I had passed the store many times on my way to work and had always noticed one sign in the front window that said, 'Cheap Used Phones.'

Inside the store, I found floor to ceiling shelves super-crammed with everything to do with telephones, from cables to phone covers. A quick scan indicated there was little logic to the place.

A small, skinny middle-aged man dressed in jeans and a checkered flannel shirt came from a back room. He had scraggly shoulder-length hair and a beard and looked more like a Vermont mountain man than a polished New York City merchant. He asked, "Anything you need?"

"I see that you sell used phones."

The man smiled. "Thousands of um."

"Would you sell burner phones?"

He laughed. "As many as you want. No questions asked."

"Okay, please give me one."

"Only one? You don't want to use those things too often."

"Why's that?"

"Big Brother is watching."

"Please give me two." Definitely, I was becoming like Stan.

The seller reached into a drawer, took out two phones, and placed them on the counter. "There you go."

"How does it work?"

"What do you mean?"

"What's the best way to use them?"

"It depends on the opposition," the seller stated.

"The opposition?"

"Yeah. The opposition comes at different levels. An example of basic opposition would be your husband. In this case, you'd want to keep your phone calls confidential between you and your lover, or whoever you don't want your husband to discover. Just turn off the sound so he can't hear it ring in an awkward moment."

The guy spoke matter-of-factly, and wasn't joking.

He continued. "In a more advanced case, there are people with tracking technologies who want to follow your movements or even cause you harm."

"Let's go with the second case."

"Sounds serious."

"It is."

"With GPS, a satellite is tracking you. These two phones don't have GPS, so you don't need to worry about that. We call them dumb-phones because they don't do much. They don't connect to the internet, so you can't be triangulated via Wi-Fi connections. But, you can still be triangulated with cell towers, so you need to keep the phone turned off when you don't use it. Just make sure you change locations after each use."

"Does that mean no one can track me?"

"Yes and no. Government agencies use voice imprint. They know you when you talk. And, also, don't turn on both phones at the same time, again because of triangulation."

"Is that it?" I asked.

"Turn the phone off after you use it, and never call the same number twice. By the way, there's no security camera in this shop and no record of this sale. And, when you walk out of this store, keep your hat low so that it covers your face. And change your jacket as soon as you can."

Talk about paranoia. This guy was over the top, but I was glad for his advice. There was no way of knowing how much technology Mira Brennen had at her disposal.

The phone seller had given a lot to remember. I paid cash, thanked him, and left the store. After walking three blocks, I stepped behind a dumpster and called Mort.

He answered, and I said, "Mort. I can't talk long. Are our friends safe?"

"Yes," he said.

"Have them call me, but they should not call from your telephone." I gave the number of my second burner phone, wrote down Stan's number, and then hung up. Upon ending the call, I turned the phone off and turned the second phone on.

I had just broken one of the rules of the guy in the store by leaving one phone on, but I had to take the risk. There didn't seem any other way of contacting Stan. Now, all I had to do was figure out a plan of action and wait for Stan's call.

* * *

I walked several more blocks and withdrew cash from an ATM. Then, I took the phone seller's advice and bought a blue lightweight windbreaker while wondering if this is what spies had to do.

Upon leaving the clothing store, my phone rang. There was only one person who would call that second burner phone.

"Are you safe?" I asked.

"Yes. We found things to send to you," Stan replied.

"Don't send it to my email." There was no way to know if anyone had hacked my account."

"Understood. How can I get it to you?"

"Call me back in thirty minutes."

I hung up and walked back to the phone store and went inside. The seller was behind his counter. He looked up.

I said, "Is there any way someone can send me information over the internet without discovery?"

The seller smiled and said, "About a zillion ways, but you could start with TOR."

"What's that?"

"The dark web."

* * *

The phone seller said his name was John Smith, which sounded fishy because of the way his eyes shifted to the side like searching for something forgotten. He spent several minutes on his computer, then printed out a piece of paper and handed it to me.

He said, "Follow these instructions. I've created an account for you on the dark web where you can share information with your counterpart."

I looked at the paper and asked, "My counterpart also needs these instructions, and I'm not sure how to inform him."

"Don't send anything via your email account in case someone is looking in."

"That's what I'm talking about."

"Where is your counterpart?"

"On the Upper East Side not far from East Harlem."

"Hand carry it," The shopkeeper said.

"I can't. It wouldn't be good if I were spotted. As you can figure out, I need to stay off the grid."

"Off the grid is my specialty," he stated. "It's the best way because of the multitude of adversaries out there."

It felt like John and Stan would get along fine with each other. "So, do you have any ideas how to get it to him?"

"I have someone who can hand carry it, that is if you are comfortable with giving me a delivery address."

I gave him Mort's address and said, "I need to call my counterpart. I'm not sure he's still there, but he needs to know that the document is arriving."

John reached in a drawer, took out a telephone and handed it to me. "Call with this one. It's highly secured, almost like making Voice Over IP calls over the dark web. It's not for sale, but I'll let you use it."

I walked out of the shop and called Stan's number, and he answered.

I said, "It's me."

He asked, "Where can I send my research?"

"Within the hour, an envelope with instructions will arrive at Mort's place. Are you able to get it from him?"

"For sure."

"What's the essence of what you're sending me?" I asked.

"Conclusive evidence that Lyra-Dominion has received significant cash injections from several illicit sources."

"Unbelievable," I remarked. "I look forward to see it. How is our young friend doing?"

"She's hanging in there. Anything is better than being held prisoner for months."

"Good news."

"Do you have any thoughts on what we do now?" Stan asked.

"Let me have a look at your research, and then I'll get back to you."

We hung up, and I walked back into the shop. Handing the phone back to John, I said, "Thank you so much. You've been most helpful."

"I'm glad to be of service. You know that the government and other terrible actors are watching every move we make."

This guy should meet Stan, as I'm sure they would have a lot to talk about. But, he was helpful.

John asked, "Can we make a trade?"

"What kind of trade?"

"Give me your two phones, and I'll give you two new ones. There's a saying in my line of work, once used, burn it."

"Are you going to throw away my phones?"

He laughed. "Of course not. They'll be recycled. In a few minutes, I can sell them again as pristine burner phones."

We exchanged the two phones, and I thanked him again and walked out of the shop.

My eyes glanced at every person on the street and every car that went by. Then, I looked for doors, alleyways, and subway entrances, places to evade capture.

I took a breath. Was I hanging out with the wrong people, like John the phone guy and Stan? I commanded myself to drop the excessive fear and to relax. Although, was that possible? My plan now was to wait until receiving Stan's information, and then decide what to do.

Then, I had an idea. I had seen Mira Brennen's calendar and knew that she was speaking at a conference in the financial district in the afternoon.

Instead of being attacked, I contemplated becoming the aggressor.

CHAPTER THIRTY-SIX

At the lower end of Manhattan are the offices of some of the largest financial companies in the world, along with the New York Stock Exchange. That is where people of power and influence do business.

I was going there to do business of a different kind.

I took the subway from Central Station to Wall Street Station, a fourteen-minute ride. Then, I walked a block south on Broadway. It was always impressive to see the tall buildings on each side of the street, making you feel small and insignificant.

I came to the entrance of one of the buildings and then stopped, and took out one of my burner phones. I found the card that FBI Agent Cortez had given me in Long Beach and called his number.

He answered, "This is Agent Cortez."

"Hello, Mister Cortez. I don't know if you remember me, but this is Sarah Zipper, the journalist from Real Media. I once called you, and we met in Long Beach."

There was silence for a moment, and then Cortez said, "I remember. I've tried to call your phone, but there's no answer."

"It's out of order. Could I ask where Luke Cotton is?"

There was another pause, and then, "He's being held in federal custody."

"But where?"

"In New York."

I sensed he was evasive. "Come on, Agent Cortez. The public has a right to know where you are keeping prisoners."

"He's at the Metropolitan Correctional Center."

That was only a mile from where I stood. It was a federal jail that held male and female prisoners. "What are the charges against him?"

"For one, homicide. He is culpable in the murder of Scott Roberts, for which you were already asking questions. And he's using coffee shipments as a front for smuggling."

"Do you have proof of that?" I asked.

"We wouldn't arrest him without proof."

"Did you find any evidence when you raided his office at Coffee Trust?"

"I can't discuss an ongoing case."

I was sure they found nothing. "And, I bet your so-called proof came from an informant."

"Again, I can't speak about that."

"Luke didn't do it," I stated.

"And how do you know that."

"You're aware that Real Media has more than a journalistic interest in Scott Roberts case. He worked with us. I replaced Scott and came across information, leading me to a different conclusion than the one you made. And, my information didn't come through mysterious informants or office records that contain no hard evidence."

"Then, who's behind it?"

"There is a company called Lyra-Dominion. They own Nyx Lines, which you visited in Long Beach, and Nyx Lines is smuggling drugs. That's the part Scott Roberts discovered. But there's more. The management of Lyra-Dominion is laundering money, which inflates their financial results."

"That's farfetched," Cortez said.

"Why don't you ask your financial experts to look into Lyra-Dominion's books, and then let me know if it's fanciful."

"Without some initial evidence, we can't get a warrant, and we need a warrant to access the books."

"There are people who can supply evidence."

"Look, Ms. Zipper, at this point, I'll consider your hypothesis, but I believe we have this case wrapped up."

"Do you really?"

"Yes. Luke Cotton will be in court tomorrow before a judge where a federal attorney is bringing charges."

I understood that the FBI had already made up its mind, and it was unlikely they would look at another theory without convincing evidence. I said, "You're doing the wrong thing."

"I don't think so."

"Wait and see."

I hung up.

* * *

As soon as the call disconnected, I turned off the phone, as instructed by John Smith at the phone shop.

Walking down Broadway, I questioned if it had been the right thing to call Agent Cortez. At least I found out where Luke was imprisoned and that he was to appear in court the following day. Did he have a lawyer?

The call with Cortez rattled me.

I claimed to have evidence against Lyra-Dominion, but did Stan have definite proof? My experience with Stan was that it was often "maybe," or "I almost have confirmation," and his evidence was often conjecture and supposition.

I needed to see his research. This wasn't a simple story about a restaurant. It was in another league from what they taught in journalism classes. This story was about coffee, and coffee farmers who worked hard for the enjoyment of others, and about greedy people who leveraged the coffee supply chain for their evil ends. And, about destroyed lives, from coffee farms to asylum seekers, and it touched everyday people across the country.

Turning into the entrance hall of a tall building, I found my way to a large room set up like a classroom amphitheater. Rows of desks descended to a stage. The room was full, with thirty to forty people attending the event.

Mira Brennen was at the podium, giving a speech. Behind her was a large poster that said, 'Wall Street Investors Monthly Symposium.' Another sign said, 'Lyra-Dominion, Mira Brennen.'

Mira was saying something about a fundamental human right, the right of wellbeing, and she was coming to the end of her speech. "We may not always get it right, but we do our best to strive for this ideal. We make a concerted effort to examine every process to determine what may keep us from achieving this ideal, and we eliminate negative forces from this process. It's holistic with the recognition that we are all one."

The way the light reflected off her copper red hair gave me the impression that a goddess stood before us, as though a halo would appear above her head.

She continued, "I believe that if every business in America worked to achieve this, we would have a better world, and wellbeing would become an actual reality. Thank you for allowing me to share my thoughts with you today."

When she concluded, loud applause rippled through the crowd. I looked around and saw admiration in people's faces, as Mira made a slight bow, and her lips moved to communicate a soundless 'Thank You.'

The people wore their business best, a sample of investment managers from formidable New York financial companies. I felt out of place wearing sneakers, jeans, a windbreaker, and a green New York Jets cap.

Mira walked from the podium to the center of the stage, where there were two chairs. A woman held two microphones and handed one to Mira, and then they both sat down.

The woman said, "Thank you, Mira, for that inspirational talk. Looking out for the wellbeing of all those around us is a challenge, especially for our work colleagues."

Mira smiled. "It goes far beyond that. Consider what will happen when we look out for the wellbeing of this great nation and the global community."

"Ah, ha," the woman said. "Do we sense a career change? Politics may be the next step."

The crowd laughed.

Mira looked at the crowd. "I'm humbled to have achieved something so remarkable. My company has accomplished so many positive things in such a short time. Why can't we do the same thing for our country? It would be an honor to dedicate my life to that."

"If you do, you will have many supporters." The woman turned to the crowd and asked, "What do you think?"

People clapped, and in a wave, they stood and chanted, "Mira, Mira, Mira!"

Mira smiled and nodded and then raised her hand and lowered it, and the people sat down. Then the woman asked if there were any questions.

There was one question after another. Someone asked Mira's thoughts on the economy, and another asked if Mira worked out and what she ate to keep a trim figure? "Pilates and broccoli," she replied to that one, which was followed by laughter from the audience.

A microphone circulated through the crowd, and I kept raising my hand, and finally, the microphone was given to me.

I stood and took off my green cap, and asked, "You spoke about Lyra-Dominion's success. In looking at the details of the companies held in your portfolio, some show unbelievable results. Excuse me, let me call them un-real results. How do you explain that? Where is all that additional cash coming from?"

There was a hush in the crowd.

Mira looked toward the back of the auditorium, saw me, and then she froze. It took a moment to collect herself, but there was a change in her composure. "It's attributed to excellent management. The people working in Lyra-Dominion are exceptional."

I still held the microphone. "As a follow-up question, has there ever been an investigation into some of your investors, particularly those representing questionable products coming from South America?"

There was a murmur in the crowd.

The host next to Mira said, "To give everyone a chance, we have a limit of one question per participant. Is there anyone else who has a question?"

The person who passed around the microphone attempted to take it from my hand, but I held it tightly and exclaimed. "Mira, I know what happened to Scott Roberts, and your part in it, and your dealings with cartels and keeping an undocumented domestic worker hostage in your house for three months. So much for the meaningless hype about wellbeing."

The microphone got yanked away from me, and the room went from a state of shock to a surge of people's voices. At the front of the room, Mira's large green eyes tightened, sending sharp spears at me.

I quickly slipped out the exit door, walked out onto the street, and took the subway back to Central Station. I briskly walked to the phone shop and went inside.

John Smith looked up and grinned. "You again?"

"I'm wondering something."

"What's that?"

"I need to disappear for a while. Do you know anything about that?"

"Lady, becoming nameless and unseen is what my friends and I are all about."

CHAPTER THIRTY-SEVEN

John locked the shop's front door, and we went out a back door into an alley.

"No cameras out here," he stated. "I made sure of that."

He led me down the alley and then used a key to open a metal door. We went inside a building and then down steps coming to a corridor that zigzagged several hundred feet.

John said, "New York City is full of underground passageways going from building to building if you know about them. If you get stuck, you can always revert to the drainage system, but we won't need to do that."

The image of walking through the New York City sewer system was not appealing. "Where are we going?" I asked.

"To a safe place. Once there, you can tell me how I can help."

The passageway was dark, and I had a strange feeling. Could the guy be trusted? I hardly knew him. I was taller than he, and the boxing and Krav Maga lessons might come in handy after all, as there seemed no way for flight. What if he came back with a couple of his friends to do me harm? Well, they would have one mean Jewish tigress on their hands. Although, I had difficulty to imagine myself as a female Rambo.

He led the way up some steps and used a key to open a door, and we went inside a medium-sized storage room with shelves lined with all sorts of canned and dried foods. On some shelves were hazmat clothing and blankets. Another rack had emergency lanterns and cooking supplies and a portable stove. A large metal gun rack was against one wall, holding three shotguns.

A microwave was on a table next to a sink and faucet. On the table was a coffee machine.

John said, "You don't find all preppers in the woods. I'm part of the New York Preppers network here in the city, and we have supplies and evacuation routes if needed."

"I didn't know that existed," I remarked.

"Be prepared if you want to survive," he said. "This place is also handy for someone like you who needs to disappear." He paused and looked at me. "What are we talking about?"

"What do you mean?"

"What are you running from?"

Should I tell him? I said, "I'm not a hundred percent sure. I'm a journalist and have come across some damaging information. The result is that people connected to a drug cartel are after me. Law enforcement may also be looking for me, but I'm not sure about that."

He looked both ways, as though someone might be watching. "The law can be worse than criminals."

"Maybe," I said. "It's a fact that the government has the most power and resources. Before I go public, I need to substantiate some information. That's why it was important to get those dark web instructions delivered."

"They were safely received. My network took care of that. I also included a couple of burner phones in the package, so you can freely talk with your counterpart. Here are the numbers of the two phones." He handed me a piece of paper on which the numbers were written.

It seemed that John's network was like the ultimate conspiracy theory group. I couldn't complain. He had been of immense help.

"Can I get connected to the internet here?"

"Of course. We've thought of everything. Let me help you."

I pulled my laptop from my computer bag and handed it to him, and he spent a few minutes connecting to a Wi-Fi network.

"There," he said. "You are now working over a virtual private network, and if anyone is wondering, you are in Germany. I also logged into your account on the dark web, and it looks like your counterpart has sent some documents."

"Thank you so much. I'm quite amazed. It seems you know your way around technology."

"Mainly phones. Some of my friends are light years ahead of me when it comes to computers and the internet. Anyway, I'll leave you to do your thing." He pointed to a door. "Behind that door is a room with cots if you need to sleep, and a bathroom. Is there anything else you require?"

"The table and chair are fine."

"Go ahead and use anything you need. It's not there for show."

"Thank you again." I took fifty dollars from my purse and handed it to him. "That might help cover costs. May I ask why you're being so helpful?"

He lowered his voice. "Some of the people coming to my shop and asking for burner phones are a different kind of clientele. They need unique assistance. I figured you were one of those, and perhaps someday you might be a candidate for our prepper's network."

It sounded like he was recruiting members, but that was okay. There was a potential story here, with John and his network, but that had to be for another time.

John gave me a key to the door of the room and told me to also use the door's thick deadbolt. At least he wasn't planning to lock me in as a prisoner, or was he?

* * *

After John left, the room became deadly quiet. I wondered what I had gotten into.

I looked at the gun rack again, and at the bottom was a drawer. I opened it and it contained two loaded handguns. John Smith would surely not come back with friends knowing I had a weapon. I took one of the pistols and checked to see that it held bullets. It looked like it was loaded. Were they real or blanks?

I placed the gun on the table next to my laptop. Was this the height of paranoia? I had never held a gun before but was reasonably sure how to use it having seen demonstrations a million times in the movies.

On the table next to the coffee maker was a bowl of different colored coffee capsules. I took a brown one, hoping it contained caffeine. After turning on the machine, I inserted the capsule, and pushed the 'on' button. It took a minute to warm up, and a couple of minutes later, I sipped a cup of coffee.

It was just what I needed.

I wondered what Luke thought about these coffee capsule machines. At least some of the capsules were labeled with countries like Brazil and Kenya.

On one of the shelves, I found a box of granola bars. The expiration date was still good, so took one and ate it while drinking the coffee. I wondered if the granola bar or coffee contained some kind of drug that would put me to sleep. Some Jews speak of 'Jewish anxiety.' Is that what I was experiencing?

I called Stan, and he answered.

"Are you and Valentina okay?" I asked.

"We're in a safe place. How about you?"

"I think so. I won't tell you where I'm at, but it seems a good place to work. You sent some files. What am I looking for?"

"On one spreadsheet are bank records showing deposits into a Lyra-Dominion bank account. These are coming from different companies registered all over the place. It seems these are shell companies."

"Does that give any evidence of corruption?"

"On another spreadsheet is a list of investors and their bank accounts. Those shell company accounts are linked to the Zapatero cartel. That spreadsheet is the key that unlocks the mystery."

"Is that all? Is it enough to incriminate Mira?"

"There's more. Phone records show regular calls to a number in Mexico. The Mexican phone number belongs to a lawyer, who represents Carlos Ortega of the Zapatero cartel. And, of course, we have Mira Brennen's calendar showing trips to Mexico City. All the pieces ad up."

From what I had learned, it was two members of the Zapatero cartel that killed Scott Roberts. "Do you have any suggestions on what we might do?"

"Take it to the FBI," Stan answered.

"It may not work. They seem fixed on a different scenario." I updated him on my conversation with Agent Cortez.

Stan was quiet for a moment and said, "There is proof here, maybe not enough to show Mira Brennen's guilt in the Scott Roberts case, but at least in money laundering."

We stayed quiet for a moment, and I said, "I have an idea."

"What's that?"

"You always said that the pen is mightier than the sword. Shall we coauthor an article?"

"I like that, but you should take the lead. I've had my day of glory, and now it's time to pass on the baton."

"Thank you, Stan, but I need your help."

"You start writing, and then we can figure out what to do with it when finished."

I paused for a moment. "Stan, can you do me a favor?"

"What's that?"

"Tell my mother and sister Naomi to go hide somewhere until I call them. The people who work for Mira Brennen threaten families. Just ask Valentina. I don't want my family harmed."

"I understand, but your mother won't like it. You know how she is. Why don't you call her?"

"I need to get to work, and that phone call might take a long time. It's best if you call her."

"She will question this."

My mother was someone who would take on the world. "Don't go into detail, but insist that they find a safe place. Let's all try and get through this thing."

"It makes sense. I'll do it."

"Thanks, Stan."

We hung up, and I set up my laptop on the table next to the coffee machine, pulled up a chair, and began to write.

I wasn't sure where to begin. For days my thoughts had been about coffee and about writing the articles for Luke and the coffee organizations.

I began to write, and several hours later, after completing a draft, I called Stan and then sent the article to him via our dark web site. Stan checked my text and made a few suggestions.

Thirty minutes later, I finished the article and then called Ernie.

"Ernie here," he answered.

"Ernie, this is Sarah."

"Where are you calling from? This isn't your number."

"I know. It's a long story."

"Zipper, do you know what time it is?"

"Eleven thirty."

"It's bedtime."

"And I bet you are still in the office."

"That's beside the point. Zipper, my phone has been ringing nonstop. You stirred up a hornets' nest this afternoon at that Mira Brennen event. What's wrong with you?"

"I'm working a story." Those were the magic words.

There was a pause. "How are you coming on it?"

"It's finished and ready to publish. In our last call, you said you would help."

"Give me the background."

As concisely as possible, I told him about Lyra-Dominion and the extraordinary financial results and the illicit cashflow from offshore companies. I also described Mira's connection to the Zapatero cartel and the link to Scott Roberts.

Ernie said, "I'm angry about what happened to Scott. Send the story, and I'll see what I can do. How can I get back to you?"

"I'll post the story to our Real Media cloud account. At the top of the article is the number where you can call me." It was the number of my second burner phone. The Real Media cloud account had a couple of levels of encryption, so it would take time for someone to hack it.

We hung up, and I waited, and fifteen minutes later, the phone rang. It was Ernie. "Zipper, are you sure about this? It's explosive."

"Positively sure. We have all the files, as well as a witness who was in Mira's house for three months. And Stan Schultz did most the research on this."

"Stan Schultz? How did he get involved?"

"It's a long story, but he was working on this way before Scott Roberts, and Stan's work is flawless." I held back mentioning the long list of conspiracy theories, but that's probably what made a journalist like Stan great, a curiosity to look below the surface and beyond the obvious."

"Then, let's run with it."

"We need to move fast because Mira Brennen's thugs are after me."

"It's too late to submit it to the major New York newspapers. They would want to vet this, and we don't have time. But the online newsfeeds are always looking for content. Let me shop it around. By tomorrow morning, it will be out there, I'm sure."

"Thanks, Ernie."

"No, thank you. Zipper, you've done great work. Now, when do we get the coffee articles?"

I shook my head. He never knew when to stop pushing. There was always a new story and a deadline. "I'm working on it," I grumbled.

CHAPTER THIRTY-EIGHT

The army cot wasn't comfortable, so it took time to get to sleep. I woke up at eight-thirty in the morning.

After rising, I went to the simple bathroom and took a shower. When I had a chance, I needed to thank John and his friends, whoever they were, for the use of this place. While I didn't feel completely safe being here, it was better than staying in my apartment where Ricco and his thugs could get to me.

I dressed and while making coffee, turned on the TV on the wall and found a business channel. The stock markets would open at nine-thirty. The futures were negative. What was driving them down?

On the TV, two well-known presenters discussed the negative opening. One was Joe Dern and the other Reba Swift, who for years hosted the Morning Market Outlook show. I focused on the news ticker moving across the bottom of the screen. One thing jumped out. 'Lyra-Dominion alleged suspicion of money laundering.'

I turned up the volume.

Reba Swift said, "And now we have Mira Brennen, the CEO of Lyra-Dominion. Good morning Ms. Brennen."

Mira's face appeared. She was not in the television studio but coming in via a video conferencing system. "Good morning," she replied.

"Ms. Brennen, this morning, an article appeared on Reuters, with allegations of money laundering in your company. How do you respond?"

"This is defamatory and malicious, an example of fake news at its very worst." Mira stared into the camera, her cheeks and lips firm, and eyes tight, as though expressing disgust and annoyance.

"Reuters is known for checking their facts," Reba Swift stated.

"Not always. Even with the best of media companies, untruths can slip through."

"Why do you call it an untruth?"

"For some bizarre and unknown reason, the journalist who wrote this article has a strange vendetta against my company and me. She harassed me in public venues, and my lawyers have already warned her company, Real Media, that this provocation must stop. Before that damaging article was posted, we were already in the process of filing for a restraining order. What she wrote is a pure lie, and we are now exploring legal actions against Reuters and Real Media and, of course, the journalist, Sarah Zipper. She has produced a ridiculous piece that is nothing more than slanderous. Society can't allow this to happen, and she will pay."

"Why would Sarah Zipper have a vendetta against you?"

"That's an excellent question, and probably one that only a psychiatrist can answer. Until now, her entire career has been nothing more than writing about foul smells in restaurant dumpsters. She has a history of sensationalist reporting where recently she faced legal problems by suggesting to rename the reputable 'Le Palm d'Or Restaurant' to 'Barf on the Table.' It shows how she lives in the gutter. Maybe she's just trying to make a name for herself, but now, she's way out of her area of competence."

"So, do you deny the accusations?" Reba Swift asked.

"Absolutely. This kind of fake news can destroy a company's reputation, and we will defend ourselves to the fullest. This is an unfounded attack, an insult to wellbeing."

Joe Dern interjected and said, "We need to take a break. Thank you for coming on our program with such short notice."

Mira's face disappeared from the TV screen. The presenter said, "That was Mira Brennen, the CEO of Lyra-Dominion. We will have more on this on the other side of the break."

I muted the sound on the TV and sat down in a chair. That news made me shaky. Mira had come out swinging, and for a moment, I wondered if it was the right thing to have written that article. It wasn't easy to bring down a wicked sorceress who was at ease in twisting truths. I should have known Mira would viciously attack if threatened.

I reminded myself that the files copied from Mira's cloud account were real. The connection of Lyra-Dominion to the Zapatero cartel was real, and it has been Zapatero members who shot Scott Roberts. To top it off, Valentina was a first-hand witness, having been inside Mira's house for three months.

Still, having top lawyers representing her, Mira would deflect any assaults.

I picked up one of my burner phones and called Ernie.

After ringing three times, he answered, "Ernie here."

"It looks like something stinky hit the fan," I said.

"Zipper, you better believe it. My phone is ringing nonstop. All the news organizations want a piece of this one."

"How did you get Reuters to take the article?"

"I got through to their night desk, and at first they refused it They wanted to double-check the data."

"So, why did they take it?"

"Stan Schultz. He has an exceptional reputation in the industry, especially when it comes to deep-dives into company financials. After mentioning Schultz, they were interested. Then, when I threatened to take the article to another agency, they bit the hook. This was just too juicy to let go."

"It looks like things will heat up," I remarked.

"You better believe it."

"Is that bad?" I asked.

"Absolutely not. Real Media is now on the map. We can take the heat. Just remember that all news is good news. Our name is out there."

"What's the next step?"

"My other phone is ringing. I need to start working the lines."

"What should I do?"

"Hold tight. I gotta run." The line went dead.

Well, that was a helpful and definitive answer. Ernie frustrated me. He was now back as a player, at least for the lifecycle of this article. He was in his element, and I imagined him answering calls from news agencies and enjoying the moment. I wanted no part of that. I didn't need him. I'd figure out what to do on my own.

I reached into my bag and pulled out the business card of FBI Agent Cortez, and called his number.

He answered. "Cortez."

"Agent Cortez, this is Sarah Zipper."

"Hello, Ms. Zipper. It looks like you took a big swing. Is it a home run or a miss?"

"What I wrote is true. Concerning Luke Cotton, you and your district attorney are up the wrong tree. I have data, and you will look like fools when this gets out." To use his simile, this was time to play hardball.

"What do you have?"

"Spreadsheets, accounts, phone records, and a first-hand witness. Are you ready to stop your silly witch-hunt with Luke and consider new facts?"

"Send them to me."

"Can I use the email on your business card?"

"Yes."

"They are on their way."

We hung up, and I went to my Real Media email account and using a 'send large files' website, I sent all Stan Schultz's files to Agent Cortez. I felt relief after posting the data. There was no need to use the dark web for this one.

I looked at the television and saw that the stock markets had opened lower by one percent. For Lyra-Dominion, it was much worse, with the share price down by fifteen percent. It meant that Mira Brennen had lost millions in the matter of minutes.

I smiled, knowing Mira would not be happy.

CHAPTER THIRTY-NINE

It was a strange feeling to know that one article appearing on a middle of the night digital newsfeed knocked billions of dollars from a company's value. It was uncertain where this was leading. All I wanted was justice for Scott Roberts, and for Luke's release from jail. And, I wanted a better life for the coffee farmers at La Fuerza.

I turned up the sound on the television. Joe Dern and Reba Swift discussed Lyra-Dominion.

Joe Dern claimed the company was grossly overpriced, inflated because of a Mira Brennen personality cult. Investors, business schools, the media, feminist groups, and politicians worshiped her. It was time to value the company on business fundamentals rather than the charisma of the CEO.

Reba Swift disagreed. She challenged my article, saying it was a hit job, and Mira Brennen was right that it was fake news, and a food journalist was trying to make a name for herself. In fact, by doing this, Sarah Zipper was giving a bad name to all journalists.

The two presenters continued on that topic, getting into a hot debate as the Lyra-Dominion share price dropped another one percent.

What would Agent Cortez do with the information I sent him? Or, was he going to ignore it and continue with the assumption that Luke Cotton was guilty? If that was the case, the FBI might even turn on me, as I was associated with Luke. I was with him in Central America and traveled with him to Long Beach.

I had an uneasy feeling. Had I done the right thing by writing that article and making it public so quickly? It would have been better to establish the facts. Did my actions have the potential of ruining the reputation of Real Media and Ernie? That was Ernie's responsibility because he agreed to release the article. Swim together, sink together.

Joe Dern and Reba Swift discussed the journalist who wrote the article, even questioning my credibility, asking, "Who is this Sarah

Zipper, and what knowledge does she have of companies and finance? Indeed, it did seem to be a hit piece."

I felt attacked, and made a quick decision. I looked up the address of the television station. It was in the financial district, not far away. I decided the best action was to go there and defend myself. The assault had to come to an end.

I put my computer in my bag and hung the bag's strap over my shoulder. I put the handgun back in the drawer of the gun rack, turned out the lights, and left the preppers' room. It took some winding through underground passageways to work my way out of the building. Once out on the street, I briskly walked to the closest subway station, took the subway to the financial district, and rapidly walked a couple of blocks to the television station.

In the building, I announced myself to the receptionist at the front desk and said I wanted to talk to the two television presenters. After speaking with several different people, the receptionist called over a security guard who escorted me into an elevator and led me to the third floor of the building.

A man with thick glasses met us. He introduced himself as the producer of the show and told me that my article had become the lead topic of the day. Indeed, they wanted to interview me on live TV.

Things moved fast, and I didn't have time to prepare, other than knowing that I needed to justify my article before it got trashed. If that happened, the publishing industry would ridicule me forever. The upcoming articles on coffee would lose their credibility, having been written by the bogus journalist that wrote the fake piece on Lyra-Dominion.

The producer led me into a makeup room, and shortly after, I sat in a chair on a studio set facing the two presenters. Three large television cameras aimed at them.

Reba Swift smiled and said, "We are on a commercial break, but in two minutes, we'll ask you questions about your article. Are you ready?"

"Ah, not really, but I'd like to clarify some things that were said earlier."

"Don't be nervous," Joe Dern said. "We will help you along."

"Relax," Reba Swift added.

A man stood next to one of the cameras and counted down the time, and then we were on air, broadcasting across the country and around the world.

Reba Swift looked at the camera and said, "A lead topic of the day is the Lyra-Dominion article that appeared this morning in Reuters. We are fortunate to have Sarah Zipper with us, the journalist who wrote the article."

Reba paused for a moment, which seemed to me as a contrived way to build suspense, the act of a seasoned presenter who knew how to make the most of the moment. Reba asked, "In your article, you claimed that Lyra-Dominion is engaged in money laundering. Some say your article is nothing more than fake news and a hit job. How do you reply to that?"

So much for helping me along, I thought. "There's nothing false in what I wrote."

Joe Dern said, "We understand your specialty is food. How were you able to concoct a story about the financial workings of a complex holding company?"

It was a journalistic attack, a way to provoke a kneejerk reaction from the interviewee, to get a soundbite to be later used in a headline out of context. "Thorough research." I simply said, not needing to elaborate and potentially hang myself, legally speaking.

The presenters waited, as though giving space for me to say more, a way to trap myself. When I didn't, Reba asked, "Aren't you concerned about legal proceedings against you? The article seems exceedingly aggressive and exaggerated."

"It's nothing but the whole truth." There was no way I would use their phrases like aggressive and exaggerated on live television.

Reba said, "Let me pick up on Joe's earlier question. Tell us how you, writing about fast food joints, had the background to take on a story like this."

I looked at the presenter but sensed I was speaking to a camera positioned past Reba's. "I was hired to do a story about coffee, particularly about hard-working coffee farmers. As I got to know the coffee supply chain, the facts about Lyra-Dominion emerged."

Joe Dern interrupted, "Our producer has just informed me that Mira Brennen is available for an interview. She was with us earlier this morning but is here again to respond to your allegations."

Before I could say anything, a monitor appeared with Mira's face. Mira was speaking over a videoconferencing application, perhaps from a studio in her company office in the city.

Joe asked, "Mira Brennen, how do you respond to the accusations that Lyra-Dominion is involved in money laundering for drug cartels?"

With a frown and tenacious eyes, Mira looked into the camera. "These are nothing but lies. My lawyers are now exploring legal restitution for the damage to my company's reputation."

I wondered if the lawyers had agreed that Mira appear on television shows.

"Sarah Zipper, how do you respond to this?" Joe asked.

I sensed the presenters enjoying. Conflict raises viewer interest, which increases ratings. I asked, "I'd like to ask Mira what she was doing in Mexico City on the first weekend of last month? Who was she meeting?"

"How do you know where I was last month or any other day?" Mira asked.

"You didn't answer the question."

"Our company is considering an acquisition."

"So, you go there on the first weekend of every third month over the last three years? It certainly is taking time to make up your mind on the acquisition. What telephone number do you always call when you get to Mexico City?"

"What do you mean?"

"I mean, the telephone number associated with the lawyer of the Zapatero cartel."

"You are hallucinating," Mira said.

"Am I?"

The presenters stayed quiet, watching the drama unfold without their intervention.

"What you allege is unadulterated made-up fiction," Mira claimed.

"Then someone should check your phone records. The next question concerns sizeable transfers coming from offshore accounts into obscure Lyra-Dominion bank accounts. It's a complex web of transactions that only an expert accountant could unravel. The sums are significant. Who holds those offshore accounts?"

"I have no idea what you are fabricating."

"The Zapatero cartel is behind the offshore accounts." I had a sudden fear that the boss of that cartel would not appreciate the Zapatero name brought into this. Ricco and his helpers were looking for me, but what would happen if the Zapatero cartel joined them? A shot of apprehension hit me like a lightning bolt. Had I spoken too fast? Still, for the sake of Scott, a case had to be made.

"I have no idea about your lunatic fantasy. It's made up."

"Mira, I don't make up phone records, flight reservations, and bank account transfers. Those are real."

"This is slander," Mira stated, her voice rising. "It's an attack on the wellbeing of Lyra-Dominion and the people of this nation." Mira's ordinarily pale cheeks had become red. Her often used and time tested slogans were suddenly becoming superficial.

I leered. "I understand you want to run for President. Talk about fantasy. That would be a disaster for this nation. What about your involvement in the murder of Scott Roberts?"

Mira's eyes hardened. "I don't know what you are talking about."

"Scott Roberts. He was investigating your company, Nyx Lines, in Long Beach, California, and he discovered drug smuggling in your company. Your right-hand guy, Sai Bashir, was making telephone calls to organized crime numbers in Long Beach just before the murder. It turns out it was the same crime group that murdered Scott, the Zapatero cartel. You know what I'm talking about. Scott was murdered."

"This is defamation," Mira yelled. "I will bring civil charges to you, your company, and everyone close to you."

It was a threat on national television, and I understood its severity. It wasn't only about legal action, but physical revenge, like what happened to Scott. Still, I had to stand my ground.

"It would be defamation if it weren't true," I calmly countered. "Why did you retain Valentina Lopez as an unpaid domestic servant in your home for three months, kept there as a hostage. Isn't that illegal?"

"I don't have unpaid domestic helpers working for me."

"Valentina would say the opposite." I knew that Mira's cook was a witness. I also wondered how many unpaid staff there were inside Lyra-Dominion's restaurant chain? Also, the restaurants might be distribution points for illegal drugs. I had said enough and didn't want to make those additional charges.

"You are living in a dream world," Mira said. "And, you will be hearing from my lawyers."

I countered, "To add insult to injury, you are piggy-backing on the coffee supply chain, hurting hard-working coffee farmers."

Reba Swift interjected and said, "Unfortunately, we are facing a hard break and need to end the interview there. Thank you both for coming on this morning and for the lively discussion."

A monitor showed a commercial being played, and a timer ticked down, indicating the show would go live in three minutes.

Reba turned to me and said, "That was certainly an exceptional exchange. Thank you for coming in, although I'd advise you to get legal help. It looks like there may be an onslaught of charges against you. The Lyra-Dominion shares went down another five percent during that interview."

"Good," I said. "I don't worry about court cases, as I have proof." At least I had proof of the phone calls and money transfers. The use of Nyx Lines to smuggle drugs needed further verification, as well as the connections to the Scott Roberts case. But, most of my claims were factual.

I walked out into the hallway of the television studio and called FBI Agent Cortez.

"Cortez," he said.

"This is Sarah Zipper. Is Luke still being held?"

"He's in the process of being released."

"So, what are you doing with the information I sent you."

"I can't get specific, but the information was helpful."

"Are you issuing warrants for Mira Brennen?"

"It's an ongoing law enforcement matter."

"Besides what I sent you, we have more. You need to see everything that was on Mira's computer. She probably wiped it clean, but we have copies. That includes phone records and bank account numbers."

"That would be helpful," Agent Cortez stated. "We already have a warrant to access all records."

I asked, "Will you arrest Mira?"

"I told you, I can't give you any information, other than she might be concerned about her future."

Enough was said. The FBI were releasing Luke, and that was a sign of how the investigation was progressing. "Thank you," I said.

"No. Thank you." Agent Cortez paused and then laughed. "What you just did on national television was gutsy. Well done, Ms. Zipper."

We hung up, and I left the building, wondering where to go. My first inclination was to meet Luke when he walked out of jail, but I didn't know when that would happen. And, he might be put in danger if I went to him. Instead, I made a quick decision to visit John Smith, the phone guy. Until the police rounded up Ricco and his team, I needed to stay off the radar. I needed an escape plan to go into hiding. How would the Zapatero cartel react? Would they try to silence any witnesses against them?

My first thought was that Stan and Valentina should join me in hiding, but it might increase the risk to have us all staying in one place. I decided to find a safe place of my own, and I wanted to talk with Luke. At some point I knew the FBI would want to speak with all of us, especially to Stan who could walk them through the numbers.

Staying somewhere in the city would probably be best, but the idea of spending extended time in that prepper's supply room wasn't appealing. John might know of something, as he seemed to be an expert in living invisibly.

I walked down the street toward the subway station, my eyes scanning cars and people. Was Ricco still looking for me? And what about Mira? In light of what Agent Cortez told me, maybe Mira was considering an escape plan of her own.

When I first heard about Scott's death, it was like being punched in the gut and knocked to the ground. Now, I felt like a fighter in the ring, who got up from the mat, ready for the next round, whatever that was.

Before getting on the subway, I put on my blue New York Yankees hat, knowing I needed to disappear. It might be for a few hours or even weeks, but I was ready.

CHAPTER FORTY

Three Months Later

I sat back on my couch and raised a cup of coffee to my lips. It was a Muninya Hill, an award-winning coffee from a cooperative in Burundi. On the package of green beans, it said, 'Beautiful sweetness. Taste caramel, grapefruit, and tamarind with lingering subtle spicy flavors.' I certainly did not sense all those flavors, but fundamentally, this coffee was downright sublime.

Enjoying this moment of relaxation, I reflected on the past three months since appearing on the Morning Market Outlook television program. After the show, one of Stan's friends loaned an apartment and I disappeared for two weeks. While John the phone guy had ideas, it was Stan's network that gave the best solution.

It turned out that John Smith was not the phone-guy's real name, and I never found out what it was. Here was someone running a shop in the middle of New York City, a few blocks from Central Station, yet he was off the grid, with no social media or telecommunications imprint. How he paid bills and filed taxes, I didn't want to know. At least I now had a way to obtain certain kinds of help, for it seemed that John had a fascinating network of people possessing all kinds of specialized technical skills. I thanked him for his help, and when walking to the Real Media offices I often drop into his shop to say hello.

After two weeks of hiding, I moved back to my apartment, and a week later, Stan moved back to his. My expensive telephone was recovered from the back alley woodpile, and it worked fine, although now I carried suspicions of being tracked by some mysterious government organization or criminal gang.

During the following weeks, I was interviewed several times by the FBI, where I told my story, going through each step from Honduras until finally appearing on the television show. I left out the part about staying in the preppers storage room.

Stan was especially helpful to the FBI with his understanding of company financials, and Valentina gave details about discussions overheard in Mira's house. Mira and Sai had talked about eliminating a journalist in Long Beach.

Jonas, the cook, confirmed listening to some of those conversations, and he described his working conditions. He had a great fear of Ricco, who threatened his family, but Mira was the most intimidating.

The FBI arrested Mira, Sai, and Ricco, along with the three accountants working in the Lyra-Dominion office in New York

The FBI also arranged for Valentina to stay in the United States. Her testimony was crucial, so they were keeping her in a safe-house until the trial. Once the court case was over, Luke planned to give her a job at the Coffee Trust offices in New Jersey.

As more facts came to the surface, there was a massive domino effect of arrests, including drug traffickers, the two men who murdered Scott, and a human trafficking network supplying underpaid workers to restaurants and sweatshops. Several people in Nyx Lines were taken to jail. Governments in North and South America had shut down the Zapatero cartel.

Ricco realized he faced a lengthy prison sentence, so he agreed to a plea bargain. It was better to be a witness for the state rather than spend the rest of one's life looking through steel bars. His testimony confirmed that Mira and Sai initiated the shooting of Scott Roberts. Scott had discovered the smuggling activities of Nyx Lines, and they silenced him.

Like Ricco, one of the Lyra-Dominion accountants saw the light, and his lawyer worked out a deal with the FBI. The source of illicit funds was revealed, as well as the entire web of bank accounts and transfers.

Because of the vast network of criminal activity connected with Lyra-Dominion, the judge did not allow bail for Mira and Sai. They waited in the Federal Metropolitan Correctional Center in New York City, the same facility where Luke was held. Ricco was in police custody somewhere in a secret place.

The Long Beach Police Department identified the location of Scott's body, and they flew it to New York, where I joined with Ernie and a host of other journalists attending the funeral service. It was an incredibly heartbreaking moment for me. Scott was a delightful colleague and I had wished to know him better. In fact, it was learning of his death that sent me on a quest in search for answers, and through that I learned that I could be self-confident in all my endeavors.

Being curious, I researched the meaning of 'Nyx'. In Greek mythology, Nyx was the goddess of the night, daughter of Chaos. Indeed, the name of that shipping line was appropriate, for Mira Brennen typified what happens when someone becomes their own law and their own morality. It turns the world to darkness.

It took several sit-down sessions with my mother to explain what happened entirely. My mom still reprimanded me for getting the family into such a dangerous predicament, but she announced that I was now written back into her last will and testament.

Fundamentally, being proud of my accomplishments, she reveled in the attention given to her at synagogue social gatherings.

For three months, the Lyra-Dominion affair dominated news cycles, and I was praised by journalists, the same ones who had put me at the bottom of the journalistic food chain. Some were even talking about a Pulitzer Prize, but I knew what was in their egoistic jealous hearts.

Initially, I gave interviews, but I could only sustain the notoriety for so long. Much of the time I hid out at my apartment and at the Real Media office, where I gladly crafted the articles on coffee farmers. The first article had gone into the Sunday section of newspapers across America, and because of my name, it was a success. Luke and the sponsoring organizations were thrilled.

I received job offers from leading journals in New York, Washington D.C., and Los Angeles, but for now, I decided to stay with Real Media. Of course, Ernie was ecstatic to receive all the attention and celebrated the flood of new business coming into the company.

As I sat on my couch and drank the cup of coffee, I considered how my world had changed. A few months ago, I had questioned my future, feeling that life had become trivial as a restaurant writer. This was coupled with the big question for everyone, what to do with the rest of your life. The visit to a coffee farm altered everything.

The day Ernie asked me to write the article, I had taken the elevator up to the Real Media offices on the twenty-first floor, walked down the hallway, and stopped at the window to view the surrounding buildings. That day I thought of them as church spires seeking the gods of materialism.

Now, the city was different. I saw the wonder of those human-made structures, the vibrancy of the population, and the hope people carried for achieving their goals. But, I also detected a darker realm of greed and oppression. Because of this, I knew I should pick up the baton handed to me by Stan and write about that sinister side, for journalists carried an enormous power to bring light and redemption. It would take time to adapt to this new reality. Yet, for some silly reason, I still had a hankering to write about restaurants and food.

The events of the past months made me realize something else. Unfortunately, there were a lot of fake journalists who bent truth to achieve some political or philosophical goal. That was not for me. My purpose was to write nothing but the whole truth.

I took a sip of my coffee, and my phone rang. It was Luke.

"Hi," he said.

"Hi to you," I answered.

"Are you still coming?"

"I wouldn't miss it."

"We fly out at nine-thirty tomorrow morning." We were going to Honduras to visit the La Fuerza farm. Valentina had given me four full suitcases of gifts and necessities for family. I packed one small bottle of non-sticky mosquito repellant for myself.

"Bring your swim gear," Luke said. "We'll accompany a shipment down to the coast and spend a few days at a beachside resort. This time we're going to the Caribbean side of Honduras."

"Thanks for the advance warning." I chuckled. At least he didn't tell me on the day of departure.

"I'm working on my communication skills."

"I can see that," I laughed.

Luke paused for a moment, and said, "I look forward to the trip, especially to be with you."

"Me too," I responded. I wished he could see my smile over the phone line.

We finished our call and I leaned back on my couch and put my feet up on my empty coffee table. The journals and newspapers had gone out with the trash.

When he used the word resort, it was best to keep an open mind. I had learned that such terms as *guesthouse* and *best hotel in town* can have a lot of meanings. The bat-infested hotel in the port town of San Lorenzo was an example of the subjectivity of describing accommodations. It didn't matter. To be with Luke was what counted.

We had seen each other frequently over the past months and had become close. When I told my mother about Luke, she responded, "Surely you can't be seeing a *goy*," which was a politically incorrect term for a non-Jew. Although, after she met him, her opinion changed. At this point, my mom had given up on the idea of a religious doctor from a respectable Jewish family. At least if we had children they would be Jewish, for mothers passed this distinction.

As far as religion, Luke and I came from different perspectives, and we openly discussed our beliefs. Luke was stuck on putting his trust in a radical Jewish zealot, who claimed to be the Messiah. He loved the Psalms and the other books in the Tanakh, which I knew well. And, he spoke from personal experience on how this relationship with God had changed his life.

Luke caused me to think more about religious *stuff*, to use his word. That was good.

We found common ground, but I stood within the tradition of *bat mitzvah*, a daughter of the commandments. That teaching had miraculously glued together my people for centuries and preserved our identity, but it had to be more than folklore or rituals. My belief was that someone stood behind the Jews, which I understood to be Adoni, the sovereign, loving, transcendent being. Who else could have kept such a people together during so many troubles throughout history?

While I did not claim to be overly religious, it was Stan who kept me connected to my roots, reminding me to say the Shema, *Hear, O Israel, The LORD our God, The LORD is One.* Every once in a while I found myself saying that, along with the other prayers.

In the end, Luke and I laughingly described our relationship as nothing more than Judeo-Christian.

I discussed this with Daniel, my bother-in-law, Naomi's husband. As a young rabbi, he would know about these things. In his yeshiva, one teaching was that Jews are to marry within the faith, whereas many Reform rabbis thought differently. Daniel found some workarounds, explained only through the wonderfully complex logic of a rabbi. While the Torah was unbendable, there was a small area of maneuverability when it came to the teachings on marriage. I love the way rabbis think, and wish I had their unique ability to reason. Maybe my father's theology books had done the trick, but my suspicion is that Daniel gave in to the wishes of Naomi who looks out for me. In the end I will never know, for